THE HONEY MAKERS

Diana Saville

Thorndike Press
Thorndike, Maine USA

This Large Print edition is published by Thorndike Press, USA.

Published in 1998 in the U.S. by arrangement with St. Martin's Press, Inc.

U.S. Softcover ISBN 0-7862-1382-5 (General Series Edition)

The text of this Large Print edition is unabridged.
Other aspects of the book may vary from the original edition.

Set in 16 pt. New Times Roman.

Printed in Great Britain on acid-free paper.

Library of Congress Cataloging-in-Publication Data

Saville, Diana.
    The honeymakers / Diana Saville.
    p. (large print) cm.
    ISBN 0-7862-1382-5 (lg. print : sc : alk. paper)
    1. Pregnancy—Fiction.   2. Large type books.   I. Title.
    [PR6069.A938H6   1998]
    823'.914—dc21   97-52109

For Margy

Acknowledgements

Acknowledgements are due to the following for permission to quote copyright material: to HarperCollins for an excerpt from 'The Life of the Bee' by Maurice Maeterlinck (used here in translation by Alfred Sutro).

The verse on page 248 is from Emily Dickinson's poem: This quiet Dust was Gentlemen and Ladies.

I am grateful to Michael Sissons, ex-beekeeper and to Carolyn Mays for their support; and as always, to Robert, which brings me to the bees themselves which we have kept for twenty years.

Honey in mouth, sting in tail.
(*in ore mel, in caude aculeum habet.*
Old Latin proverb)

Who collects honey and roses must bear
the stings and the thorns.
(Old English proverb)

It is dearly bought honey that you lick off
thorns.
(*Cher est le miel qu'on leche sur épines.*
Old French proverb)

PROLOGUE

From the darkness of the hive, the queen has emerged shyly into the clear fresh light of a May morning. Long and slender, she carries her wings folded neatly on her royal back. She is a young queen and still a virgin though only for a little longer, for today is her wedding day and the most important day of her life. Today, this May morning, is the day of her nuptial flight.

For a bride she is riotously attended. A throng of honeybees tumbles around her, alert to the ceremony that is due any moment now. On the brink of her destiny, the virgin pauses, teasing a little—does she flirt?—patters her delicate legs for a second, then she suddenly turns to face backwards, spreads her gauze wings, and soars forth on her wedding flight.

She has a good, racing start, but the males follow immediately, jostling for position, frantic and lustful for a royal mating. Who knows? She might be easy prey as sometimes it takes place near the hive. But this queen is strong and agile. She withholds her royal favour and flies further into the warm blue sky. Her lovers, full of honey, begin to fall back except for just one, a proud athlete, faster than the others, whose lust has made him heedless of his own fate. Chasing furiously he reaches

1

her. With his organ puffed out, his air sacs inflated, his wings vibrating, he clasps and enters her.

Poor winner and loser, what a terrible mating. Amongst honeybees, her marriage is always his funeral. His wings relax, his sacs collapse and his abdomen opens. The poor empty athlete spins over and hurtles dying to the ground. Still trailing his remnants, the freshly fertilised queen returns to her hive. She pauses at its threshold to clean and rid herself of his embarrassing debris. Then dusted and polished by her attendants, she seeks the sacred darkness. In three days her life's work of egg-laying will begin.

CHAPTER ONE

Elfie Lyle left the baby Jesus staring vacantly from the centre of the canvas and closed the window of the studio. She cast a last automatic glance over the tops of the solvent bottles to check on their seal, then walked through the door to greet her first sunlight of the afternoon. The courtyard was mellower than at lunchtime, as the shadows had lengthened from the rose over the arbour, the bay trees in pots and from a pair of *putti*, burglar-alarmed at their toes, for which Hugh was asking £4000.

She crossed the yard and pushed open the back door of the showroom where Susan was beginning to close for the day. The sleek antique furniture was tethered like a stable of polished racehorses around each side of the room. The various woods exhaled the smell of beeswax and an eighteenth-century must. A knowledgeable nose would also detect the scent of war against woodworm.

'Mind out,' said Susan who was starting to manoeuvre her Hoover along a clear run of carpet.

'Sorry,' said Elfie automatically although she was well out of range.

The two pearl-grey Italian whippets began to tremble in their basket by the office desk. The more emotional of the two, Bertram of

Thinghill Witherstoke, whom she preferred to call and he to answer to, Bertie, gave a whimper.

'Any sales?' She fondled a whippet ear to instil fortitude.

'Two gold-card carriers after the davenport in the window. They want five hundred off and have retired hurt for a council of war in the teashop down the road.'

'Better keep open until they come back,' said Elfie, jumping sideways as Susan made a purposeful lunge with her Hoover. Bertie gave a second moan.

'They won't be back till tomorrow,' said Susan contemptuously, who had long since mastered the psyche of customers. Time was the only weapon in their limited armoury and one of pitiful stature beside their Achilles heel of desire. She could discern the latter at a hundred paces and was fond of quoting George Herbert's 'Love and a cough cannot be hid'.

She now threw a glance of patronising pity in Elfie's direction. She might have worked here for seven years and been married to Hugh for five, but her understanding of clients remained woefully unreliable. However, in fairness, she had to concede that Elfie was a picture restorer rather than a saleswoman and the manipulation of lust was not her responsibility. Elfie with her cool Botticelli brow would know nothing about lust.

Susan looked at her more closely. The pale

brow was a little furrowed.

'Going home to see the new heir and grandson?'

Elfie nodded. 'Hugh says he's very pleased.' She added, frowning: 'I hope he's there to greet Meredith before I arrive.'

She was a little frightened of her stepdaughter, Meredith. The disparity in their age was too small and that in self-confidence too large. It was an imbalance that the passage of time had failed to correct. Indeed, she feared that the advent of Meredith's son might effect a widening of the gap.

'Well,' said Susan, 'just smile.'

'As I always do.'

The whippets arched the exquisite curve of their necks whilst Elfie bent to attach their leads. Then, stepping fastidiously over the Hoovered section of the carpet, Bertie and Como followed her black leather pumps out of the showroom.

She nosed the Fiat out of the reservation, through Sheep Street and down the main stone artery of the Oxfordshire Cotswold town. Clusters of early tourists were huddled in front of the house agents' windows. They dreamed there in silence. Of a cosy and coddled future, of Albertine roses round the door, of a retirement spent gazing forth from five-barred gates. No retirement for Hugh, she thought. Dealers never rested in peace, and Hugh was in any case neither restful nor peaceful.

Leaving the town by its rear exit, she drove sedately through the lushness of May greenery. That sharp green of perfect early fertility, no longer chlorotic like April, not yet sere like August. It was the time of year she loved best, when everything was in peak vegetable condition. Driving slowly because she was reluctant to arrive, she wished also to linger in this countryside with its wide horizons, especially welcome after peering at a dark canvas all day. The sky flooded light over the open landscape and the late afternoon air was soft. Either side of the lane the untrimmed verges were foaming with cow parsley, waved gently back by the passage of her car and then subsiding in its wake. Beside her the whippets lay curled up on the front seat, their thoroughbred legs intertwined, their sensitive noses occasionally woffling a little when a draught of some juicy smell blew in through the open window.

Still dallying, she turned left at the signpost, braked at the bend, then picked up speed as the road began to dip a little, leading to the wooded combe. It was here, under the brow of the hill, that their house lay, though she always thought of Rooke House as Hugh's. She turned right into their drive, still heading downwards as the stone farmstead stood beneath the lane, and through the gap in the trees, she saw that Meredith's car was indeed ensconced. It looked new: a Trooper, a good colour of khaki mud, set high above the road level so that she could peer down her small Scandinavian-sized nose over the human ants of the highway. The perfect choice for cross-country treks over Wimbledon High Street near Meredith's home. She noticed with relief that Hugh's Volvo estate was beside it and that the central courtyard of the farmhouse and barns looked wonderful in the slanting six o'clock light.

She opened the door of the car, and she and the dogs clambered out to glance round for a second before she entered the house. The stone arch to the courtyard was festooned by trails of the longest-tressed wisteria, white and violet. Today the scented petals had started to come fully out. The sight, as always, renewed her. Feeling calmer, she turned, went back up the paved path and pushed open the rear door. She heard their voices in the kitchen and stretched her mouth to smile.

'How lovely,' she announced.

They turned to face her. Hugh was standing, taut and upright by the elm dresser. His daughter, big and languid, was propped up against the refectory table. There was a momentary displacement of air in the room to accommodate Elfie's entry.

'How lovely,' she repeated, 'Meredith, how very nice to see you.'

Smiling, Meredith, gave a little wave with the fingers of her right hand. She did not move out of the space she had established, thus forcing Elfie to advance and enter it to kiss her. Her stepmother then perambulated to the other side of the room to kiss Hugh hello.

'Christie's OK? You're not too tired?' It was her usual question. He would be sixty-four this year, though his energy always surprised her.

'Fine. I bought them.' He had been to London for the day to assess a few rugs at the auction.

'And He? Where is He?' said Elfie.

Meredith lifted a slender wrist and thrust her long fingers into her thick honeyed hair to shift it from her forehead. How slender her wrists were in contrast to her big breast-feeding body. She was all glamour and fecundity. The potency of the combination filled the room. She now slid her fingers out from her hair which fell massively forward again, and pointed to the floor beside the sofa.

'Oh' said Elfie. 'What a pet.'

Reclining in his collapsible chair, the two-week-old infant lay at peace on his bed of sleep. Elfie drew near, knelt in reverence, then paused to watch him in silence. As inscrutable as a Buddha, his eyelids were tightly closed over his floating thoughts and feelings. Now and again his tiny hands pushed at the air, as slow and incoherent as those of a man under water. A shadow brushed his face, a memory perhaps of his amphibious entry into the world. Then he sank back in peace.

Elfie inserted a finger into his furled fist. Its

palm was moist, not yet toughened by the air that grown-ups breathed.

'Hello,' she said softly to him. 'You've got an awfully long way to go.'

'He's called Albert.' It was the first time Meredith had spoken since Elfie's arrival. Her voice was unhurried, a convent product but with the brassier patina of lives since lived.

'Does he open his eyes?' Elfie had forgotten what babies were supposed to do and when.

'Oh yes. Big ones. Like Pa's.'

'Nice name,' said Hugh, topping up his whisky with a splash.

'Have you picked him up?' asked Elfie.

'Good God no. Might drop him.'

'Don't be silly. You're quite dextrous with porcelain.'

'Not wriggly.'

As if to prove his point, Albert shifted in his miniature deck chair and gave a cry, then a second, and third until he had built up a good continuity. Bertie and Como, whose curiosity had so far overcome caution, backed off to the far side of the room. Recognising a shift in the pecking order, they suddenly looked aged and stressed out.

'Food, sweetie?' Meredith went over to the chair, unleashed Albert from his strap and lifted him up. Then, easing herself well back into the Provençal cushions on the sofa, she raised the hem of her safari shirt and fitted the child onto her noble veined pumpkin of a

9

breast. She gazed serenely at Elfie as she did so, afloat on hormones.

'I think I'll just check on those rugs,' said Hugh. 'I shouldn't leave them rolled up in the car.'

'What are they?' asked Elfie. Her eyes were magnetised by the resplendent vision before her. Meredith looked like a lioness with her honey hair and tawny shirt and trousers. She could have accommodated at least three or four more cubs on her breasts. A pride could live off her milk.

'A couple of fine floral Kashans and a very decent Kerman. More than 480 knots to the square inch.'

'Got one to spare, Pa?' asked Meredith casually. 'Christening present?'

'Absolutely not. It's my bread-and-butter stuff.'

He spoke the truth in this. He could rely on the fact that the middle classes still bought Oriental rugs even through recessions. In the bad times, he might keep the same items of furniture for six months or more, long enough anyway for him to grow fed up with their presence. He might not have to feed and water them, but they still consumed rent, salaries and his peace of mind. The rugs, however, were different. Items of higher mobility, they moved quickly in and out.

He put down his glass and started to walk out of the kitchen, the soles of his shoes ringing

10

on the cold slabs. The whippets did not like lying down on the paving because their hairless tummies were sensitive to the chill.

'I'll come with you,' offered Elfie, funking a session with Meredith on her own.

'No,' said Hugh 'they're not heavy. Stay and talk to Merry.'

He walked nimbly through the door, too fast for her to protest. Resigned, she took out a bottle of white wine, poured herself a drink and began to set the table for dinner.

'I suppose I can't offer you one,' she said to Meredith. 'It'll spoil the milk, won't it?'

'Bit of an old wives' tale, that.' Meredith spoke lazily, holding out her hand for a glass, 'but don't lay for me, not with Albert. I've got to get back to the family.'

She was referring to George, her husband; her first child, Mona; her second, Florence; also her nanny. They had a weekend cottage, fifteen miles away.

'Oh,' said Elfie, not disappointed that she would be sharing supper alone with Hugh this evening.

'We just dropped in to show Pa the grandson and heir.'

Hugh now returned with two rolled-up rugs under each arm. He saw Meredith was still feeding and disappeared to deposit them in the hall and fetch a third. The room felt as if a force ten gale had blown in and out.

'Lovely to have a son as well as daughters,'

11

offered Elfie. She meant it and was annoyed it emerged as a platitude.

'A son is a mixed blessing,' said Meredith. 'He either turns out queer or you get a daughter-in-law. It's got to be one or the other, though I suppose if you're really unlucky you'd get both.'

She lifted Albert and shaped him over her shoulder for what Elfie supposed was a ritual burp. She was sure she had been burped as a baby in the 1950s.

'Let me,' she said, holding out her arms. She went over to the child and lifted him from Meredith's hands to position him over her own shoulder, arranging a strategic handkerchief in advance. Twelve inches from top to bottom, his boneless form adapted to her nooks and crannies, his cranium pillowed snugly against her neck.

Hugh returned with the third rug. He saw his wife with the baby and his dark gaze flicked momentarily away.

'This is the nicest,' he said, rolling it out over the paving stones. Unfurled, the silky Kerman revealed its indigo and grey-pink palmettes against a fawn backcloth. It was clearly the product of an old and highly refined civilisation.

'Hugh,' said Elfie, 'not now.'

Neither Hugh nor Meredith paid any attention. Both stared at the rug, the one replete with a good purchase, the other hungry

12

to acquire.

Exasperated, Elfie walked out of the kitchen, through the cool hall and into the drawing room. There she stood in front of a slim eighteenth-century looking glass. Her reflection was fuzzy and blotched. None of Hugh's mirrors was much good at doing its job, their age and elegance supposed to be self-justifying. However, she could make out the shape of her fair face and the baby's narrow back in his white stretch jumpsuit. She watched herself put a cheek against the downy surface of his vulnerable head, softer than fur, warmer than silk. She turned from the reflection to the reality of his small face, so close to hers she could see the transparencies of his lids. He parted his lips—was it wind?—but it was only to form a small yawn. He must have needed to draw a sip more oxygen down to his lungs.

Elfie closed her eyes. My stepdaughter doesn't just have one, she has three of these, she reflected. Then her mind moved idly to the painting of the baby Jesus on which she must work tomorrow, indeed for weeks, as she had today and yesterday. The thought occurred to her that even the Virgin Mary was given an infant, and she with only the Holy Ghost.

*　　　*　　　*

After closing and locking the shop, Susan had returned home which meant the end house of a terrace on one of the newer estates. It was a resting-stage for a coven of divorced and single mothers. Evicted by misfortune from their first way of life, they strove here to make temporary nests before emerging for a second try. Several bids were often required before a successful lift-off could be achieved.

Bags in one hand and keys in the other, she opened the front door to the horrid but inoffensively decorated hall—'flash of pastel' as she knew it was called in the trade. She could hear movement on the other side of the partition. Nick, her elder child, must have returned from an afternoon's delivery trip to Warwickshire. At eighteen, he and old Walter were responsible for the successful transfer of Hugh's antiques from the showroom to local buyers. He was lucky to have the work when most of his mates were on youth-training schemes and Susan was anxious it should be immaculately fulfilled, as the job had potential. Though her own circumstances might be sadly reduced, her energies were usually directed into enlarging his.

She found him bending down in the kitchen, sending a rapid practised eye over the contents of the fridge. Only four and a half cubic feet large, it lacked the capacity to fuel him. He needed one at least double the size.

'Oh Mum,' he groaned when he saw her. 'How can I work out on this?' He indicated two bare shelves and a frozen moussaka which was all that remained of his raid.

'There's more here,' Susan replied apologetically. She was laden with plastic bags from the supermarket at lunchtime.

'I haven't got time to wait.' His normally cheerful, handsome face was stricken. The absence of enough to eat always reduced him to palpable despair.

'You can't heave about with all that food joggling inside you,' but she brought out a large beef pasty from a bag and handed it to him.

'They tell us that chicken and fish are best to train on,' he said with a grimace.

'I wish they'd shut up. I can't afford to keep you.'

'You can't afford not to keep me.'

They looked at each other for an uncomfortable second. As they had both bumped into the truth, she changed the subject and heaved her shopping onto the kitchen table.

'Did you get the right address this afternoon?' she asked.

'Up a lane, turn right, over a field, through a cutting, down five potholes and goal.'

He had been delivering a seventeenth-century chest with oyster veneers; new handles, replacement bun feet, but otherwise good. He was learning about the trade as he went along. Like his mother, he was alert to the stepping stones in his job.

'You did strap it thoroughly? No rocking?

You know what can happen. You know that—'

'Mum. Been there. Seen the movie. Know the ending, thanks.'

'I wish you wouldn't use that silly outdated phrase.' She felt suddenly irritated. 'No one at your age has the faintest idea of how things end.'

She spoke thinking of her husband, Charles, who had been killed in a road accident six years ago. Seen the movie. Know the ending. Sometimes she agonised over the irony that her son was driving for a job, a fact which had given her nightmares at first. Ah yes, she knew the endings of things intimately. What made it worse was that Nick was so like Charles: the flat, strong-boned face of a rugby player; the sixteen-and-a-half-inch neck; the broad shoulders; the sturdiness of character; the willingness to tackle.

She now heard sounds in the tiny hall, put her head round the door and saw her nine-year-old daughter, Jessica, peering from outside through the letter box. As Susan opened the front door, she noticed she had a packet of fluorescent pink and green sweets in her hand. This was not a matter for approval and these looked odder than most.

'Here,' said Susan, investigating the one Jessica was about to put in her mouth. It appeared to be the top half of a finger. A repulsive indentation suggested a nail.

'Don't,' said Jessica, dropping her bag and

blazer on the hall floor.

'What on earth—'

'Nose-pickers.'

'Oh no.' Susan put her head back and sighed. It was trivial but somehow symptomatic of the ghastly habits she had picked up from her school.

When Charles had died, she had no choice but to withdraw Nick from his boarding school. It was unable to provide bursaries for the sons of newly indigent widows in recessionary times of falling rolls. Nick, however, had sufficient good temper and robustness to survive. Susan was less certain of Jessica who had known no other than the ritual antipathy of her comprehensive school to a gentler way of life. She gave every sign of settling for thoroughgoing cryptic colourisation as a method of survival.

'What's this for, Jess?' asked Nick as she escaped into the kitchen with her bag of sweets. 'Oh yummy. Makes the knockers grow?'

'Shut up.' Jessica covered her bony chest.

'Nick,' warned Susan.

'Oh, great.' He grabbed a nose-picker and put it to its official use. 'Got some to spare for the team?'

'Stop. They're mine,' yelled Jessica, thin arms flailing against the chimney-stack of her elder brother's torso.

'Don't encourage her,' said Susan, trying not to smile.

17

'I'm off anyway.' Nick gathered up his kit which had been scattered over the kitchen floor in his haste to ransack the fridge.

'No,' said Susan, 'one last thing. Here's the delivery list of addresses for tomorrow. I may not see you in time to go through them.'

Nick scanned it, frowning. There was a partner's desk for an office in Stratford. A marquetry centre table to Nuneham Courtney. He also noticed with interest Martha Dacre's name, which meant a relatively local trip. His heart rose at the thought that he might see her fantastic daughter; then sank at the thought of delivering the stone sphinx. It was her second this spring, and the effort and indignities of transporting the first remained in his mind. He sighed, thinking he had better do this one separately. One false move and it would smash any chaste ladies' furniture in the van.

'I don't know the man the table's going to,' said Susan. She added delicately: 'I didn't awfully like the look of him. He said he had leopard-skin drapes.'

She glanced at Nick, the repository of all her hopes, a deal of anxiety, so much of her love. Such a decent, strong, good-looking boy. He didn't have a girl at the moment. She dreaded the thought that he could attract the wrong sort of attention. Male genitals were so importunate and you never knew whose were on the prowl in this trade. Rich, acquisitive old men and their impressionable boy companions

18

made a commonplace sight, snuffling for truffles in the showroom.

'Take care, won't you?' she ended up saying lamely.

'What she means is "Mind your Bum",' said Jessica.

*   *   *

'I have a sphinx coming tomorrow from Hugh Lyle,' announced Martha Dacre. She sat with one knee crossed over the other, smoothing a Lancôme cream round her green eyes to rejuvenate the cells.

'A second?' Her husband, Philip, glanced at her. He was changing his tie and trying to solve a clue in the *Financial Times* crossword at the same time.

'They look better in pairs.'

Philip stared forcefully at the clue, but his concentration had fragmented. He wondered whether to raise a protest. He was hesitant. They were dressing to have dinner with friends. They were already late and it seemed an unfortunate moment to throw a spanner in the works, especially one that could poison the whole of their evening.

Martha peered intently in the mirror before continuing.

'I think I'll get them to place it so it peeks out of fronds. It'll look more real that way.'

'Instead of seeming what it is, you mean. Yet another lump of overpriced stone.'

19

There, he had let it out of the bag: his thrift, lack of taste, resentment, lower-middle-class upbringing, all the characteristics she cherished in him. They would undoubtedly be late for dinner now.

'It's not frightfully expensive, if that's what this is about,' she said evenly, but he saw her raised ankle rotate briefly. Born into a family where the women had tree trunks for legs, Philip had sometimes wondered whether he had married her for her slender expressive ankles. But it was their irritability he remarked more often these days, not their slimness. He took a deep breath and decided to re-run this conversation to a happier destination. The sphinx was booked, his wife was spendthrift, his marriage a challenge; he might as well accept this trio of truths with a good grace.

'Where will you put it?'

'I want both of them to flank the exit from the little white garden.'

He looked back at the crossword clue, reflecting. 'You know it's near the beehives.'

'Yes, I wanted to discuss that with you.' Her tone had a determined thrust.

He put the pink newspaper down carefully on the grey and white chintz sofa. Care had infiltrated itself into a lot of his gestures these days.

'They're a bloody nuisance,' she said violently, flicking her ankle back and forth. He noticed she had painted her toenails a dark red.

'Those two nasty little wooden hives spoil the view. I want you to get rid of them.'

Philip felt a tremendous urge to take some precipitate action. Instead he walked over to the *toile de Jouy* curtains, pulled them to the very ends of their pole, opened the window and leaned out. It was half-past seven and there was evening sunlight over the tops of the trees in the garden. The bees would still be flying at this hour, collecting golden pollen from the huge blue ceanothus he could see in the distance. It would be a fine honey crop. He wished he could stay here watching them instead of having to trail out to dinner on his first day off this month.

He turned back to face the room and his wife.

'Martha, we've been through this before. My job is demanding. I like the bees. I need hobbies.'

'Children have hobbies. They write essays when they are little called "My Hobby".'

'No, grown-up men have hobbies. They need them more than children.'

'For Christ's sake, can't you fish or something, like proper men? You could massacre a few salmon in your spare time like Daddy, couldn't you?'

'Get out of the house, you mean. Look, I'm away from the house ninety per cent of the time anyway, out of the country often. I like to spend the remaining oddment here.'

He employed a reasonable tone. In his youth

21

as a management trainee in a large company, he had been taught to talk disputes through. He had learned to master the art of an unexcited debate. Now, some thirty years later, he believed himself immune to hysterics. He had been the butt of a thousand tantrums throughout his life: unevenly distributed of course, there being a handful of wobblies in his current work as a management consultant and nine hundred or so at home.

'I'm sure we can sort things out,' he said smiling. 'You with your sphinx and me with my bees.'

She gazed at him coldly before slipping a grey silk shift over her dark and mutinous head. It slithered over her slender body.

'I might move the hives,' he offered, watching her quick movements in the mirror as he adjusted his navy and fawn paisley tie.

He saw her throw her eyes to the ceiling. Martha's idea of compromise was nothing less than annihilation of her opponent.

'In return,' he continued 'for no more stuff from Hugh Lyle.'

'His wife,' said Martha 'is restoring an eminently purchasable painting of the baby Jesus, Mary and some angels.'

You, my darling, wouldn't recognise an angel if it approached you bearing a lily in its hand, he thought as he opened the panelled door.

'Do buck up,' he said. 'I've been ready for ages.'

CHAPTER TWO

After Meredith's departure, Elfie returned to the kitchen and completed laying the long rectangular table for Hugh and herself. Theirs was a restful kitchen with ochre lime-washed walls and a hint of stencilling near the ceiling which was a relic from an era that had come, exploded and gone. This, an error of judgment, showed the one concession to modern fashion. Otherwise, the kitchen and the scullery had been left unscathed, a stubborn monument to the past, a time warp in a world where catalogues launched a thousand new kitchens and accessories by the month.

Moving about this placid interior, fulfilling the ritual flow of tasks for the meal was normally a source of satisfaction, though not this evening. Tonight she was working herself into a state of fresh distress. 'She doesn't deserve Albert,' she said out loud to the dogs. But funnily enough, that didn't seem the cause for concern. What really rankled was that, as she and Hugh had waved the Trooper goodbye, he had said to her: 'Rupert's turn next. Time he married and had a family.' *Rupert's turn next.* The phrase had required a ten-minute incubation period before starting to eat her like some awful disease.

It wasn't that she had anything against her stepson Rupert, who was Hugh's elder child. In fact she quite liked him, actually far preferred him to Meredith. Indeed, if she looked at the issue objectively, she would agree that, at thirty-four, she would wish him to be a happy husband and father. But *Rupert's turn next*. Here was a queue forming in which she had not been granted the chance of a place.

She thumped the food onto the kitchen slab and surveyed it sadly. French beans, free-range chicken breasts (no cruelty to animals here), cherries, yoghurt and molasses. Stuffed with potassium and calcium, the meal positively reeked of health. She then went to the dresser drawer and took out the bottles of vitamins C and E that she normally gave Hugh. Oh, such a fortunate husband and what a wonderful wife. Thanks to all she had fed him, his appearance was that of a man who might have been eight years younger. He was in far better form than when she had married him. Lean, unlined, fit, a swordsman. Clever Elfie to have accomplished the job of all younger wives: that of rejuvenating their husbands. But why bother, she thought furiously to herself, and then immediately felt ashamed. The spurt of temper began to ebb, leaving only a sad mist as an aftermath. Poor Hugh. It was no fault of his that his wife should have changed.

A scratch at the door reminded her that the little tortoiseshell cat had not yet been fed. About to open it, she was interrupted by the telephone.

'Is he in yet?'

'Oh Mrs Marley,' said Elfie. 'I'm so sorry. He's just slipped out. He'll call you back shortly.'

She put the phone down. 'Hugh,' she yelled.

No answer. He had absconded. She opened the kitchen door. 'Hugh,' she called again. There was an unhelpful silence. The cat, a rescue job called Baglady, flattened itself around her ankles, not a difficult task as she had been run over when younger, the event leaving her permanently hungry but also as squashed as a flounder. Elfie picked the cat up and wound her around her neck.

'Hugh?' Her voice hit the stone walls of the courtyard and bounced back to her. Sod the Marley woman. She'd have to find him.

She picked up the mobile telephone, left the house, walked under the stone arch though did not linger this time, across the lawn, and into the little knot garden, an essay in hard surfaces and clipped evergreens. It was a very controlled garden and she had decided some time ago that she no longer liked it. Last year she had scattered fistfuls of annual poppy seed into the gravel. It had germinated in the warm, moist earth and erupted into waves of silky mother-of-pearl flowers. 'A bit messy isn't it?' Hugh had said.

She now looked about her. He sometimes sat on a stone bench here, though it was empty this evening save for a wagtail in frantic motion.

'Hugh,' she called again, but there was still no answer.

She walked out of the garden, falling over Milo, the golden pheasant who had jumped out of a bush and started pecking at her heels. Thus collared by the cat and hobbled by the bird, she carried on with her search. In the evening stillness, broken only by the pheasant's ugly squawk, the soles of her feet scrunched over the gravel path. The noise of its surface underfoot was the reason it was supposed to be a good burglar deterrent, though Elfie had protested when Hugh had planned a moat of gravel round the house.

'Give over,' she yelled at the pheasant as he ran to keep pace, jabbing at her ankle. He had pecked at the eye of his small brown wife a month before and blinded her.

She checked her little period garden, the vegetable plot where she broke off eight sticks of asparagus, and was about to give up when she decided to peek into the hedged enclosure off the lawn. The waterlily pads would be waxing fatly over the formal pool.

'Caught,' said Hugh as she erupted through the yew hedge.

'You. All alone and hiding? What's up?'

'I'm tired.' He hid his left hand behind the stone bench.

Elfie sniffed. 'Hugh. You haven't been smoking.'

'Just a little one, so small it's invisible to the

26

naked eye.'

'Hugh. You promised me months ago.' *Why bother?*

'It's the first I've had for years. Stop staring at me as though I'm addicted. Look, I know what to do with my hands without a fag in them.' He stuck the butt in the side of his mouth and waved his hands around.

'Bags of charm won't get you out of this one.' But she spoke without conviction. She decided against having a row.

'You've got to ring Mrs Marley. She's called you twice this evening about that William and Mary chest on a stand.'

'Can't it wait,' he groaned.

'Get it over with.' She passed him the phone.

He looked quite exhausted. The neural energy that had driven him all day had collapsed in the face of a buyer. Watching his face, Elfie recalled that on the rare occasions that he saw Meredith, he was often like this. She felt a pang of guilt for her secret outburst against him this evening, though the melancholy remained. *Rupert's turn next.*

Settling down with Baglady to listen, she kicked the golden pheasant away and waited in the hope of distraction. No saleswoman herself, she was usually entertained to watch his technique in play. Hugh dialled the number. Even from three feet away, a large and hostessy presence could be detected oozing out of the receiver.

27

'It is a desirable piece,' she heard her husband say. 'The top around 1690. The stand of course is only nineteenth-century but expertly and authentically made.'

There were patterings of demur on the other end of the line. They sounded larger than life. The telephone could be relied on to amplify all emotions or their absence.

'£4600,' he confirmed. 'It is in perfect condition.'

He is wearing his antique voice, thought Elfie. It usually amused her. Confident and with the slightest stain of superciliousness, not enough to offend, just the right amount to impart credentials. This is the man I married, she thought as she listened.

'What?' Hugh was affecting surprise. 'Including delivery?'

Elfie knew this routine as well as he.

'No, I'm afraid not. £4200 is the most I can concede.'

This was the moment, the negotiations leading to close of sale. Poor Mrs Marley. Hugh did it hundreds of times a year; it was probably her first and last go.

'To be frank,' said Hugh, 'I'm not worried if I sell it to you or not.'

Elfie stared at him surprised. Here was a new departure. Either he was suffering from burn-out or this was brinkmanship of the most flamboyant kind. Business was still distinctly spotty and buyers of this kind weren't always thick on the ground.

'Good. That's fine. Many thanks. As soon as my office receives a cheque, they will arrange the delivery to you.'

He pressed the button on the phone to cancel the call.

'There you are. She fell like a plum.'

'Pushing your luck.'

'And whilst we're on the subject, make sure Susan warns Nick to wrap the goods thoroughly in the morning. It may rain tomorrow. I heard the forecast in the car coming back.'

'Where are they off to?'

'A flashed up piece to Nuneham Courtney. And a stone sphinx to Martha Dacre.' He added significantly: 'Her second.'

'She's been getting a lot recently.'

'Why don't we have them to dinner?'

'Because I don't like her.'

'Try a bit harder, can't you? She's a good customer.'

Elfie grimaced. In the equation she made between guests and the washing-up they created, Martha Dacre was found wanting.

'I'll ask them to play tennis if you like. That way we shan't have to talk.'

'You're a good girl. Sorry I was a bit short this evening.'

'You're always like that when Meredith comes.'

'I scarcely ever see her.'

'Is that why?'

Hugh got up and stretched. 'Lord,' he said, 'I'm tired.'

*   *   *

Later that evening in their bedroom, at ten o'clock which was earlier than their usual bedtime, Hugh stepped into the right leg of his navy pyjamas and then the left leg and slowly clambered into bed. It was a big old oak affair with linenfold panelling and grapes and birds and ancient fertility symbols which they had slept in for two years. Furniture had transient tendencies in this house and swaps were forever imminent, a cause of protest from Elfie in this particular instance, and, less vocally, in general.

She too had undressed. About to slip on her old cotton nightgown, she paused. Naked, she picked up her silver brush and began to stroke her long, straight fair hair. The strands clung electrically to the bristles before floating on gravity to her bare shoulders. She turned to her reflection in the mirror but watched him in its depths rather than herself. She was surprised he was not looking at her. She put the brush down, switched off the main overhead light, a crystal Victorian shade, and walked over the worn Shiraz rug to her side of the bed. Hugh had rolled over to his left to reach for a book in his cabinet.

'Not reading tonight are you?' she said. 'I

felt like talking.' She slid under the sheet. It moulded itself to her naked form, clinging rather more closely than when she wore her nightgown.

'Just a little read.'

'A little talk.' She wound her left foot around his ankle and hooked it towards her.

He began to put down his book slowly.

'We could,' said Elfie, 'just have one.'

'What?'

'You know.'

'No, I don't know.' He spoke with some irritation.

'A child.'

'A child?' The book slid down the bed. 'Elfie. We agreed.'

'I know but—'

'I explained that at my age—'

'A little one, so small you wouldn't even notice it.' She spread her hands six inches apart to indicate its size.

Hugh frowned. He opened his mouth and then shut it.

'Well, three inches then.' She pursed her lips charmingly.

'Perhaps one day.'

'You'll be older still then. And so shall I. One day.'

'Who knows? I might adapt.'

'Then when? Tomorrow?'

'Elfie. We've been through this before. I'm too old. A grandfather, not a father. We agreed

31

even before we married.'

'I know what we agreed. But all these stepchildren. These step-grandchildren. Who do they turn me into? Always a bridesmaid, never a bride.' She tried to speak reasonably.

'Sweetheart—'

'Don't sweetheart me.'

'I'd be seventy-five when it was ten,' he said plaintively. She stared at him. Why did he think she stuffed him brimful of vitamins and minerals? *Why bother*?

'Look.' He held out his right arm in the hope that she would fall into her habitual position in its crook, but the reflex did not seem to be operating with its usual fluency. 'Let's go to sleep and talk about this some other time, shall we? Come on. Sunny side up?'

'When?'

'Soon,' he promised.

She gazed with disbelief at the arch-procrastinator she had married. For soon, she might as well read never. If he waited long enough, she would wither on the vine.

'You did agree. Remember?' he reminded her.

She was silent, but did indeed remember.

CHAPTER THREE

The wedding of Elfie Weston and Hugh Lyle had taken place five years ago in a registry office during a freezing snap in January. At their ages, marriage was as much a matter of policy as of passion. Hugh was then in his late fifties, Elfie twenty years younger, and both had experienced a disappointing past.

Hugh and Vendela, his first, and half-Swedish, wife, had divorced when their two children were growing up, though he told Elfie that the marriage had long since collapsed. It was his great misfortune that his wife had experienced the sexual revolution after they had married and then only with other men. Like so much in life, it was bad timing that had wrought such unfortunate effects. At this stage Hugh was chairing a large and quoted printing company, a preoccupying job that had forced him to practise masterly inactivity in his home life. For a long while he had no time to see, then had refused to see, then seen but decided from pride to overlook the erratic comings and goings of his vivacious, fox-furred wife. Many years later, with the benefit of tranquil hindsight, he had thought she was probably a bit mad, though he had not realised this at the time, since it is always easy to mistake madness for vivacity. But, anyway, mad or sane, it was her final departure with a polo-player from Argentina that brought their long era of semi-detachment to its inevitable and explosive close.

The event was not unconnected with the loss of his job when the company was merged with another; and the dual misfortune made him resolve to move out of London in search of a more tranquil way of life. War-wounded but still resilient, he looked about him for something to do. It was at this time that an uncle died and left him a small and sickly antiques business in the Oxfordshire Cotswolds. Hugh's first impulse was to sell but since it was unsaleable he followed his second which was to nourish it with the cheque from his dismissal.

It was a rash decision, but he proved right to assume he would be successful. Raised by parents who placed nice furniture in the category of good manners—an automatic accoutrement for gents—he had developed an effortlessly educated eye for choice pieces. Now, many years later, it was that eye which would earn him a living. Refinement of his knowledge followed swiftly. He learnt the difference between banding and stripping, tallboys and lowboys, a spade and a scroll foot. In country furniture, he could tell apple from pearwood, cherry from plum and beech from birch. He spoke about breakers and sleepers, and referred to runners and lookers. He knew that right and wrong were not aspects of morality but the terms for original and faked pieces. From modest and agonisingly slow beginnings, the business had started to prosper, flaring finally into life during the champagne era of the eighties, for all collecting was destined to rise as well as dip according to the state of the economy.

It was at this stage that Elfie had embarked on completing the occasional commission from him to restore a painting. He had met her at a New Year's Eve party, where he had immediately recognised her as his type, though not his usual experience. Darkly complexioned himself, he knew himself to be compulsively drawn to fair women; though Elfie was no Junoesque blonde like his first wife, but high of brow, a frail, chaste and shrouded beauty of the Renaissance, with hair folded on the crown of her head, and falling to her shoulders. Trained originally at the Courtauld Institute, her credentials were impeccable; her face pure; and her character controllable. The contrast she made to his fickle ex-wife Vendela was in itself an asset. For the first time, Hugh felt he had met a younger woman who could provide a second, but safer marriage. She could restore his trust in its success.

A woman in her late thirties is neither pure nor demure and Elfie was thankfully no exception, as Hugh well knew. A full generation below him, she had clocked up a fair mileage in men, though there had been some fallow times and a prolonged static period devoted to the same married man, Anthony, an obsession that only ended when she realised he would leave neither wife nor children. The addiction, so consuming and remorseless in its prime, had finally dwindled

35

into a transient regret when she passed a Roman head like his in the street. It was at this twilight stage, emergent from a long period under the sea, that Elfie met Hugh.

Up until now, Elfie had resigned herself to a lifetime of spinsterhood. Of course it was no longer termed that nowadays, for women were not permitted to regard themselves as victims. Instead it went with a proud carriage and was called freedom, independence, feistyness in the blind doublespeak that transformed all negatives to positives.

But Elfie's married sister, Judith, and their mother too, both haves rather than have-nots, recognised a negative when they saw one and Elfie was too honest not to agree with them. She admitted that she would prefer to be married, perhaps even, shameful thought though it was, perhaps even a little for the sake of the event as well as the condition. After all, marriage was a staging post in life and one she would be pleased to pass. However, she was aware that the chances of doing so were shrinking, for the quality of men was likely to grow poorer and the choice smaller as she became older. Worse still, her work confined her increasingly to the world of upper-class Bohemia; no more interesting, just more spoilt, more silly and markedly less heterosexual than most. There was no doubt that starting from scratch in her late thirties to make a match would be even tougher than it had proved a decade ago.

When Elfie first saw her future husband, he was standing patiently before her in a queue beside a damasked table, awaiting his portion of summer pudding, a disorientating choice for a New Year's Eve buffet and one, moreover, which must have come straight out of a freezer. The queue was slow-moving. To pass the time, Elfie was calculating how much money her hosts had wasted on their pompous curtain swags and how much better she would have spent it, when a shoulder blocked her line of vision. Dark, aloof and right-angled, no dandruff, no scurf; her interest started stirring. She swivelled sideways for a better view and what she saw looked cheering. Silent and apparently alone, or unattended anyway, a handsome profile was examining the silver teaspoons.

'Are they Hester Bateman?' asked Elfie.

How awful: it had sounded like showing off. Knowledge was often more suitably kept private and at a party it could seem a vanity offence. But she had suddenly recognised the cool oval of their shape, the work of a rare woman silversmith working in the eighteenth century, and Elfie had spoken in sudden pleasure before pausing to think of herself.

The shoulder registered surprise, by turning in stages towards her, rather than in a single fluent movement. Almost immediately Elfie wished she had stayed silent. It would have

37

been nicer to have met so racy a prospect on another evening. Tonight she was not at her best; red-nosed from a cold, pink-eyed from contact lenses and flaunting a pre-period pimple just like any teenager, an irritating event at her dignified age. Elfie had begun to flush when she noticed that the profile of the hawk face was smiling and its eyes were dark and warm.

'Not bad,' said Hugh. 'Well actually, that's rather good.' And she realised the compliment was meant for her and not the spoons.

By the time she had started to work for him, at first only occasionally on a painting or its frame, then more frequently, they had been together for three months. Quite long enough for her to recognise his energy, short temper and high standards; indeed, for a man who had knocked about the world, he had retained an awful lot of sharp edges. None of which would make him easy to live with, but she did think she could love him and thought she could love him even more if her reservoir of emotion had not been so enormously drained in recent years. So utterly damn well exhausted wondering how often her married Anthony was fucking his wife, whether she should murder her or poison him, whether he or she was the greater wimp—he, for staying with his wife; she, Elfie, for staying with him. And meanwhile those years had ticked by: one, two, three, four, prime time years spent in learning the art of patience, recrimination and self-denial. Years when her universe was filled and all her potential was blocked by the single figure of one unworthy man. To the east, west, north and south there had been nothing but Anthony. Dear God, such a fool she had been, to have sacrificed herself on the altar of any man.

Hugh, in contrast, did not seem to exact any sacrifice. They shared the same knowledge, similar tastes and complementary work, which seemed to add up to an identical outlook. Nor did his possessions demand any sacrifice. His children were grown-up and his cat, an ageing relic of his first marriage, was an undemanding moggie. In addition, he had a beautiful yellow-stone Cotswold house and a garden he adored. He even had an income and no alimony, which alone would have signalled perfection. Nor was his age the slightest barrier. Indeed, he had made strenuous efforts to be 'new man' rather than an older man: in the first eight months they lived together, he cooked 10lb of strawberry jam, 26lb of gooseberry and 2lb of sloe, the latter still, as it happened, uneaten in the larder. He was tender, loving, grateful and faithful, as he had originally been with his first wife. Though he drove a hard tempo at work, at home he was a happy man and an accommodating husband.

An accommodating husband though a reluctant father. He had explained to Elfie before they married that he felt too old for children now. 'Do you understand?' he had asked anxiously. 'I do understand, truly,' she had replied. 'Do you mind? Is it too much to deny you?' he had pressed her. 'Just being with you makes me happy,' said Elfie.

It was actually true. In the first years of their marriage they had both known much happiness, not ecstatic because passion does not often have a second wind, but grateful and blessed with the flavour of an Indian summer. They had worked together on their garden. Hugh had added old statues, a nineteenth-century figure of Pomona bearing a tray of apples, and a bronze Mercury on his way to give someone a message beside the formal pool. Elfie had collected antique plants: scented Victorian violets, patterned Paisley pinks and the double Queen Anne's jonquil—a pinched puff of yellow with such a heavenly perfume, though it had a frustrating habit of dying off. Then when the striped tabby died too, Elfie stamped their second marriage with a pair of Italian whippets who looked as if they had just stepped delicately out of a four-hundred-year-old painting.

Such happiness and gratitude until recently. Until, perhaps, though it was hard to nail the turning point, until Meredith became pregnant with her third baby. Was it only then she had realised that Meredith had a future whereas she, Elfie, was surrounded by the past. Suddenly everywhere she looked was old: the house, the dogs, the plants, the garden, her paintings, his furniture, Hugh, and soon indeed herself. Suffocated by the past, she yearned to replace it with the future. For the previous five years, her body had produced those chemicals that give joy. Now these endorphins had seemingly left her to dance attendance on another person's body.

Whose happy body and where she did not know, nor did she care. All she knew was that she had passed the first staging post in life and it had not proved enough. All it had done was to give her an unforeseen hunger for that second milestone, which was motherhood. Who would have thought it? The compulsions of birth, marriage, motherhood and death. I must be a patient and understanding wife, Elfie told herself, I am the luckiest of women and must stand by my promise. But looming behind Hugh, she could see the long, cast shadow of Anthony and those four years of pointless patience. Only a fool makes the same mistake twice.

CHAPTER FOUR

'We're taking it to Martha Dacre.'

Nick had to shout for the second time above the noise of the van. Old Walter was growing not only forgetful but deaf.

Walter blew through his lips and rammed his

woollen cap further onto his head. It was evident he had chosen this morning to have one of his funny turns, short periods when he seemed to absent himself. On these days Nick had to work very hard to fire Walter into action of any kind. He would usually turn the cranking handle once or twice by asking Walter two questions about his past. The first about Doreen with whom he had a roll in the hay at the age of twelve, which was a memory still guaranteed to spark a brain cell sixty years later. The second, even more inflammatory, was normally about his wife with whom sexual relations had been extinguished thirty years ago. These two questions, when asked in conjunction, almost always generated more than the sum of their parts. But neither overture had worked this morning. It was clearly going to be one of those funny turns which could only be brought to a close by a good fat tip. Martha Dacre was an unlikely source for a donation.

Nick remembered the last sphinx he had delivered to her only a couple of months ago. It had been pouring with rain and she had kept changing her mind where this bloody mythical creature should go. He had tugged his trolley this way and that, conscious that her daughter Tabitha, whose skirts were trimmed to the level of her teasing crotch, was watching from the window.

'Take 'ee down 'ere,' commanded Walter,

directing operations with all the aplomb of one whom age has kicked upstairs and who has acquired a young underling. The trolley had eventually been grounded in the mud and he, Tarzan, had been forced to send for humiliating reinforcements.

If only, Nick thought now, if only Dad were still alive and I could have stayed at my old school, I'd have stuffed Tabitha at the age of fourteen, instead of learning on 'ten-fags' Donna—a reference to a classmate who would go the whole way for half a packet of cigarettes.

'She locked me out,' said Walter suddenly.

So that was it, realised Nick. Walter's wife, Maisie, would sometimes push him out of the door first thing in the morning and bolt it behind him. It was her method of sending him to work, whether to potter in the Lyles's garden or in the antiques van. He was, in fact, well into his pensionable years, but Maisie demanded more than his pension. On his long travels together with Walter, Nick had learned a thing or two about domestic tyranny. Maisie, an *éminence grise* whom he had yet to meet, was the most exigent of housewives, on account, Walter had once lugubriously said, of the burden she suffered in life with her back passage. 'Eat neatly, Walter,' she would warn at mealtimes. 'Out,' she ordered if he began to cough. 'Drive slowly—*five miles* an hour,' on those rare occasions when they were in sufficient harmony to embark on a car journey,

Maisie in the back wearing a felt church hat, Walter the chauffeur of their old straw-yellow Fiesta.

Nick glanced at him sympathetically. All he could see was Walter's profile: a nutcracker jaw with his pipe clenched in between, rigid as a spirit level. He realised Walter must be terribly depressed. Even his accent, a barometer of his mental wellbeing, had disappeared. Waxing and waning, it was prone to develop its ripest rusticities in his manic phase. This morning, however, it had been crushed out of existence. Oh God, thought Nick, I'll have to let him direct operations again today.

He turned the van left into the drive to Mrs Dacre's house. Its pretty seventeenth-century stone façade with its three storeys of round-topped windows was visible through the white flowering crab apples that foamed over the gravel entrance. Pulling up outside the coach house, which was used for garaging, he jumped out of the van. Temperamentally unable to saunter, he walked with deliberate sturdiness to the front door. Aware of the possibility of mocking Tabitha-shaped eyes at the window, he felt muscle-bound as sometimes happened before a key rugby match.

'Ah,' said Martha, opening the door.

He noticed a blur of loose grey trousers and a navy-ribbed top, but he was trying to focus beyond her into the hall.

'Follow me,' she ordered, but confusingly

advanced towards Nick, forcing him to step back suddenly. There was an outraged screech as he trod on the Burmese cat's grey tail. He had failed to notice it at Mrs Dacre's ankles, a matching extremity to her flannel trousers.

She led him purposefully round the side of the house, past the canal pool and under the rose arches spanning the path that bisected the back lawn, out of the far end and into a small hedged garden with swags of grey foliage and white flowers. It seemed leafy and bowery, scented too. He noticed that the sphinx he had brought last time was half-hidden to one side of the exit.

'We didn't put that there,' he blurted out.

'No, we moved it,' she said.

It occurred to him that his blood, sweat and humiliation had been for nothing, but then he was just a humble delivery boy: it was his to do or die until he made it to the ruling classes, when he would bloody well make sure he could wreak vengeance on his substitute.

'Adam,' she called. 'Felix.' Mrs Dacre turned back. 'We have some help for you this time.'

Two bare-chested, brown-backed boys emerged from the garden. Lissom gods, they must have recently emanated from the party pages in *Tatler*. They half-grinned at Nick, he nodded back; rival teams, but two against one, gentlemen versus the tradesman. They followed him back up the path to help manhandle the sphinx from the trolley. Walter will have a complete breakdown, thought Nick, when he sees this lot. No directing us now. The three of them rolled the stone beast, already slabbed on its trolley, carefully from the van's electric tail-lift onto the ground and wheeled it back along the path.

'What a fearful excursion,' said Felix to Adam.

'Wait for me,' called Walter, stumbling along behind.

To his right, at the entrance to the swimming pool enclosure, Nick could see a blouse on the ground. Was it Tabitha? Topless?

'Here,' said Mrs Dacre, as they reappeared in the white garden. A woman of few words, she was pointing under a tree, on the opposite side of the path to the first sphinx. The three boys rolled the trolley to the location and began to transfer the animal to its new lair, Adam and Felix at its head, Nick at its rear, literally handling the lion's share. Sweat began to pour off him at the weight. His neck expanded another half an inch under the pressure.

From behind, he could hear Walter. He had freaked out completely.

'Snowy, flowy, blowy,
Showery, flowery, bowery,
Hoppy, floppy, croppy,
Breezy, sneezy, freezy.'

he was reciting.

They corresponded to the months of the

46

year, and at the very worst moments of his life, Walter ran their soothing, incantatory flow through his mind like the beads on a rosary.

Oh Jesus, thought Nick. I hope they don't think this nutter is my father. He thought of saying 'my father is dead' but it didn't seem entirely appropriate.

'That's quite charming, no, perhaps a little bit more to the right. See? he has a good and a bad profile,' said Mrs Dacre as her little team of oxen placed the statue on the ground. She stepped forward admiringly and brought a branch or two of a silver, willowy shrub over its muzzle. She bent to pick a white aquilegia and held it fastidiously to one side and then the other of the sphinx, wondering where she should plant it. The men were panting. The sun had come out from the rain clouds and it was hot.

Martha alone failed to hear the sudden intense buzzing in the air. By the time she looked up, a throbbing jet of bees had entered the little white garden, invading its space tumultuously, flooding its four corners, their thousand million transparent and sunlit wings vibrating furiously, directing their flow first towards one sphinx, then the other, then finally to Nick, in preference to his two sweatless companions, alighting on him, taking wing, throbbing and then settling again.

He stood, rooted, despairing, knowing he must stand solid and impervious, a statue

47

himself. The sound rang in his ears like a tinnitus. He heard Martha's little shriek, then the quick patter of her feet down the path. He heard 'Oh Christ' from Adam and Felix, who had retreated to a safe distance. He thought sadly of Tabitha. Then he heard Walter: 'Hoppy, floppy, croppy,' he was saying triumphantly. From within the veil of bees, Nick could hear his accent had returned. Walter, a failure with the wife, was a master of bees.

'Stand 'ee still,' he ordered. 'Fetch a box, you bumblepuppy,' he told Adam, as the bees began to form a cluster.

Abandoned but for Walter, Nick remained motionless. Beside him the blank stone gaze of the sphinx turned outwards, indifferent to the bees settling on its face. Beyond, Martha and Felix watched aghast. Walter alone seemed relaxed. Fumbling slowly in his pocket, he brought out a box of matches and re-lit his pipe. He sucked, it flared, he spat, he sucked again, inhaled deeply, then blew the smoke into the clearing. He repeated the process to excess. What's he up to? wondered Nick.

'Bring it here,' said Walter to Adam who had returned nervously with a box.

Puffing like a steam train, Walter advanced on the bees which had now grouped, a black beard on the nearest sphinx's face. In his right hand he held out the box. His left steadied the pipe in his mouth. He blew a stream of smoke.

The river of vapour floated into the swarm, around, above and below. Wreathed in clouds, the bees began to stir, they shivered apart with unease. They hummed messages of anxiety to one another. A few stray fearful workers sought refuge in the box, then more, then a swelling retinue.

Walter puffed on: in, out, in, out, the mighty engine behind his rib-cage rising and falling. The docile trail of bees flowed forwards. You old miracle worker, thought Nick. Adam, Felix and Martha, the latter fanning herself lightly, peered perplexed from their haven. Before them, the little brown man continued. Like an ancient ritual masque, the pageant unfurled in its slow mysterious way, with the pied piper cajoling the swarm of bees inside his box.

*　　*　　*

At the same hour in Wiltshire, Judith Coles was interrupted by a telephone call from her sister, Elfie, during lunch. Her husband, Giles, immersed in his newspaper, paid little attention, but on its periphery he registered a series of exclamations and clucks. Large and rumpled, he tried in vain to huddle further into his chair, knowing his wife would demand his audience at any moment now.

'Poor old Sis,' said Judith out loud to herself, replacing the telephone receiver in its cradle on the kitchen wall. She returned to sit at the lunch table.

'Poor old Sis,' she repeated to her husband who was invisible behind the *Telegraph*. She noticed that *The Times*, his preferred professional choice, had been dropped on the floor.

'Mmmm,' Giles agreed. His was a valiant attempt to prevent a discussion about human problems. He had learnt over the years that little supportive noises might be sufficient to save him from having to think.

'One does have such sympathy for them both of course. Poor Hugh as well as Elfie. It's an awful dilemma.'

Judith eyed the sheet of the newspaper that faced her from Giles's side of the table. Page three of the *Telegraph*. A man had locked his wife in a box. She donned her long-distance spectacles and read it for a moment, then re-launched.

'What do you think, Giles?'

It was a heavyweight missile. He winced but held the paper steady.

'Well,' he began. 'Not quite sure really.'

'I think,' said Judith ruminatively, 'it is probably a surprise case of *Torschlusspanik*.'

The doodlebug of a noun rocketed towards him and managed a hit. His paper wavered.

'And what, pray, is that?'

'Literally, panic at the shutting of the gate. In Elfie's case, terror that the womb is closing down. It's pre-pre-menopausal.'

Giles had been going to lay down the *Telegraph* in total submission, but the mention of the menopause stiffened his resolve.

'It stems from the fear that the opportunity to have a child will be lost forever. Giles, are you listening to me?'

'I am indeed. It sounds awful.'

'What have I just said?'

'Something about the menopause. As always.'

'God almighty.'

Judith rose in exasperation and seized the newspaper. Most of it came away easily, though he was left with a small triangular patch in his right fist which had tightened as a defensive reflex. He let it flutter to the floor and surrendered. He looked at his wife. She was pyramidal, including her head. She had never been sexy, nor even graceful like her sister, Elfie, whose femininity was a mystery to him, but she had been a good bossy wife, a good mother and she had continued to feel right to him for thirty-five years and he hoped for another fifteen, no, say twenty-five if they were lucky and his job as a country solicitor didn't finish him off too early with all its need for new-fangled competitiveness.

'OK.' He abandoned his burrow. 'What do you want me to say?'

'I want to know who you agree with.'

'Well.' Giles began carefully since he wished to avoid taking sides, especially about in-laws

51

which could lead to the rocky foothills of a row. 'I do understand both points of view. But anyone who marries an older man knows the score. You remember the old chestnut?'

'What?' asked Judith.

'The wife as a young man's fancy, a middle-aged man's companion. And an old man's nurse.'

He settled into his ladderback chair, ash with a rush seat, one of a matching set, all purchased from Hugh for £1800 when they had moved six years ago to their Wiltshire house near Aldbourne. It still rankled with Giles that he had not been offered a family discount.

'To some extent it still fits,' he continued, 'especially with serial monogamy. After all, this is the age of the specialist.'

'Hang on. I've been a jack of all trades and a master of none as far as you're concerned.'

'Too true,' he agreed affectionately. 'No bloody good at any of them.'

'So you sympathise with Hugh?'

'No. I didn't say that. I never sympathise with Hugh. All I mean is that Elfie was grown-up and knew the situation.'

'And she should have adjusted.'

'Yes.'

'Why not Hugh? Why shouldn't he adjust? What if she had a little accident?'

It was a subversive thought and not at all like Judith. He was surprised at her. His legal brain rebelled.

'It wouldn't be an accident.'

'But how would you react if you were Hugh?'

'I don't know,' said Giles. 'Honestly, I don't.'

It wasn't actually true. He knew he wouldn't like it at all. Married to Judith for this length of time, he would hate to imagine another wife driving her ruthless course through his credos and fixations. Judith was quite bossy enough but at least she played straight.

'Well,' said Judith, rising to her feet. 'All I can say is that it's a problem and we ought to cheer her up.'

'Don't make the mistake of interfering.'

'I'm not. All I have in mind is a jaunt next week to the Chelsea Flower Show with us. She can applaud Andy's first big display.' Judith and Giles had two children, Lucinda, a cookery book editor, and Andrew, five years younger, who had designed a collection of garden furniture.

Giles screwed up his features, his upper lip nearly touching his long overhanging nose.

'She can come, but it means we'll have to ask Hugh.'

'I can't exclude him.'

Giles's face switched to outright grumpiness.

'Right. That's settled then.'

She stood up and looked around for the next promising object to organise. Surveying the debris on the lunch table, she remembered some leftovers that needed to be eaten up from the fridge. She walked over, opened its door and peered in. There were a couple of yesterday's pilchards in sauce, the rind of a slice of Cheddar and half a peach. She scraped a small patch of mould from its surface, transferred all the delicacies to a pretty plate and ferried it ceremoniously to the table.

'Bin,' she said to Giles. 'Where's the bin?'

He closed his eyes and opened his mouth, his expression one of duty. As she leaned over him with the food, he brushed his lips against her ample breast.

'No, Giles.'

'It's only a nuzzle,' said Giles. 'Or is it sexual harassment now? Or even rape?'

*   *   *

'I am warning you,' Martha shouted after Philip, but he had escaped into the garden, desperate to exchange his wasp of a wife for his soothing bees. It was nine o'clock on Friday evening, nearly twelve hours after Walter had teased the swarm into a box in the white garden. Walking down the path, Philip smiled to himself, enchanted by the ingenuity which had inspired the old man to blow smoke from his pipe to coax them into captivity.

Entering the white garden, he looked about him for the box which the bees had entered. There was silence here compared with the tumult of this morning's invasion. It was dark and cool, perfumed with a heavy scent from the arching wands of smilacina. White honesty lit up the black corners. He noticed a single snowy aquilegia flower lying, picked, on the grass beside the new sphinx and wondered why it had been so rudely dropped and neglected. The box was nearby, upside down, mouth to the grass though tilted up on a stone so that the bees could fly in and out. He picked it up and closed it, remarking before he did so that the insects had already begun to form a wisp of comb, the first stage of the palace of wax they were destined to assemble.

Holding the box he went to fetch a wide flat board from the potting shed and then made his way to the new hive he had set an hour before on the boundary of the garden, far from any of Martha's artistic or social activities. This at least would be safe from her bile, which was more than could be said about the first two hives. He had explained yet again to her that he could not move them until winter when they would be semi-dormant. That if he did so now, they would simply return to their former location, taking as a marker the surrounding trees, flowers, pebbles, indeed the entire programme of their old map. But Martha had no wish to understand. He anticipated a summer of excoriation. She would be much happier if he concentrated on his other hobby: rose-breeding, something that amused her for its decorative potential and its dinner-party value.

It was a calm evening with dark clouds and little wind. He bent down to the new hive and placed the board at its entrance, tilting it so that it was raised towards the mouth of the hive, forming a wide drawbridge over which the bees could advance upwards. Their instinct was to walk up rather than down. He paused for a moment, making sure that all was in order and the board stable, connecting with the entrance to the hive. Then he upended the bees' box onto its flat wooden surface. He shook it as casually as if he were trying to drop heavy fruit from a tree. The huge cluster tumbled out, unsuspecting, dazed, bewildered to hit a new strange world. Philip shook the box again to detach the remaining stray bees. He knew they wouldn't sting him at the moment. There were times when they were savage and menacing, but not now, not after swarming when they were peaceful, even ecstatic, still laden with the honey they had taken from their own hive, the golden booty they had plundered before seeking their next home.

Philip watched closely. This was always an extraordinary moment, one of the great noble mysteries of beekeeping, or indeed the natural world. Would they enter the new strange abode? Spread out on the board to form a radiating fan, the bees had started to align themselves so that their heads were facing the hive. He watched the little signallers at the entrance. Their heads were dipped, iridescent wings fanning, their bottoms lifted. Then suddenly, with feverish swiftness, the message spread. The dark ranks of bees, in their thousands, bowed their heads and raised their abdomens. Philip, lying on the ground, saw the little white spot beneath the tail, each bee celebrating and signalling with a display of its small white spot, thousands upon thousands.

The prodigious mass began to move, at first slowly into the mouth of the hive, then in an unstoppable wave. He looked for the queen who was always hard to see. Somewhere—shy, fearful and seeking darkness—she would be guarded by her handmaidens.

He could not see her and knew the chance to find her was now past as the bees were pouring into the hive. Within moments they would be housed in their new city. They would transform it into a crystalised mansion of mathematically precise spaces; a kaleidoscope of hexagons, perhaps one hundred thousand, each fragrant, cleaned, rigorously organised. Philip found their obedience to their destiny awesome, as always.

CHAPTER FIVE

Although Elfie was genuinely fond of her sister, she had hesitated before accepting her proposal to visit the Chelsea Flower Show. Later she wondered why. It wasn't that she doubted its entertainment: she and Hugh attended most years. Nor that she lacked an interest in her nephew Andy's display of seats. Was it rather that she had enjoyed a sufficiency of other people's families recently? In her present mood, she feared that Judith's son was coming too swiftly into focus after Hugh's daughter. You old sourpuss, she thought, and pushed all reservations aside. As always, the show should be tremendous fun.

Andy had wangled them tickets for the private viewing on Press Day. They had planned an early arrival but in the event were all delayed.

'You're late,' said Elfie when they came to pick her up.

'A little local difficulty,' answered Judith at which Giles shot her a warning look. She decided not to add that Giles had caused a half-hour hold-up because of his failure to achieve a motion, the omission of which always reduced him to unease about the day ahead.

It was therefore later than expected when the trio set off, all of them nursing their own private anxieties, Judith worried about Andy, Giles about himself and Elfie about her future.

Giles in particular was in a huff. He longed for a man's company, even Hugh's, but his brother-in-law was at the call of a client in Cheltenham and would be unable to join them until the early afternoon. He had no choice but to sit it out with the women of the family until after lunchtime.

*   *   *

It was eleven o'clock when they emerged
blinking into Royal Hospital Road, near the
site of the great Chelsea showgrounds.

'These are the boring bits,' said Elfie as they
pottered past the tools, books and sundries at
the entrance. She paused while Judith tried to
haul Giles away from a Japanese tractor mower
which was the size of a tank. Giles had always
pined for a ride-on. It was humiliating to admit
that they lacked a lawn large enough to require
it. Two changes of gear and it would have
crashed into a border and been forced to turn
round. Should they move houses? he
wondered. With a name like Giles, he felt he
deserved a tractor mower. 'How big is your
garden?' the salesman enquired on the stand.
Giles waited until his wife and sister-in-law had
moved safely out of earshot. 'Oh, quite a few
acres,' he said.

Elfie waved Judith goodbye and set forth for
the marquee, her favourite part of the show
where the nurseries displayed the gorgeousness
of their wares. It was always other-worldly here
for the flower arrangements could manage to
escape the constraints of the garden.
Intoxicated by the very first stand she
encountered, she gazed in wonderment at the
dark globes of purple alliums mingling with the

milky plumes of some smilacina.

'It's bloody ridiculous of course,' said a journalist who was scribbling behind her. 'The one needs sun and the other moist shade.'

Elfie spun round to snub her ingratitude, but she had already fled in search of the next victim.

Meanwhile, Judith was walking her circuit of the showground to track down Andy. She paused to consult her little map. She would have to march along Northern Road, past the conservatories, and down Western Avenue and into Southern Road where most of the garden stonework, statuary and furniture were assembled. She felt her heart start to race in empathy for her only son. Little Andy had been shy about his seats; the artist had shrunk from unveiling his canvas before even an indulgent family. She caught sight of Elfie who had emerged for a breather from the moist heat of the marquee. Elfie was beckoning. Damn, thought Judith, whose only interest in the show pertained to her son, but she dived back into the tent in response to the summons.

'Do look,' said Elfie, pointing to a huge sheaf of deepest violet velvet streptocarpus. 'Isn't it fit for a nineteenth-century French interior?'

'Lovely,' agreed Judith, pausing a tactful second before the stand, its plants cascading like a bishop's mantle, 'but it's really crucial we find Andy.'

The two set off together this time, past a line of conservatories, berthed like glittering yachts at rest. Giles was to be glimpsed in the top storey of a double-tiered glasshouse, lying back in a recliner and sipping a drink. He saw his wife and sister-in-law in the throng below, sat up and waved happily from his crystal palace to their ant-sized figures below. He had entirely forgotten about his inability to pass a motion that morning. In fact he was on cloud nine in his eyrie in the sky. 'How big is your house?' the conservatory saleswoman had asked him. 'Oh. Some acres,' Giles had replied.

By now the throng was thickening, clearly swollen by a fair proportion of members of the public. Some, like themselves, had networked to attend on a privileged day; others were nosing around in advance of the evening's gala preview at £150 a ticket. The judges and spectators were jotting little notes in their books: good, bad and failed, they wrote with a flourish. Ticks and crosses flew around the arena, gold, silver and bronze awarded and withheld. Some nurserymen had turned pale.

'Can you see me shaking?' asked Melanie Hall, a specialist in period plants from whom Elfie bought regularly. Both she and her husband looked grey. They had risen at dawn the previous day to assemble their stand and had slept the night in their van. 'Never again,' groaned Melanie. 'She says that every year,' said her husband.

Two stands along, a knot of people were gathered around an exhibit of more dubious taste.

'This one is, let us call it, an open communicator,' said a public relations rep, displaying a scarlet rose with a golden boss.

'What a darling flower,' exclaimed an American woman over a brown rose. Dressed in sunglasses and a black blazer, she was fanning herself with a swatch of urn catalogues. Elfie noticed that urns were everywhere, resplendent for the hostess with the mostest. She looked round to nudge her sister, but she had long since deserted, exasperated with the slowness of her pace.

Walking through a line of espalier apples with nice stretched-out arms and legs, (not sad thalidomide plants like Hugh's cordons), Elfie now found herself in the area of the show which was devoted to gardens. She leaned over the gate of the first to enjoy its horrors. Proudly presented by a national newspaper, it had a thatched shed, Shinto arch and a Barclays bankful of orange azaleas. A woman beside her took off her panama hat and fanned herself in disgust. 'It's simply dreadful,' she said to the newspaper's gardening correspondent, who was seated glumly by the entrance, clutching a besom broom.

'Don't blame me. We just bought it,' he said tetchily.

'What's that thatched shed for?' she pointed.

'It's to hide our thatched gnomes in,' he replied.

In the foreground, a man in short navy bermudas and a woman in green trousers were putting the finishing touches.

'What's that plant called?' asked Elfie, pointing to a creeper with a flurry of ultramarine blossom.

'Don't ask us,' said the girl. 'We haven't the faintest idea. We're the garden designers.'

'It is *Parochetus communis*,' said a reedy, androgynous voice from behind Elfie, 'and it shouldn't be blooming now. What have you done to the poor darling to so upset it?'

Elfie wandered on, alternately appalled and enthralled. The exhibits seemed to be growing ever more outrageous, each mirage replacing the last. Here was the grouse moor garden, complete with heath, shotguns and an amazed bird.

'What is this?' asked Elfie.

'We are upgrading the suburban image of heather with the gardening public from the shires,' replied a man in wellies and a wax jacket.

Though a valiant attempt, it was the neighbouring stand that had drawn even more visitors: a Bach fugue garden laid out by students who had decided to manicure a score in box.

'*Das stimmt nicht*. They have got that wrong,' said a Middle European voice of the professorial type. '*Es geht so*: tum-te-tum-tum-tum.' He beckoned the leading student over to sing the corrected version into his unappreciative ear.

'Pedant,' muttered a photographer who had voted it the most photogenic garden of the show.

'Seen anything of Judith?' asked Giles, suddenly appearing at Elfie's elbow. He was prominently displaying a leaflet for a £60,000 conservatory. Behind it were more serviceable little brochures on moles, aphids, capsid bug, leaf miners and hoppers, each apparently with its own publicity representative. Giles was also carrying a box of compost marked 'Lion Droppings'. 'It includes the armpit smell,' he said. 'A great deterrent to deer.'

'I didn't know you had deer.' Elfie was startled. It was hard to imagine in a high-walled village garden of an eighth of an acre.

'Oh yes,' said Giles, disappearing again. He had indeed become slightly confused by now about both the nature and size of his own garden, fantasy having merged with reality since setting off early this morning.

The experience was becoming surreal. In a daze, Elfie joined the huge clot of people standing by the grandest garden of the show.

'I say,' said a woman in a £200 cream straw hat from Harvey Nichols.

'I've got hay fever,' wailed a little girl with a sneezing fit.

'It's all these frightful flowers,' said her mother to Elfie.

She shouldered her way to the front row and gasped at the Persian garden spread out before her. A leaflet of explanation was thrust into her hand. Designed on a great right-angled cross, it symbolised the four quarters of the universe divided by four large rivers. The walls were surmounted with narrow beds of flowers and covered with glazed tiles. A tree laden with fruit like the golden apples of the hesperides hung over the water.

'Rivers,' said Elfie. 'For goodness' sake. What will they do next?'

'It's hubris of course,' said the woman in the hat.

'How do you make the tree fruit now?' asked a man at her elbow.

'Secret,' said the designer. He wondered if the Araldite would hold the apples firm until the end of the week.

Elfie, impressed but exhausted, slipped away. She felt as if she had been hallucinating for the last couple of hours. She found she had now reached the periphery of the show. The dozens of little gardens overfilled with blooms, belvederes and bombast had ended and here was a London street. She turned to resume her search for Andy and Judith and stared straight into the eye of an elderly man sitting by a striped canvas partition. She instinctively looked down and saw that he, and a younger

65

companion, were in fact exhibitors. Spread around them, no plant higher than a few inches, was an elaborate design of clipped dwarf shrubs in greys and greens, graded to produce a charming, aromatic mosaic. Beyond the gaudy partition of the neighbouring stand, the show now seemed like a raucous carnival whirling above this moment of calm.

'Wonderful.' She clapped her hands. The two men, who were now standing, gave a small polite bow and presented her with a leaflet.

'Thank you so much. This is the best thing here today.' The men nodded again. Speech was clearly not their language.

As Elfie turned, she suddenly saw Judith and Andy. Giles was in the background, facing away from them, fanning himself with his brochures. Judith's face was red. It was wearing a brave smile.

'Look at our clever son.' She pointed vaguely in the direction of some seats.

'Where are they all?' asked Elfie. 'These?'

She could see two nearby seats, respectable wrought-iron jobs in that chic colour of gunmetal blue, as good as a freemason's handshake in all the smart Gloucestershire gardens, and trickling everywhere by now.

'Not those drab little jobs,' said Andy scornfully. 'They're on the next-door stand. Mine are here.'

His gold ear-ring sparkled in his right ear and, as he turned to point, she saw the sun flash

66

from his bared midriff. Peering more closely, she traced it to a small gold bangle in his navel.

'See?' His arm embraced a collection of what appeared to be painted plaster statues but it was hard to discern their theme. Giles's fanning accelerated. He cast a yearning look at the neighbour's blue iron seats.

'Andy has taken casts of his own seat,' explained Judith. 'His theme is the seat as sculpture. Clever, isn't it?'

The pyramid of her outline seemed to embrace him like a mother hen spreading over chicks.

'Face facts,' said Giles crisply. 'There comes a time when you have to sit down on a seat.'

'Dad. Everyone makes those.'

'Yes,' said Giles, 'because everyone can sell those. Has anyone placed an order for these?'

Giles's sense of reality, so notably absent for the last few hours, had suddenly been restored to him. The truth, gritty but bracing, emerged from the mists of fantasy. It provoked him to action. He walked over to the litter bin and dumped his mower and conservatory leaflets. He kept those on aphids and leaf hoppers. Pests would always be with him.

Andy looked furious. He felt outrageously misunderstood. A country solicitor in a rut, what would his father know? Giles's sense of reality took another step forward, a large one. As he looked at the expression on his son's face, he could see another tap for a loan heaving up over the horizon. He feared he would have to shell out for his children until they were forty at least. Ah, the unfairness of it that he should have a son with artistic and vegetarian leanings. Everyone else's child was a merchant banker and a carnivore.

Judith thought: how enchanting children are when they are little, how problematic when they grow old. The ages of thirteen to twenty-six in sons could be dreadful. Andy had another year to go before he escaped the trough. She must protect him from Giles's impatience until then. Their expectations of him had been too high and disappointment was the reason that clouds had temporarily shaded the sun. She remembered Andy's face when he was four years old: its busyness; its large, eager eyes; its transparencies of emotion. She thought of the loggerheads of parents and sons.

Elfie looked away and in the distance noticed Hugh walking towards them. Surprised, she glanced at her watch. It was two o'clock, past lunchtime. She waved at her husband who had stopped to admire a stand. Perhaps I am mad to press Hugh for a child, thought Elfie. What Hugh says is perfectly true. If I had a baby now, by the time he reached Andy's age, which is only 25, Hugh would be 87, or more probably, dead. What do I do?

'Thank God. Hugh,' said Giles, relieved to see his brother-in-law in the distance. He felt he had suffered a sufficiency of women and children. Another male—adult, seasoned, hard-headed—was what he required.

'Oh God, Hugh.' Judith suddenly remembered that, with all her worries this morning, she had forgotten to have a talk with Elfie. She turned away from her first chick, Andy, to her secondary chick and put a mothering arm around her sister. She drew her to one side, out of reach of the men who were in any case unawares, Andy still smouldering, Giles walking towards Hugh.

'I meant to have a word with you earlier,' Judith whispered. 'The answer to your problem might be to have an accident. You were one, after all. Talk to Mummy.'

'I don't know what you mean,' said Elfie, trying to wriggle out of her sister's grasp as Hugh bore down on them with a shower of leaflets. Christ, Judith, she thought: nosy, blundering, tactless, no grip on subtleties. She ought by now to realise that well-meaning thoughts were by definition destined to be ill-received.

'I thought we might update our tractor mower,' said Hugh, bestowing a brochure on Elfie.

In the background, a muscle spasm passed over Giles's face.

'By the way,' Hugh added, 'You know Meredith has been here. She was leaving just as I arrived.'

Elfie stood still, listening. She forgot about

Andy. She felt the memory of Meredith and Albert stir within her. She was surprised to find her core of need was still solid and intact: it would seem to be a survivor. Judith's whisper rustled in her brain: an accident.

CHAPTER SIX

Elfie's parents, Lydia and Ronnie Weston, lived in a village near Ludlow. Over the last thirty years, they had moved from Reigate, to Gloucestershire, and now Shropshire. Retreating north and west, they had plotted their blue line through the Tory counties of England, liquifying capital en route by moving into smaller and smaller houses, though larger and larger gardens which was madness. Lydia feared they had not reached the end of their moves but the prospect of a last stage oppressed her. A bungalow beckoned, a low-lying snake in the grass, waiting to trap them in their tottery old age when frailty had made them too weak to resist.

Lydia had an aversion to bungalows, which seemed a waiting room for death. In their prime, Lydia and Ronnie had lived in a three-storey house, then traded down to two, but a bungalow was one and therefore preceded the last stage when they would sink underground, when down was a prelude to out. She had been given a reminder of this yesterday afternoon when Ronnie had told her that friends in a neighbouring village were moving into a single-storeyed house. He was clipping the rogue yew in the hedge into the shape of a rabbit as he spoke.

'So you see, some people are sensible.'

'Foolish, is all I can say. I give them a year.'

'Gloomy and doomy as usual.' Snip, snip, he pointed the rabbit's ears more sharply.

'Not at all. Rather them than us.'

'You never liked them much anyway,' he grunted as he bent down to reach the scut.

'Quite. Good riddance. Stuff both of 'em into a bungalow.'

Stuff 'em all actually, but please God spare us. Then she thought how awful that fobbing off death should have become so elaborate and poisonous a pastime. Peculiar too in the circumstances. Here they were, the pair of them, in their early eighties and still complete. Their full quota of organs and most of their own teeth.

This problem had stayed with her overnight and she was still pondering it this morning as she picked up her needlepoint and walked out to the terrace. It was a bright, fresh day to sit on the lichened seat and watch Ronnie at the end of the garden planting two trees. He was really too old, poor darling, and had been forced to bequeath the digging to Cyril who was almost too old as well. However, Ronnie still wanted to put the trees in himself. Like the Queen, he

71

recognised a ceremonial aspect to planting trees, which consisted of one royal shovelful of earth followed by interment.

'Why trees?' she had asked. 'We're not the ones to benefit. You're mad to plant trees at your age.' She corrected herself: 'Our age.'

'Hope doesn't get less because one's old,' he had explained. 'A long life doesn't mean more hope or a very short life less.'

He had looked fondly at the two infant trees he was holding in his hand, twin sweet chestnuts for the eastern and western boundaries. Far too big, certainly, but she thought they would look quite wonderful for the inhabitants of this planet in the Year of our Lord 2100. If her own and Ronnie's immediate successors in the house didn't dig them up meanwhile, of course.

'Hope is in the trees,' he had said simply, inspired by the 400-year-old giant chestnuts he had admired at Croft Castle.

Lydia could not see this, but then Ronnie was an optimist and she a pessimist, which was presumably why they had married. How long ago it seemed: in the hot summer that preceded the outbreak of the Second World War. She felt she had been married to him from time immemorial: through bombs, blitzes, Harold Wilson's grubby little government, the miners' strike. They had fought and survived all these and no man or woman had put them asunder, but now death and a bungalow threatened.

Her needle moved arthritically over the canvas of the cushion cover in her hand. Rich pink oriental peonies, shaded and golden-bossed, floating against a navy background, her own design like all her cushion covers. Now and again, she moved her feet up and down on the ground as though she were walking. It was important to keep the circulation uncongested. One didn't want traffic jams in the calf. They could lead to a bungalow.

As she worked, glancing up frequently at Ronnie's stooping back in the distance, she thought that if only Elfie and Hugh had a baby, she would feel rejuvenated. Judith's two children were now so grown up, they scarcely counted as offspring; in any case, they only made duty calls once a year at Christmas and were in no haste to provide her with great-grandchildren. But if Elfie were to have an infant, it would give a great cyclical surge to Ronnie and herself, a little diversion before death. It might prevent her daily scan of the obituary columns:

BATESON—JACK, On 28 May, passed away (of what?) *at Rawnsdale Nursing Home, dearly loved husband of Beatrice Anne* . . .

DALTON—On 28 May after a brave fight (against what?),
MOLLY, aged 82, dear mother of Anne, Robin

and Thomas . . .

WESTON—on (precisely when?—would it help to know?),
LYDIA, after fobbing off (what?), *gloomy and doomy wife of Ronnie,* (beloved?) *mother of Judith and Delphine, who has never forgiven her for the name and prefers to be known as Elfie . . .*

Yes, doubtless, a grandchild would help to disperse all that. 'You would like a youngster to play with, wouldn't you?' she asked Ben, the old cocker spaniel who had plodded after her onto the terrace. He looked up at his leader's voice; weepy-eyed, grey round the muzzle, and thoroughly gaga. 'Well I would anyway.'

She paused in the middle of her diagonal stitch. Absurd, it should be impossible to discuss it with Elfie who dismissed all interest as intrusion. Not at all like Judith who usually wallowed in a boisterous and intimate chat. Though even she, after hinting at problems, had been boring and clammed tight shut. Well, if my daughters won't tell me, I must take courage and demand an explanation, thought Lydia, next week when Elfie comes. What's the point in having a full set of teeth and organs but no guts.

*   *   *

74

It would have been preferable, thought Elfie, if Hugh had not offered to drive her to Shropshire, but had left her to go alone. There was a country house sale of antiques in the Marches, a bit abstruse perhaps, he had added, but he was keen to attend. She had considered switching the day of her visit so that she could shake him loose, but it would look churlish at the last moment. It would also seem suspect. Elfie was conscious she was beginning to concern herself with plausibilities rather than truths.

They set off on the Friday following the Chelsea Show, leaving Susan as usual in charge. It was a brilliant day with that clear crystalline light of early summer. The ground was hard and dewy as though there had been a good sharp frost overnight. As they drove along, Hugh thought to himself that they should spend more time together. Their old companionability had leaked away recently, and he was anxious to restore links. He yearned to demonstrate that, though adamant in one direction, he was flexible in all others and attentive to her needs.

'Happy?' He took her right hand in his, keeping his own on the steering wheel.

'Mmm.'

'Nice for just the two of us to be sneaking off for the day. We should make more trips together like this.'

'You're going to spend today working.'

'I'd love you to come.'

'I can't just drop in on my parents and push off.'

'Of course not. Not today anyway. All I mean is we should make a point of enjoying the freedom of just a twosome.'

'Mmmm.'

He glanced sideways. It occurred to him that his efforts were fruitless. It was water he was pushing uphill, a substance as resistant as it was elusive.

The drive took two hours. After a pleasant exchange of platitudes about the journey and the weather, Hugh left his in-laws and drove over to the sale. He rarely attended such occasions now, and then only on his own behalf and never for the ring. In any case, he had never belonged to a ring, that illegal group of dealers who struck an agreement before an auction that only one should bid, thereby avoiding the inevitable increase in price if the professionals bid against each other. Hugh was too much of a loner and had arrived too late in the trade. He had never been accepted as one of 'the boys', nor had he wished it; indeed, his aloofness and independent contacts had been a matter of chagrin to the others.

He parked his car in the field reserved for vehicles before the large old manorial farmhouse, a grey timbered affair at the stage of ripe decay. An aged spinster had died here a few months ago, having mouldered the last ten

76

years of her life amongst the family inheritance. Such a situation was a not uncommon one, and Hugh had some idea of the type of business even before he glanced at his catalogue. Yes, all was for sale, the usual curate's egg of surprising extremes: from job lots of broken flower pots to some nice brown Georgian, including a George I walnut settee and a desirable long-case clock. The middle range was largely shipping furniture which once upon a time he would have bought and transported in containers to Europe and America. In the early days the pantechnicons used to pick his stuff up every Monday, a weekly arrangement that had set him up for life. Now he was rather more selective and specialist.

Once upon a time, too, he would have enjoyed an auction like today's with its triple appeal to the gambler, the salesman and the collector within him. Now that he was in his sixties, he found such occasions infinitely more poignant. It wasn't simply his age. It was also the fact that sales had become more ruthless. Nothing was held sacred. He remembered a fragment of James II's heart in a box which had been sold at Bonham's two summers before. Not that he expected human remains here, but anything more suitable would be scavenged.

He now stood in the middle of the throng and stared round the large marquee where the late Miss Stella Dunn's intimate possessions were exposed, catalogued and numbered to the world. Here was the residue of a whole lifetime, to be picked over, scrutinised and assessed by nosybeaks and vultures. Was this all that one left behind from one's tiny pilgrimage on earth? He picked up a fur cape; it was small, fit for a pair of thin, depleted shoulders such as only the very old possessed. She would have worn this every Sunday morning at the church which he had noticed a mile down the hill: a quaint affair with little pointed angels at the four corners of the plinth beneath its central spire. He noted a large collection of stuffed birds, many of them exotic, little iridescent humming-birds, poised eternally in flight against a sheaf of grass. They, poor things, had predeceased Miss Dunn by a century at least, doomed to be preserved in perpetual purgatorial motion.

On the far side of the wall, overhanging some railings, was a group of ancestral tapestries: faded, even bird-dunged in some cases, they depicted the four seasons though age had long since turned summer's green to autumn's rust. He noticed a fifth: the Rape of the Sabine Women. Funny to think Miss Dunn had lived on close terms with that. But then familiarity took the sting out of even the most eccentric experiences, and people too for that matter.

He sighed and then pushed his sentiments aside. The professional in him now stood up to be counted. He walked over to a walnut chest of lovely colour and patination, pulled out the drawers to assess the grain and direction of the lining—nice that it was oak. Checked the top wasn't reveneered which would reduce its value and satisfied himself that the handles, keyplates and bracket feet were original. He then moved over to the longcase clock and raised his eyebrows. Here indeed was a matter for surprise. The lovely thing before him was untouched and perfectly proportioned. Long and slender in outline, it had a slim 42-inch door and a fine herringbone inlay. He opened its top and ran the tips of his fingers over the brass engraving on its face. Such elegant spandrels. His touch was sensitive as though he were reading Braille or making love to his wife.

Methodically for an hour he continued to scan other items of furniture like a laser. Then, armed with a paddle with which to announce his bids, he settled down to wait. The auctioneer who would be the life and soul of the party for the next few hours, had called for attention. The celebration of the last rites had begun. Miss Dunn was on her way.

*   *   *

Right, thought Lydia, as she waved goodbye to Hugh. She had also despatched Ronnie to the shop to buy two *undented*, *unrusted* tins of tuna for lunch, ten mushrooms but only if *very* fresh, and two pounds of *good* apples. He had only just left after converting all the underlined superlatives on her list to bad. With a house now empty of men, she anticipated the talk with her daughter.

'All right, Elfie?' she asked consolingly, passing her daughter a coffee. She thought she looked pale.

Elfie smiled back, though with little conviction.

Of late she had found it affecting to see her mother and father at these intervals. The signs of age seemed to proceed in fits and starts. After a rapid onset ten years ago, both parents had then appeared to have settled into that steady trough of old age when longevity is taken for granted. A little osteoarthritis, slightly raised blood pressure, a degree of diabetes in her father's case, all these had been accepted and embraced. Age was only a paper tiger. Or was it? Elfie had the feeling of movement below the surface, unseen, like subsidence. At the edge of the canvas, the spaniel was clearly on his last legs. The whippets, fastidious to excess as always, gave him a wide berth.

Mother and daughter, alike in bearing and gesture rather than looks, walked through the house and out of the French windows to the garden. Lydia steered her to the seat and table. They sat down side by side, looking out at the grass. If she faces me, thought Lydia, she won't talk. Two greenfinches were pecking at the nearby bird table, their strong bills cracking seeds. They were nesting in the ivy on the little cottage, the presence of the ivy in itself a bone of contention: Ronnie maintaining it pulled the house down, Lydia claiming it held it up.

In front of them the grass was uncut and looked neglected.

'Gardener has got a hernia, blast it,' said Lydia. 'It's hard to get gardeners. For what we pay, you have to take them with hernias.'

'Mean isn't the word for it. You could pay a little more.'

'You in *your* position might think that. But not us in *ours*.'

Elfie awaited the onset of her familiar and therefore reassuring flow. The price of Cyril, the gardener; the age of the car; how their outgoings regularly exceeded their income. Her mother was trundling round her ancient and enjoyable run.

'For a start,' said Lydia, 'this retail price index is nonsense. Anything *I* want to buy inflates by ten per cent a month.'

'Don't save your money for us.'

'We're not keeping it for you. We're keeping it for us. The cost of a good death is dreadful.'

'Stop talking about dying.'

'I wouldn't except at our age there's nothing else that's as big ahead. Except—' Lydia felt the words coming. They seemed balder than intended. She took a gulp of coffee to swallow

81

them but, too late, for she heard them escape. 'I just wish you'd hurry up and give us a grandchild,' she spluttered. 'I know it's not my business but I'll be dead soon so who cares what I say now.'

There was silence. The greenfinches hammered away. Oh God, she thought, one shouldn't hide one's clumsiness behind the skirts of old age. She remembered Elfie's sensitivities as a child. No one changed in life. She looked round on a tide of remorse. Elfie was staring down.

'I can't. Hugh doesn't want one. He won't change his mind.' She spoke explosively, the wall of reticence broken.

'Hugh. Hugh doesn't *want* one. *Hugh*.' The name was expelled in a gasp of breath. All Lydia's emotion converged on her son-in-law who was standing in the way of her grandchild. 'Hugh,' she repeated. Who the hell did these men think they were? Just bloody bystanders to the event. She looked at the cocker spaniel whom she had had castrated in his second year.

'Hugh.'

'Shut up,' said Elfie. She resolved not to air the topic any further. Other people's emotion exhausted her more than her own.

'*Hugh*. That he should have reduced you to a supplicant. My own daughter. For my own grandchild. Hugh.'

'I should never have told you. Just stop going on about it.' Elfie's eyes filled with tears.

'Just fucking well have one anyway,' said Lydia.

Elfie noticed a biscuit crumb on the right side of her mouth. She was simultaneously shocked by the swearword, which was the larger gobbet to drop from her mother's mouth. The old shouldn't watch television so much. All that violence and bad language set an appalling example.

'By now I'm probably too old anyway to have one just like that.'

'Nonsense.' Lydia banged her fist on the table, the blue veins on her hand standing out with her vehemence. 'You lot make far too much fuss about it. In the 1930s, one in every five women had children in their forties.'

'How do you know?' Elfie was startled.

'I looked it up,' said Lydia slyly, 'when I knew I was going to have you. You were an accident, remember? On that holiday we took after the war in France. Why we called you Delphine, remember?' She looked hard at her daughter. 'I DIDN'T WANT YOU,' she added to make quite sure she understood.

'Oh,' said Elfie. 'Oh you didn't, did you.'

'Loved you when I got you, of course.' Lydia patted her hand. 'Why don't you have an accident? Easy as pie.'

This is irredeemably coarse, thought Elfie fastidiously. I'm the only person with a sense of responsibility towards my husband's needs.

She nonetheless persisted. 'How did it

happen? I've forgotten.'

'I was given a wonderful new foam. It wasn't so marvellous. I became pregnant.'

Elfie stared at the garden. She had last sat here in March when bulbs were pushing through the soil and the resting-buds of herbaceous plants were erupting into leaf. All were now in full swing. It was invigorating to think of her own life force, unique and quintessential, thrusting through the barriers of human science.

'And Daddy? What did he say?'

'After the initial shock he adjusted. Men usually do.'

'Do they indeed. Hugh's different.'

'Oh is he?' Lydia was sceptical of the notion that one man should differ from another. Age levelled out most differences and death the lot. 'And why doesn't our lord and master want one?'

'He says he's too old. He's already got heaps of grandchildren.'

'Too old. He should be in his second wind by now.'

The idea that Hugh had his fill of grandchildren infuriated Lydia afresh. Wrath spurred her to action. She got up and walked round and round the terrace, banging her shin on the spout of the watering can. Her generation, she realised, was the last to have any fight in them. One needed a Second World War every twenty years to put stuffing into

84

people's spirits. Men of straw, the lot.

There was the puttering sound of a slowly driven car coming up the lane. It braked to turn into the garage. It was Ronnie, creeping along cautiously in order to keep a safe hold on his driving licence.

'Don't you dare say anything to Daddy,' warned Elfie. 'And as for Hugh, I'll kill you if he learns I've discussed it with you.'

Elfie could see the ripples spreading onwards and upwards. Throw a tiny pebble in the pool and a flood emerged.

'Just remember,' said Lydia, 'marriage is a conflict of interests and the one who is the more determined usually wins.'

'The rest of us think it should be give and take.'

'Quite so. Give and take. Believe me, it evens out in the end.' She turned away. 'Got the food, Ronnie,' she called out to the giver who was now climbing the three steps to the terrace.

*   *   *

They sat in silence on the journey back home, Elfie at the wheel, Hugh with his eyes closed, though evidently not asleep, in the passenger seat. Gardens and orchards flashed past, the last stray apple blossom shining in the dusk, the vague shapes of sheep just visible, breathing quietly and at rest beneath the canopies of trees. She glimpsed a pig in one garden, rotund and peaceful. The road sang and hummed different tunes as they travelled its changes of paving. Elfie thought of her father planting big trees, his choice of giants that would exceed his life span which must soon draw to a close. The last acts of a long existence. She thought of her mother's hunger for a grandchild, spurred by the same need.

'Elfie.' Hugh had stirred. 'It was rather sad today.'

'Yes.'

It was simpler to agree. She did not want to talk about the sadness of his day, when hers had experienced its own share of emotion. She thought of her own accidental existence and marvelled at the arbitrary and unpredictable ways of life. Extraordinary that she should prove so unstoppable. The primaeval swamp was everywhere, clearly within her as well as without if she acted swiftly.

Hugh put out his hand to touch hers on the wheel. He felt suddenly vulnerable. She let his rest there because she felt sorry for him, sorry for them both that they could not reach an harmonious agreement about a matter of importance. The conflict of two differing needs lay between them, a gap in age and attitude that could not be breached by the making of jam. She felt tender towards him because she now knew that she would no longer be fobbed off with the deception that he might consider a child, when it was manifest he neither would, nor, perhaps, even could. She glanced at his face, dark, older, more lined when at rest than in movement. Him, or me? she had wondered, who comes first? Poor dear Hugh, she thought, as she felt the calm weight of decision settle within her.

*   *   *

That night, she tucked her new exquisitely contoured and tailored diaphragm into the far reaches of her drawer, and made love to Hugh for the first time without any form of protection. She knew there was little chance of conceiving at this stage and saw it as a trial run, a test in part to see if he were aware of its absence or presence. It was a Wednesday night, outside their usual schedule that had evolved over the last few years, but she was keen to re-establish the more spontaneous rhythm of their first year together.

She felt close to him, welcoming his dark face moving above hers, the familiar weight and shape in her arms, the strange intimacy within her. She felt profoundly stirred and excited. They repeated as they had so many hundreds of times their repertoire of movements. Her hand rested between his shoulder blades, whilst he pulled the core of her towards him, dipping his face into her neck and lemon-scented hair. She felt the thump of his heart against her rib-cage, the breakout of sweat on his skin beneath her hand, and she came, which was the trigger for his response, the kicking movement, the slow groan. They lay entangled. The green smell of wet grass came in through the window and she could hear the newly emerged ash leaves rustling outside. A tawny owl, affirming his territory, was hooting to his mate.

CHAPTER SEVEN

A week later Hugh's son, Rupert, was eating a supper of tomatoes on toast in his sister Meredith's big Wimbledon kitchen. He had arrived with the christening present of a large cheque for his new nephew, Albert, and had expected a decent dinner at least in return, but the evening had turned out unforeseeably otherwise. The nanny had a night off, his brother-in-law was stuck in Colombo and he, Rupert, was the only captive grown-up for miles. As a result of helping out, he had half his nieces' bathwater over his tailor's dark grey suit and few thanks from Meredith.

He had finally succeeded in lulling Mona, the three-year-old, to sleep with a reading of *Winnie the Pooh*. He had started to enjoy his own funny noises as Piglet and Pooh but, as he listened to himself, he feared he was sounding increasingly like Alan Bennett. He saw his destiny if he failed to find a wife and children quickly. The bachelor uncle, in quaint, camp orbit four times a year around his sister's children. The trouble was that Kristina, whom he happened to be in love with, was recently divorced and in no haste for re-entanglement.

'She wants none of it. No strings attached at all,' he said to Meredith, helping himself to a dollop of HP sauce.

'That's mine,' said Florence who, at six, was the eldest. Though it was nearly nine o'clock, she was still up and eating with them which was one of her *droits de* senior.

'This is for you.' Meredith pushed some Lea & Perrins towards Rupert. 'That other ghastly stuff is what the nanny lets them have. Their values go to pot from the age of two these days.'

'Their style, I think you mean, not their values.' Privately Rupert doubted whether his sister could distinguish between the two. 'Anyway, I like HP sauce. It gives me the feel good factor of escaping from the kennel.'

He attacked his tomatoes on toast with renewed vigour, though the good feelings to which he had referred were already tainted by the foreboding that there might be nothing more to come.

'No,' he said, 'Kristina wants none of this.' He gestured around the kitchen, embracing the domestic clutter of toys, Albert at the breast, the HP sauce, and Amos, the golden retriever on his rug.

'*Moi non plus,*' said Meredith suddenly.

Rupert looked up in surprise. 'But I thought you loved it. You do nothing but breed. Sorry—.' He stopped himself en route to glancing at Florence which would have given the game away. '*Avoir* bags of *enfants.*'

'Daddy wants us—and more of us,' said Florence, her enchanting face radiant with the satisfaction of trumping the grown-ups. She beamed from one to the other, her long fine fair hair trailing over her pyjama jacket shoulders.

Meredith raised her eyebrows and pushed her mouth forward. 'She has a friend at the Lycée. I forgot.' She turned to her daughter. 'Florence, why don't you run upstairs and check whether Mona is asleep. I'm sure I heard a little cheep.'

'She's asleep,' said Florence, determined not to release her hold on the tiller.

Meredith shrugged. She judged her tough enough to listen without a shield. Nothing could dent the me at the heart of Florence's six-year-old world.

'It's true.' She looked down at Albert who had fallen asleep at the nipple. 'George wants four. Never mind the quality, feel the quantity.'

'He can afford them.' George was a merchant banker.

'That's what it's about. He wants to show he can afford them, and a Norland nanny in a

90

brown uniform. Never mind me.'

Rupert felt irritated. The speed and range of women's resentment was gigantic.

'Come on, Merry. This is crap. You've never struck any of us as the little woman. You wouldn't go along with all this if you didn't want it too.'

Sod it, he thought, the pretence. It was always women who had control over this area of life. Look at Kristina.

'Crap,' interposed Florence. 'Crappy, crappy.' She looked expectantly from one to the other, awaiting the silent awe that usually ensued whilst grown-ups wondered how to deal with this sort of word. None was forthcoming. Meredith's attention was locked on herself. She was silent.

She is smouldering in her padded cell of Wimbledon, thought Rupert. With a second cell in the Cotswolds—where was it?, he tried to remember—ah yes, Great Rissington, a pretty grey stone cell overlooking a very English green. He had a sudden vision that she would do a bunk one day like their mother. He glanced at Florence. It was awful to foresee patterns threatening to repeat themselves.

'Ridiculous isn't it,' said Meredith. 'Here's me burdened with three and a fourth likely. Whilst my resentful old stepmother is steaming for one.'

'How do you know?'

'I just know.'

'Pa doesn't want any more.'

'How do *you* know?'

'He told me when he married.'

'He doesn't tell me anything. He just talks about carpets and chattels.'

Rupert was unsurprised and not displeased. Hugh had always been more forthcoming to him. Merry was her mother's daughter, he his father's son, a division entrenched by the break-up of the marriage. Conversely, it had drawn brother and sister slightly closer for the first time in their lives, temporary orphans. The relationship had stuck. They had little in common, but their experience *à deux* of a shared past prevented a total drift apart.

As he reflected, he registered a snuffly noise from behind.

'I'm not asleep.' The sudden unnecessary confession came from the doorway. Mona was standing there, blancmange pink and rumpled. Her pyjamas were pale yellow with little black Indian temples.

'Pooh and Piglet are,' said Rupert warningly. 'Fast asleep. They have flaked out utterly.' He added, 'They know which side their bread's buttered on.'

He closed his eyes and snored encouragingly to set an example—but, a mere amateur, he had already sent the wrong signal.

'I want some bread and butter,' said Mona, reminded of food rather than sleep, and seizing at this expedient straw. 'And honey too.'

She put a thumb in her mouth and walked in a wobbly line to Rupert's chair where she made imperious up-signs with her arms to indicate her desire to be lifted.

'She likes men,' said Meredith. 'She doesn't see much of George. He seems to be away three months on the trot sometimes.'

She rose to fetch the pot of honey. The bread was already on the table on a large wooden board with a carved wreath of wheat round its perimeter.

'Watch me do a handstand,' said Florence, driven to desperate measures by the loss of her power-base.

She did a cartwheel instead at a 45-degree angle to the floor. The kitchen though spacious was not adequate to her needs. Her foot touched the edge of the wooden table in its downwards arc and toppled her over. Her face puckered; she thought about crying and then did so.

'What a baby,' said Mona, placidly feeding honey soldiers into her mouth. She sat in perfect calm at the eye of the brewing storm she had caused.

Albert woke at the noise and decided to join in.

'Oh God,' said Meredith.

An hour later, Rupert left. Mona was back in bed, Florence and Albert too, whilst Meredith was already undressing as he called goodbye from the hall. He had mopped honey from the floor and put the plates in the dishwasher. He had been prevailed upon to do his Pooh and Piglet voices once more and thought it would probably be a year before he called again. He reckoned that his christening cheque for Albert had been large enough to buy him his absence.

As he let himself out of the door, he noticed the large Isuzu Trooper stabled on the drive. It was all ready for tomorrow's school run, preparing itself for its gallop over the rustic potholes and hurdles of Wimbledon's suburban tarmac. He walked in the warm night to his own car, thinking that he was thirty-four and out of sync with the lifestage of his own age group. He felt isolated and lonely. Tomorrow he faced the usual high-pitched demands of running a futures fund. He sat in the car and rang Kristina on his mobile. The evening had left him detumescent and exhausted, but he wanted to wish her goodnight. She should be back in her small mews house by now. There was no answer. The bitch. He felt the need to say, 'Watch me do a cartwheel, Kristina,' but there would still be no answer. I want to be George, he thought to himself. Well, George without Meredith anyway.

CHAPTER EIGHT

It had been arranged that Martha and Philip should play tennis at the Lyles' on Saturday afternoon. Although invited only a week ago, the guests, as so often happens, had meanwhile become unwanted: a convenient idea now seemed merely bizarre. Hugh regretted that he had ever agreed to his wife's ridiculous suggestion. A dinner party was the preferred treatment for a useful client and if Elfie didn't wish to talk to Martha, she should have lumped it. That was the essence of trade.

Hugh was in a bad mood anyway, one of those black intolerant episodes when people seemed uniformly stupid and the world inclined to malevolence. The main van was off the road so he had been forced to commission another to pick up the pieces from the auction. Then Nick had knocked a small piece of veneer from a desk he was transporting. And yesterday a well-known captain of industry had bought three statues for his garden: the *putti* from the courtyard, a boy with a dolphin for his pool and a happy blackamoor beneath a sundial. They were good prices and it should normally have been a moment of satisfaction but, even as Hugh pocketed the cheque, he felt the old niggle of resentment that had never entirely left him. He was reminded that, a former small captain himself, he was now relegated to serving the needs of these movers and shakers. Hugh felt the gulf between them. It occurred to him that an outsider might deem him equal but different from such clients. It would be nearer the infuriating truth, thought Hugh, that he was unequal but the same.

As it happened, Philip would also have preferred to cancel the afternoon's tennis. He regretted it was impossible: a mixed double was a fixture, a good-natured occasion, requiring tolerance from both sexes. Yet it seemed inappropriate with the Lyles. In all his dealings with Hugh, at the rare drinks evenings or garden parties, three in as many years, he had detected a note of condescension, the *de haut en bas* of the old guard public schoolboy of his generation for a self-made meritocrat like him.

'This is daft,' he said to Martha on the journey. 'Why are we going? I don't even like him.'

'Because I think we should know them better,' she replied curtly. 'Besides, I want to see their garden in daylight.'

Because he's smart, thought Philip. Because you can talk walnut and silver with him whereas I can only talk about swirly patterns on the carpet and moquette three-piece suites. He was surprised to find that he disliked Hugh quite strongly. Previously his feelings had been diluted by the fact that he was only going to see him in the anonymous crush of a throng. He thought now that perhaps it was appropriate that hand-to-hand combat should be arranged for this afternoon. He glanced at Martha beside him. She was wearing a cap-sleeved white silk shirt, slim shorts and a long, loose white cashmere cardigan. A white band held her dark hair back from her brow. He could smell her perfume in the new car they were driving. It was feral, a man's scent, *Eau Sauvage*, which dated her but had doubtless returned to vogue. He snatched another brief look. This was life-style tennis, all right. She had been critical of his old white cellular tennis shirt. Philip began to brace himself for the afternoon that lay ahead.

'How lovely,' Martha exclaimed when they arrived. 'Such a good idea.'

She kissed Elfie on, or rather beside, both cheeks and passed her a net of twelve balls. 'One can never have enough of these,' she crooned.

Philip noticed how charming his wife had suddenly become: how quick and penetrating her manner, how absorbing her interest in those whom she wished to colonise. He extended his hand to Hugh who took it and nodded. His shirt felt scratchy.

'How very thoughtful,' said Hugh as Elfie had accepted the balls in silence.

'Oh look, what a wonderful golden pheasant.'

'He's a pain in the neck,' said Elfie, 'but Baglady would like to meet you instead.'

From a safe distance Martha inspected the little tortoiseshell cat which had wandered over. It was immediately apparent her shape was in some way odd.

'Is she all right?' she enquired tenderly.

'Fine. A bit flat as she was run over when

young.'

'Poor darling,' said Martha but refrained from picking her up.

There was a squawk at ankle level.

'Oh no, Philip,' said Martha. 'You haven't trodden on him.'

'I couldn't help it. He got under my feet.'

All four stared at one of Milo's long striped tail feathers which was lying detached on the ground.

'Sorry about that,' said Philip.

'Don't give it another thought,' said Elfie. 'It's his own fault. I'm always tripping over him. He will peck at one's heels.'

'Quite,' said Hugh. 'These ornamental jokers can be like that.'

Elfie shot him a look. Somehow, he had managed to convey the fact that his guest wouldn't have heard of a golden pheasant. She had a little premonition she was going to have a Hugh-shaped problem this afternoon.

'Shall we move on,' she said rapidly.

Leaving Milo and Baglady behind, they walked from the back of the house and through the secluded knot garden on their way to the hard tennis court. Martha paused, pressing her hands together. By way of reparation, she moved up another octane in ecstasy.

'So clever,' she said.

'It is partly based on a pattern shown in a sixteenth-century oil painting called *Spring*,' replied Elfie.

'Do I know it?' Martha frowned intelligently.

No, thought Philip, but he recognised that the ball was already in play.

'It is Dutch, by Lucas van Valkenborch, and shows two women either side of baskets of flowers with a formal patterned walled garden in the background.'

'Ah, yes,' said Martha.

Hugh looked thundery. He had just noticed the whippets had been scratching at the gravel paths in the knot garden. Both men were silent, impatient with the prattle. Philip was desperate to play, get the game over and shove off. His arms ached with the static load of inactivity.

The tennis court was screened behind high hedges of hornbeam. They spent the first ten minutes or so warming up, until the self-consciousness of running about in front of strange people began to fall away. Even Philip, as he relaxed, thought to his surprise that this was a civilised way of spending an afternoon with acquaintances. The air was mild and the sun warm enough to cast hazy shadows on the court. He remarked the different styles of the women, Elfie graceful with her long reach, his wife smaller, a ball-thumper to compensate. It was a year since he had played with her and was struck afresh by the strength of her hitting, but then she kept herself in trim, playing on most summery afternoons with friends. He noticed that both women were calling their husbands 'darling' a lot.

'Could you toss me the ball, darling?' called Martha.

Oleaginous, Philip considered, relishing the private use of a word he would never have the opportunity to utter in public.

'OK. Shall we start?' It was a command rather than a suggestion by Hugh.

He felt tense. He had a headache on waking this morning. Usually he prided himself on his agility, but he wondered briefly if he seemed old and past it to the others. He eyed Philip across the net: a sturdy, fair, determined sort who reeked of management training. The firm handshake, the demeanour deceptively geared to seem open, even when they sacked you. He was reminded for the second time this week of the takeover which had made him redundant. He remembered the fellow who had told him: a rubbery blokeish type with an open manner. Hugh felt a little spurt of energy as he looked across at Philip and danced lightly on the spot to await his serve.

The ball flew forward. Hugh opened his shoulders, he drew his arms back. His sixty-four-year-old tennis muscles were clenched. He awaited the satisfying thud in the middle of his racquet, thunder after lightning. Nothing. The ball had passed through him.

'Lovely,' called Elfie disloyally.

Hugh gave a curt nod of acknowledgement this time, and then again, for it happened twice.

Despite a subsequent rally, the first game

100

fell to Philip. It was now Hugh's turn to serve. He lost. At two games down, a sense of discomfiture began to prevail on his side of the court. He was followed by Martha who also fortunately lost but it was by now becoming apparent that Philip was playing uncompromisingly to win. The set looked destined to continue in the same manner as it had begun. The men had squared up.

At van-in during Hugh's service, the ball floated between him and Elfie.

'Yours,' he muttered.

'No. Your side of the line.'

'Keep your eye on the bloody ball.'

The 'darling' count had sunk to zero.

Martha looked quizzical as Philip took the first set at six games to two.

'Shall we have a pause?' offered Philip with the largesse of victory.

'No,' said Hugh.

'I think,' whispered Martha to her husband, as they returned to start the second set, 'I think it would be better-mannered to yield a little more.'

'Good manners never require condescension,' he replied.

'Oh God,' said Elfie charmingly as she fumbled the ball in the net. It was love-three.

Philip groaned with sympathy. He had bent over backwards to send her a chivalrous sequence of shots throughout the match. Elfie and Hugh walked to the net on their way to change ends. As Hugh bent to tie up the shoelace on his right foot, he said to Elfie, more loudly than was necessary for the distance his voice needed to travel: 'He has all the need to win of a grammar school boy'.

She froze, her eyes flicking instantaneously to their guests on the other side of the net. Martha was looking down; she registered nothing. Elfie glanced at Philip. For a split second he returned her gaze. He has heard, she thought, just as he was meant to hear. Hugh can be such a bastard and a fool. Her chest felt tight. She looked back at Philip, prepared this time for longer, but he had turned away. There is no alternative, thought Elfie returning to the court, but to go through the motions of the rest of this afternoon. Finish the game of tennis calmly, take Martha round the garden, offer them iced tea and sandwiches, say goodbye calmly, and then murder Hugh. Is it worth it? she wondered. The row and its nuclear fall-out would persist for three days—three precious fertile days, she reflected, turned to tundra.

'Ouch.' She was startled out of her reverie by an exclamation of pain from Philip who had been mugged by a ball from his wife. A circular patch of skin on his thigh went white and then slowly flushed red.

'Oh Lord,' called Martha. 'Poor you. It shot off the side of my racquet.' Her face was cool beneath her white visor.

Philip's eyes met Elfie's again as he ferreted

out the ball which had rebounded into the net.

'Target practice?' he whispered. They exchanged a conspiracy of smiles before a flurry of strokes recommenced.

'Your game,' called Elfie.

Finish it, decided Philip, thumping a weak forehand from Hugh into the corner triangle of the baseline. He was determined not to yield to the pressure of his host's remark. Biff, bang, wallop, he said to himself. He could feel Martha's gaze scorching his profile. 'I told you,' she had whispered when they had exchanged balls.

Undeterred, he now took the match with a flourishing smash.

Hugh shrugged minutely, once more an expert of the nuance. 'Really very well done,' he said as he shook hands at the net. He spoke encouragingly, as though to a thirteen-year-old boy. He had at last regained control of his competitiveness and was pleased to have found a mode of expression suitable to the occasion.

'I'm afraid I don't know about the effortless ascent of Parnassus,' said Philip, apparently all smiles and relaxation now. 'They didn't teach us that at grammar school. They just taught us to get there.' He left a tiny pause. 'They said it was the result that counts.'

He knew, even as he said it, that he was going a sentence too far, but the adrenalin provoked by the episode had propelled him beyond caring. It occurred to him there would be hell to come from his wife who had an appetite for the *petit drame*. Two matches on one Saturday afternoon, he thought. Oh God, marriage was such an acrimonious pastime.

Though hell was postponed by tea and a charming perambulation of the garden, it erupted in the car on the way home. However, the imposed delay had caused an exaggerated plunge in temperature, cooling the heat of fury to the ice of contempt.

'I really cannot believe,' said Martha, 'that you could be so utterly foolish.' She sat with head turned away, her posture one of rigid aversion.

'What do you expect? For me to go belly up in submission to the vanity of a fool?'

'It was mortifying.'

'For him?'

'For me.'

'You.' Philip hooted at a driver who had overtaken him on a bend. He felt infuriated that his wife was siding with Hugh rather than himself.

'Me. To be married to a man who has no idea how to behave.'

'Jesus Christ.' Philip smacked his hand on the wheel, once, twice. He had forgotten how quickly she could slide into an assassination of his character, like a seal into the water.

'I want you to apologise.'

'My God, if there's any apologising to do, it should be him. Anyway it's trivial.'

She is mad, he thought, a megalomaniac of pettiness. A simple tennis match and she thinks two meteorites collide. But he knew in an hour his anger would have abated and he would be left with a sense of despair at the gulf between them. Until now, he had maintained his marriage in a state of repair by two methods. First, by not taking issue, and secondly, by paying the bills which he saw as marriage rates, just like water rates, whose payment keeps the system flowing. Both methods had ensured a quiet life, but for the first time, he wondered how long he would continue.

CHAPTER NINE

Elfie was weeding in the little period garden she had planted two years ago. She liked to be alone here, especially in the early evening, as now, when the light fell aslant on the flowers, enriching their colours. This was her favourite part of the garden, a sanctuary and hers rather than Hugh's. It was a small secluded spot, south-facing, sheltered from the wind and hot when the sun shone, its warmth gathered up by the stone walls of its enclosure. Low hedges of lavender and santolina edged the beds, violet and lemon when they flowered. In spring it was filled with stately crown imperials, with pulsatillas and dusty auriculas. Then came the striped tulips and, after, the double bonnets of

105

aquilegias. Now Elfie awaited the full June burst of fringed and laced pinks. Already many had opened and were filling the air with their heavy scent of cloves.

She weeded methodically and with enjoyment. It was a nice task at this time of day. They were easy weeds with shallow roots, and it was one of the few jobs to give quick and immediately visible results. She sat on the brick basketweave path that flowed between the beds, and fed the weeds head first into a large bag beside her. She noticed a patch of groundsel was invading the fringed Scottish pink 'Cockenzie' and bent forward to the rescue but her attention was only half attached. She gave a little tug, yet it was the tennis match that still occupied her mind.

She had made a conscious decision the other night to avoid a row with Hugh. This was no new challenge for Elfie, but an old and familiar one. As in most marriages, where one partner habitually makes a fuss and the other smooths it over, she had become an expert in her field: the manipulation of their roles. She therefore knew in this particular case that she must tread carefully to avoid any suggestion of reproach. Hugh with a bad conscience and a black mood could be detonated by the slightest criticism. Elfie had therefore opted to act as the magnet for blame. 'Perhaps I was silly to suggest a match,' she had sighed. 'Yes,' agreed Hugh, 'bloody stupid,' but surprisingly added: 'So was

I. Pity but there it is. No doubt Martha will direct the stream of her favours elsewhere. Still, you win some and you lose some.' To Sonia Bannerman, his chief rival down the road, he suddenly thought, less philosophically. She had learned her trade on the third floor of a well-known department store, which caused him to frown.

Elfie now dropped the groundsel into the bag and moved mechanically on to the double campanulas, the milky white and blue peach-leafed bellflowers; widely grown in the eighteenth century, she loved these especially. For a few moments she concentrated on the simple task of clearing the ground around them, then paused and sat back on her heels, folding her loose blue cotton skirt around her knees. The sense of unfinished business still nagged at her, the feeling that she owed Philip an apology. She rubbed her fingers on a violet flowerhead of French lavender and sniffed the sharp oil reflectively, hoping its scent would clarify the problem in her mind. She assessed the possibilities. One stood out. In the confused falsities of their departure, the Dacres had left their net of twelve balls behind. It seemed to Elfie that she could use this as an excuse: return them and apologise at the same time if the opportunity presented itself. She was herself agreeably free of Hugh's orbit, for, in the never-ending search for new customers, he had bought into the big London fairs this month and would not escape for a couple of weeks.

It occurred to Elfie that if she made her visit on Saturday, she would stand a chance of seeing Philip rather than just Martha. If he was there, she would apologise; if Martha alone, then simply return the balls. She felt pleased to have decided on a course of action and not a little curious about its outcome. Hope he'll be there, she thought to herself as she returned to her weeding, refreshed by the prospect of an encounter. Meanwhile, she would tie up the deep rose-pink everlasting pea against the stone wall. It made a good background to the Madonna lilies, Bede's symbol of sanctity.

*　　*　　*

Philip was in London and visiting the offices of a company which was on his list of overhauls. He was now sitting at a table, explaining the concept of business process re-engineering. The chief executive and five senior managers were listening intently, the sixth with some cynicism.

'Business process re-engineering,' she said. 'BPR. I've heard it's short for Big People Reductions.'

'No.' Philip shook his head and raised a friendly smile at this piece of borrowed smartness. He remarked the contrast between the severity of her dark suit and the scarlet gloss of her lipstick. He recalled her name: Fenella Wickes. Immediately on entering the room, he had noticed her short skirt, her legs crossed high above the knee, her heel spikes. The type of woman who emitted mixed messages. A type who was plentiful and he abhorred it. The cow was looking at him now as though he were the pedlar of some quack remedy.

'No,' he said again. 'Workforces often need to be slashed, but this is not conventional downsizing, as we used to understand it.'

He could hear himself talking: the familiar bilgewater words and phrases, 'concepts', 'interpretions', 'cutting time and costs', 'boosting revenues'. He could hear the level, even tone he adopted on such occasions, a learnt mode of speech to reinforce the clarity of his explanations. 'A good mind will tunnel through a problem,' he was droning, 'leaving a route by which others will follow.' He shivered suddenly for the airconditioning in the room was cold.

The men in their grey suits leant forward in their anxiety to beat all competition. One tapped his teeth with a pencil. Poor orthodontics, Philip noted. He should find a better dentist or pay more.

He wondered about the nature of the team in front of him. Should he raise the latest management consultancy wheeze? It was the mode to devise teams of managers whose brains worked in complementary ways? The system was based on the split brain theories of the 1970s, which established that the left and right hemispheres of the head showed different qualities.

In principle, a model team of businessmen would comprise the logician, whose upper-left brain dominated his pattern of thinking; the administrator, largely at the mercy of his lower-left brain; the collaborator who was controlled by his lower-right brain; and the visionary who had an upper-right drift. It was fiction rather than fact since human beings were too messy and divergent to be so accurately pegged—but the degree of predictability was surprising.

Fenella Wickes, an upper-left type decided Philip, bent forward. The skin in the V of her open-neck shirt was lightly freckled.

'How do we restructure in full flight without crashing to the ground?' she asked crisply.

'According to surveys, nearly seventy per cent of large companies say they already have or are about to take part in BPR,' said Philip. 'Only seven per cent see it as a serious risk to stability.'

In a way he regretted knowing the questions and the answers. He had heard them so often that there were times when he would have preferred by far to record his message. But in effect, this was what happened on these occasions: his voice tape played and that inner core of him, the part that was absent and secret and sceptical, listened along with his audience. He wondered how many people he had been responsible for sacking in the past few years. Blood in the offices meant blood on his hands. The woman had been right to quote BPR as Big People Reductions. He didn't like her but she was right. It was inevitable. He wondered idly whether he had been wrong about her: maybe she was a lower-right sided manager instead, quick to recognise the personal aspect of problems. What junk, he said to himself. It must be the unease at home that had induced such introspection.

'Let us define the core processes that need changing,' said the chief executive, his one vanity a Jermyn Street haircut.

'Right,' said Philip and prepared to play his tape.

*　　　*　　　*

A last-minute failure of nerve did not prevent Elfie from setting forth on Saturday. It was the first time she had visited the Dacres' house which was nine miles away. She took the whippets with her to make the return of the tennis balls seem incidental to an outing. If dogs couldn't neutralise the embarrassment of an occasion, then nothing else would.

Nobody was about on her arrival, but the Lexus in the open barn held out the prospect of Philip at least. Feeling self-conscious, she knocked at the old studded wooden door once, and after a long wait, twice. She could smell the scent of a huge frilly pink rose that festooned the façade. A Burmese cat, silky and well-fed, emerged from a shrub under the window and arched passionately against her ankles, its tail held stiffly erect.

Elfie was on the point of turning away when the door was opened by a sleepy beautiful girl in her late teens. She seemed to have difficulty keeping her tilted grey eyes open. Elfie announced herself and asked for Philip—or Martha. The girl blinked, then bent to gather up the cat which had switched its allegiance to her ankles instead. She was barefooted. Even her feet were beautiful, or maybe, thought Elfie, just youthful. The demarcation line was often blurred.

Elfie trailed her round the outside of the house, until the girl pointed down the central path of the lawn, the journey proving too exhausting for her so early in the morning. Elfie continued alone, beside a canal pool, then under the rose arches which were starting to bloom, past a swimming-pool enclosure on the right, and a small white garden on the left. Oh God, of course, there were the famous sphinxes. 'Have I told 'ee what I did to the bees?' Walter had enquired of her the other day. 'Twice,' Elfie replied, then repented. 'You were so clever, Walter,' she said and prepared to listen for a third time.

This place is trouble, she now thought to herself. She swung her net of balls in her right hand: stupid thing, a hostage. It was silly to come, perhaps better to go. She had looked for Philip, he wasn't there, leave the blasted balls on the doorstep. She had rehearsed a little speech; it had puffed up in her mind, but it now felt too big for the occasion. Absurd to take things so seriously. These small breaches of manners were unimportant and scruples were misplaced. Acquaintances were regularly made and then shed, because someone went and 'did' something, and another took offence. Her footsteps faltered in sympathy with her doubts.

'Hello.'

Oh shit, she thought and turned round.

'Elfie. What are you doing?'

He was advancing towards her, laughing, dammit, he was laughing at her.

'You've not come to ask for a return match, have you?' He pointed at the balls.

'You left these behind. Martha left them.' She felt terribly silly. The little speech she was carrying in her head splintered in fragments in the face of laughter. The words, broken free from their moorings, were strewn irretrievably about her head.

'I shall hide them from Martha,' he said, taking the balls.

'I met your daughter.' She meant to imply that he could hide neither the tennis balls nor her visit, but it seemed too conspiratorial to

113

explain. She added, 'I came to say sorry.'

'I know,' he said. 'Forget it.'

'It was rude.'

'Rude? I haven't heard that word for twenty years. It was my mother's favourite word. How nice and old-fashioned.'

Teetering from one sensibility to another, Elfie now felt nettled rather than silly. She had braved it to come and the apology she had proffered was being rejected.

'Well,' she paused. 'I'd better go. I've left the dogs caged in the car.'

Indeed, she could hear a faint barking in the distance. The cat was probably sunning itself in front of their window, licking itself in indolence, stretching a teasing leg forward, smiling at them between each balletic movement.

'Don't go,' he said, stepping forward as though he wished to catch her, although it was merely to place the balls on a seat. 'It is really very kind of you to bother.'

She hesitated and looked at him with a moment's doubt. She noticed, as she had before, his blue-grey eyes with dark lashes. His face was lined but less masked than it had seemed the other day.

Her dithering now appeared to arouse his impatience. 'Come and see what I'm doing. Quick, I can't leave it. I think you might be interested.'

Though reluctant, she walked beside him

114

until they reached a junction. To the right, the path led to a vegetable garden and a large area of rosebeds, routinely rather than romantically organised. Ahead was a patch of rough grass with the famous beehives on the boundary. To the left, where he turned, two working glasshouses.

She looked around in silence as they entered the door of the first greenhouse. A few pots of roses, all cluster-flowered, were standing on a slatted bench. The air was warm and still, and there was a green smell, the familiar scent of all plants under glass, exhaling their ripe vegetable essence.

'I hybridise roses,' he explained. 'Or rather I try to do the odd one in what little time I have. Catch as catch can, actually.'

Elfie looked at him enchanted. 'I've never met a rose breeder before.'

'Oh no, not me. I only do a few a year. In any case, that's too grand a term for what is always chance.'

'But controlled chance.'

He glanced at her and shrugged. 'Like everything, or so one hopes.'

Turning back to the bench, he took one of the potted roses. Its flowers were shaded through hues of lilac and pink. She noticed a plastic bag tied over a bloom that had been robbed of its petals and stamens.

He pointed to it. 'This is the mother, the seed parent,' he said. 'I chose it because it was

115

the most perfect flower. A flower without a blemish. Its petals were still folded so it was unlikely to have been pollinated.'

Elfie leaned forward and peered through the outside of the little plastic cover. The mother rose was visible: plucked of all but her stigmas, perfect and immaculate. She could sniff the scent of the other flowers on the plant. They smelt lightly of apples.

'And this,' Philip continued, picking up a dark red velvety rose, a single stem which had been cut and placed in a jar. 'This will be the pollen parent, the father. I cut it last night and kept it indoors to protect it from insects.'

He bent forward to examine the flowerhead. He was privately anxious that in his brief exit from the greenhouse, an insect might have slipped through the door to plunder his booty; but no, the rose was its exquisite virginal self.

Elfie came close. She stood beside him, watching intently, her shoulder brushing his blue cotton shirt. She was only a few inches shorter.

'Look.' He was pointing with a pair of tweezers to the anthers, the stamens of which were male. 'The anthers have split open. See their pollen?'

She had little knowledge of botany, but could see the minute orange grains. She stared in fascination as he gently detached the crimson petals from the rose. They made a soft velvety potpourri on the bench. He then turned

116

back to the lilac rose, the mother. She saw him lift the small plastic bag from the head of its chosen stem.

'Now look,' said Philip. 'This is the big bit. It's done very simply.'

With the utmost sensitivity, he took the dark red rose he had just denuded of petals and applied its anthers to the newly uncovered lilac rose. The male organs brushed across the female, probing as delicately as a visiting honeybee.

'The stigmas are sticky.' He was speaking quietly as though louder decibels could disturb the plants. 'The pollen adheres.'

Elfie was silent. She and Walter had often pollinated the marrows in the vegetable garden, but it was prose compared with the poetry of making roses.

'If the cross takes and the hip swells, I'll sow the seeds in the autumn,' said Philip, tying the plastic cover carefully back over the head of his pollinated rose. 'There are usually about twenty of them. They'll bloom in their first year, though it may take two years before we know for sure if they're good or bad.'

He had resumed his normal voice and practicality. 'If they're rubbish, well. If not, if one's a quality rose,' he looked at her casually, 'we'll call it—what's your real name? You can't have been christened Elfie.'

'Delphine.'

'Hmmm. We'll call it Elfie if you like.'

She brushed back the hair that had fallen over her forehead, partly out of embarrassment caused by a compliment which she did not entirely want. She now moved away, nearer the door to indicate the withdrawal of herself.

'I suppose you know the rose gardens at Mottisfont Abbey,' she said smoothly to deflect the conversation to a third party. 'Someone told me it's the most beautiful rose garden in England.'

He laughed. 'I go there every year. You wouldn't like to come would you?'

The conversation had returned to her too quickly and she hesitated for a moment. Outside the sealed, silent world of the glasshouse, she could hear the dogs were still barking. She welcomed this evidence that another life was seeping in again.

'Well,' she paused, 'I'm not sure when.'

Now that the theatre was over, she felt a bit faint from the heat and still air. She fidgeted to open the door.

'Do. It's wonderful. You mustn't miss it.'

He was advancing, keeping pace as she retreated. Following her outside, he closed the door of the glasshouse behind him, checking its seal was intact. He had one more cross to make. She was still doubtful. Hugh would not wish to come, nor would he wish her to go.

'What about Martha?'

'Martha's not around much in June. It's her busiest month. Ascot, Wimbledon, even

Henley. Bags of social and sartorial obligations.'

He paused. He was on the brink of asking the mirror question—what about Hugh?—but instinct deterred him. It was for her to decide, not for him to enquire. She had still not said no, so he gauged that some degree of calculation was taking place.

'Would Thursday afternoon be convenient? Or even evening?' he offered delicately, adding, 'It's open some evenings for the roses.'

Hugh will still be away, thought Elfie. It was extremely tempting. She had always wanted to visit the garden. They had old French roses that one could find nowhere else.

'Perhaps,' she said, walking backwards again. 'I'll ring you.'

'Ring me here,' he said, pencilling in his London office number on a scrap of paper. 'I'll be here early in the week.'

After she had left, Philip returned to the glasshouse and looked at the precious newly pollinated seedhead inside the little bag. When mating the chosen rose, he had imagined the race of the pollen grains to the egg-cell in the ovary. It was an uncompromising contest in which there would be one winner whilst all the rest were losers. Already by now the pattern of the child roses had been determined: their colours, the hairs on their leaves, the thorns on their flesh. The marvels of the future bounded by a single hep. However, Philip now regretted

119

his offer to call its offspring Elfie. He had meant it lightly as a thank-you, but his gesture had crashed to the ground under the weight of its own corn. In any case, the promise would be difficult to enact. He grinned at the thought that he had yet to christen one Martha.

CHAPTER TEN

So they have gone to Mottisfont. How nice to be outside on a sunny day. It was almost a week later and Susan had a left-behind feeling as she stood staring out of the plate-glass window of the showroom at the pavements of tourists. There were times when she felt like the frozen spider at the centre of some web whilst all the world whirled around her, frantic with purpose and movement. A receiver, not a doer, her immobility oppressed her. Even Walter saw the world on his travels with Nick. Her only transit took her from her little home to the showroom every day, to and fro, there and back.

Occasionally, her day was brightened by a whiff of pheromones like Philip Dacre's who had called for Elfie. More usually they were middle-aged women. One had just bought a walnut desk which would give her legatees a little nugget to quarrel over. She had sold it at the usual ten per cent discount which would still allow Hugh his thirty per cent margin. It was not like the old days when he would charge a two hundred per cent mark-up. Before the recession there had been plenty of slack. One for the taxman, one for the buyer, and one for me, as the saying went.

She returned to her little desk and began to write labels. Hugh deplored the luvvies style which prevailed: *a darling little table, very rare and of perfect conformation*. Antiques for idiots, as he called it. In contrast the house style was sober and factual. *A good walnut secrétaire chest on chest*, she wrote in a firm black ink. *Note that top and bottom were made at the same time. Pigeon-holed top drawer, lip moulding to all drawers. Bracket feet restored and handles replaced. Good colour and patination. Early 18th century.* She paused, checked her instructions again and added *£15000*. She knew he would accept a ten per cent discount but no more.

The sound of the door opening made her look up. One day my knight will come but not from you lot, she thought assessing the flock of tourists who had just entered the shop. Two potential buyers to eight lookers, she reckoned, four times as many sheep as goats. Several were foreign and bore the unfettered air of the holidaymaker. The English, in contrast, were characteristic introverts. Classy antique shops repressed them even more than museums. Silent of foot and hushed of voice, they crept round on their knees.

'No ice cream in here,' Susan said in her most headmistressy manner. She rose from her

121

desk to usher an unruly French family trio to the door. Outside, the child turned round and made a gargoyle by pressing his nose against the windowpane. He then pulled out a banana and did a monkey dance. His mother smacked him and he emitted a French howl of pain.

'Really, not vairy Cotswold, is it?' said a Scotswoman sympathetically to Susan. She was wearing a Pringle jumper. She smiled up at her husband, also Pringled, with whom she had driven down from Perth two days ago. 'We are vairy Cotswold people, you know.'

'Can I help you,' asked Susan, 'or are you just browsing?'

'We were admiring that wee davenport in the window but we don't think we'll buy it today.'

'It's very—' she began, when her elbow was taken by a tall blonde woman in a well-engineered coat.

'*Bitte können Sie mir diese Bezeichnung* "Chippendale" *erklären?*'

Susan frowned, but helpfully. The Pringles seized the opportunity to melt quietly away.

'Could you very kindly explain Chippendale?' repeated her husband. 'You English are so good at antiques—and also fruit cake,' he added encouragingly, twinkling through his rimless spectacles.

'Thomas Chippendale lived from 1718 to 1779,' began Susan. 'He had a rococo style of decoration.' She stopped to think that she must pull her mind together. If Hugh were asked this question, he would show all the hauteur of the savant. 'Gothic and Chinese ornament, too.' She paused again. 'But more moderate than his drawings, you understand.' What a muddle I make the poor fellow sound, she thought despairingly. 'Come and look.' she said in desperation.

She took them over to a set of Chippendale-type chairs, marvellously carved in low relief. As they passed the basketful of whippets, she was reminded that she was a keeper of dogs today, as well as of tourists, as well as of history.

'See the pierced back splat,' she said, pointing with her index finger. She stroked it lovingly to express adoration at its shrine. The right attitude was crucial in this job for it was her reverence that would inspire theirs. Buyers were often insecure and confidence on the part of the vendor was the first essential.

'You do see how very elegant they are.'

Looking at them, she saw it afresh too. A late shaft of sunlight glanced through the window, burnishing the mahogany of the fine old chairs, making their faded needlework seats glow. So what that they had passed out of the hands of umpteen dealers, each of whom had taken his cut as they moved through. Someone had sat down and made them, cut and disciplined the wood into its simple and airy lines. Someone who lived in that age of fitness and proportion, when a man of good sense could pay his respects to both God and

Mammon with a clear conscience.

I have a lovely job, thought Susan. Here I am, earning a living from selling well-crafted objects to people who appreciate them. And these two are going to buy, I know it. Yet half of her was stubbornly reluctant to be grateful and the reverie of roses refused to go away.

*   *   *

They stood in silent expectation at the garden door, absorbing the view along the gravel path which led to a central pool and fountain with dark sentinel yews. It was six o'clock and, after a week of hot sun, a canopy of low cloud had suddenly blown in late that afternoon from the west with a merciful pricking drizzle. In the soft grey light, a haze of blues, pinks and lemons glowed in the borders beside the path. A warm fragrance rose from the flowers and even the foliage, the more intense for being cradled within the four high walls of the square garden.

They followed the central path, slowly breathing the drenched perfume. Pausing at the circular pool, beside a pillow of pink globes of blossom, they looked along each of the four axes. Roses everywhere, billowing laxly over the corsets of box kerbs, festooning the tops of apple trees, weeping like cherry blossom over an arch. Tall white campanulas and spires of foxgloves spiked their flowerbeds. Here was 'Duchesse d'Angoulême' with its pendant seashell trusses. There, 'Mousseline' with milky petals and mossy buds. Flowers surfed around them, some with the plush depth of velvet, others crushed into thin folds of tissue paper. There were crimsons and violets and greys and white. Even the scents were manifold: wafts of cinnamon, then raspberries, now drifts as fresh as green apples, next smoky like myrrh.

'Nice isn't it?' said Philip smugly. It was satisfying to introduce her to an experience he already owned.

'Pretty nice.'

'Nicer than you expected?'

'Even nicer.'

'Really rather jolly?'

'Very jolly.' She began to laugh, taking his cue.

But 'it's paradise', was what he wanted to steer her into saying. It is paradise, but he was too inhibited to say it himself. He chose to say nothing. In silence he stood and looked about him at this marvellous product of old civilisations. He thought of the Chinese and the Persians, the Myceneans and the Romans, the many and great nations of the world who had bent their minds to the making of roses.

They walked slowly without speaking along one of the paths, stooping to look at the faces, and stretching to catch each of their scents. They began to drift at different paces, and, as they separated, locked into their private worlds. Within a short while Philip had lost sight of Elfie. Indeed almost of anyone, for the visitors to the garden had by now thinned out, deterred by the onset of drizzle. Freed from the need to be companionable, he took out his notebook for jottings. Every now and then he paused to write. By the time he had walked through the arch into the second garden, he had forgotten about Elfie. Other more whimsical names filled his head. All those crazy names of roses, all the Souvenirs and French Duchesses. That fantastic drum-roll of 'Gloire d'un Enfant d'Hiram'. What chutzpah.

By now the rain was falling in long penetrating strands. Indifferent to the wet, he carried on until a sudden downpour sent him ducking for cover in one of the tiled summerhouses. There he found that Elfie had preceded him, a green squashy hat crammed on her head. Her face beneath looked ecstatic.

'Sorry,' he said, feeling a touch responsible for the weather.

'Don't,' she exclaimed. 'It's wonderful.'

'I know it's a bit keen to go on in the rain,' he said, feeling the need to excuse his enthusiasms, despite the fact that she seemed to share them. 'It's just that all these roses have their own personalities.'

She looked up interested. 'You mean from their different colours.'

'Not just colours. Names too. One is like the girl next door, another like a flighty, expensive woman. A third, a bit mumsie.' He had a sudden childish expectation of being ridiculed. He had not experienced it for years. 'It's a silly notion, I know.'

She laughed. 'Not at all, except half of them are called after men. Presidents, generals, even Napoleon's hat.'

He smiled, feeling he had encountered some fellow feeling.

'I suppose it was coming here that made you start your own rose breeding.'

'In a way, yes, except that this place is so daunting, the unattainable ideal. I just tinker in an amateur way with the details. But even so, to make a perfect rose seems to me a worthwhile ambition.'

She surveyed him and frowned. 'I can't make you out. You flout one of my pet theories. That people are consistent.'

'They *are* consistent. In their choice of spouse, home, their politics, their temperament, their work. Anyway, what's it got to do with me?'

'My point is that making roses isn't the kind of thing I would expect from someone in your kind of work.'

'Perfectly consistent,' he said, groping for a simple and not too revealing explanation, 'I started it, don't you see, because it's the opposite of my work.' He glanced sideways at her. 'I need hobbies.' He remembered Martha saying 'children have hobbies.'

'I do see that,' said Elfie. 'You'd need relief

127

from your work. I do anyway.'

He felt encouraged to go on.

'It's not just that.' He spoke slowly. 'A lot of what I do destroys what other people have built up and care about. I need the feeling that I'm making something nice.'

'Not making war in the office.'

'Not war anywhere,' he said and hesitated, 'though I doubt if your husband believes that.'

'You shouldn't have beaten him with such obvious relish. You rubbed salt in it. You're all such little boys. Hugh is the little boy from—' She suddenly remembered the potted biography he had once given her: b. 1931, Clegg Hall, Cheshire, ed. Harrow, University College, Oxford. 'Well, never mind where Hugh's from. You were the little boy from—where?'

'9a, Kershaw Road.' He spread his hands and grinned. 'The boy done great.'

She laughed. 'I wasn't expecting you to be so exact.'

'I like to be exact about it, even down to the "a".'

It was true. He liked to think back to his childhood, to where he had been and to where he had come from. To his dad who had worked on the railways and grown sweet peas in his spare time. To 9a Kershaw Road, an artisan's semi in Somerset.

Outside, he could hear the rain drumming on the roof tiles above their head.

'I know Hugh's—' Elfie paused on the brink of saying 'a snob'. 'A fool' would have been more appropriate to the little incident but she settled for 'old-fashioned' and rattled on quickly, '—and it was awful he said what he did, but he can't help it and it arose out of an experience in his life that I won't go into.'

'I have had my experiences too,' said Philip. 'Mine are quite as formative as the next man's.'

He was half-amused, yet underneath annoyed that she kept referring to the event. So minor and he had annihilated it surely a week ago. Women could make such meals out of scraps. 'Don't brood,' he said suddenly. 'You brood too much.'

'You think everything can be solved by action,' she replied, then hesitated, looking out over the shimmering rain-soaked bushes with their blurred colours. 'Well, it can't.'

He turned his head to watch her. She looked round at him too. For a little second they eyed each other reflectively, recognising two different ways of living, irreconcilable yet perfectly complementary.

The light was dim in the small summerhouse and the right profile of her face as she stared at him was in blue shadow. Her skin was fair and soft, still damp over her cheeks. Wet strands of hair were plastered to the collar of her jacket. Her upper lip was full with a smooth bow. He wondered whether she needed to use cream on the lines around her eyes like Martha. It seemed to him wrong and narrow that he could only use Martha as his terms of reference. He thought he had got out of the habit of sitting in isolated places on his own with a woman he didn't really know. He could restructure companies but no longer make small talk with ease in the rain in a tiled hut.

'Look,' he said with relief 'there's some blue sky over there. This is a heavy shower and will move on.'

But she did not seem to feel the same unease. She wanted to talk and explore. She was a brooder, he thought again, a ruminant who was happy to chew the cud.

'How old is your daughter?' she asked.

'Tabitha? She is nearly eighteen.'

'Very beautiful. Once upon a time a father like you would have automatically commissioned a painting of such a beautiful daughter.'

'She is like Martha.' He knew himself to be the outsider in their domestic trio and his pride in his daughter's grace had been tempered by that fact. Still, she was exquisite, though he had never thought to have her painted. He could renovate businesses but he did not come from the portrayed classes. Martha did but he didn't; over that and so much else, there had been times when she had tried to make him feel half-civilised.

'Do you have children?' he asked. 'I've forgotten.'

'No.' The monosyllable came as a full stop.

He sensed the lines of easy communication on her part had suddenly been withdrawn. Her petals had started to close and she no longer desired to talk. In his schoolroom, there had been a plant called *Mimosa pudica*, the sensitive plant; if you touched its ferny leaves, they shrank and folded in fear of damage. As a child, he had tormented it and it had died. He now realised, as he sometimes did in a crucial business meeting, that he had chanced upon the hub of a person's universe. Occasionally it was their area of strength, more often of vulnerability. There was no doubt which in her case.

'Well,' he said, eyeing the patch of blue sky that was moving closer but not fast enough for his needs, 'it's a rum business.' He felt a protectiveness for her, but also the need to take shelter under a meaningless platitude. He had his own worries without hers too. They lay in wait for him, in the city and at home. He wanted to keep them out of this summerhouse. Here, for an hour, walking through the scented spendthrift blossom, he had felt like a free man.

He now rose and walked to the entrance. Although the blue sky was not yet overhead, the rain, thank God, had stopped. He felt an instant release of tension. He could escape to be on the move again.

'I think I'll just go and find a rose called

131

"Gloire d'un Enfant d'Hiram" again. This is the only time I ever see it. I've never been able to track it down in a nursery.' He set off along the path.

Elfie stood up and went to the open doorway. Under the bushes, she could see there were pools of wet petals, glistening and slippery on the earth. Shafts of late sun glanced off them in broken patches of new overexposed light. The fragile festoons of pink and crimson-violet blossoms over the arches of the central bower dripped pendulously towards the steaming ground. She watched Philip's back receding down the garden. She had recognised his sudden need to escape. It was familiar and not just from Hugh. She recollected it in Anthony, the last married man with whom she had sat alone in a park whilst his wife and children floated round the periphery of their lives.

Watching Philip now, she thought she should not have been so abrupt when he had asked her if she had children. Too quick to rebuff his enquiry, she had driven him away. Not surprising he should bolt. Yet, though locked in her own reaction at that moment, she had also experienced a flicker of understanding for his. She had sensed he had looked within her for a second.

She wondered what kind of relationship he had with Martha. Was it as disconnected and unsharing as he had implied? He had told her in the car he had married her three years after he had returned from Harvard Business School. She had been the daughter of his second boss. It was, thought Elfie, the classic route of self-improvement, a short cut that ignored the problems that might accrue in middle age when the goals of success and happiness could prove mutually destructive. When unlimited dreams proved after all to be perfectly finite and therefore ashen. No wonder he had wanted to breed a perfect rose, she thought with some dryness. She could see his head and the top of his blue Oxford cotton shirt looming over a fat red rose, his light jacket slung over one shoulder. A surprising, likeable man. His dreams had turned to the natural world around him, to his beekeeping and his garden, the pacific and beneficial pursuits of honey and roses, the rhythmic pleasures of the seasons.

She left the summerhouse and instead of following him, wandered back along the gravel paths to the first rose garden. As she passed a border, she noticed the sunlight gathered behind the petals of a bush massed with creamy flowers. It glowed richly as though irradiated with a warm gold. Raindrops, caught in its deep folds, glittered like taut round jewels. She paused for a moment, then walked on and stood just beyond the door-arch in the old brick wall, where she dipped her nose in the peach and apricot folds of a rose which was climbing around her head. She inhaled deeply and gasped at the intensity of its scent after the rain. Was there ever such a fragrance?

She stood still at the arch, gazing out at the whole sumptuous saturated picture. Many of the roses were once-flowering and she was seeing them at their period of evanescent perfection. It occurred to her to wonder whether anything would have happened to her before they bloomed again? Absolutely nothing was the likely answer.

CHAPTER ELEVEN

It was a temperate summer of comfortable sunshine alternating every so often with a few days of rain. Even the nights were warm. The wheatfields started their shift from green to gold, and in the garden the pinks and mauves of high summer began to mature to the crimsons and yellows of the ripe season.

The honeyflow from honeyplant blooms was heavier than the previous year, providing a succession of the sweetest nectar. The bees from Philip's hives toiled ceaselessly. The workers, driven and intense, feverishly gathered and ferried their harvest from each flower, from millions of blossoms of white clover and marjoram, from thyme and blackberry. They foraged at a frantic rate, for each honeybee was only able to carry a drop of nectar, sometimes from two miles distance, so the wearying succession of journeys had to be continuous. Those workers who had emerged from their cells just before the beginning of the heaviest flows were dead within six weeks, exhausted by the desperate effort of fetching and gathering.

Within the hive as without, the unremitting activity continued. Each drop of nectar, which was more than half composed of water, was now evaporated and distilled into a limpid and fragrant honey by the thousands upon thousands of fanning wings. Then, finally, as each pale gold cell of honey ripened, it was sealed with wax by the capsule-makers. Sometimes, on a Sunday evening before returning to London, Philip would sit near his hives and listen to the hum of the honey-making. Its ambrosial, resinous smell filled the warm humid air of the summer night. He guessed he would have at least fifty pounds of honey from the new hive he had established in May and much more from the others.

When the blackberry flowers fattened into fruit, the last of the heavy honeyflows began to come to an end. The weather was still kind, so the worker honeybees continued to tolerate for a little longer the huge fat velvety drones. These males, who had been bred solely for one of them to impregnate a new queen, had spent their summer in slothful luxury, gorging themselves on the hive's vats of honey, soiling the combs, sleeping and eating in heedless indifference to their coming fate. But as the air began to chill and the honeyflow to dwindle, the massacre of the swaggering males took place.

The carnage was grim. Unable to support their indolent passengers, the pitiless workers dragged out the bewildered, unarmed drones, two or three seizing each body. The enormous, clumsy creatures struggled to break free or hunch themselves against the blows, or attempted to use their claws to remove their assailants, but the dogged workers were remorseless. They tore away their wings, bit off their antennae and broke their legs. They cut through their stomachs and stabbed them with poisoned stings. A few managed to struggle free, but their death was delayed by merely a few daylit hours. Impelled by instinct to return to their hive in the evening, they were greeted by a new wave of warrior workers. Some of the males perished at once from their wounds, others a little less injured lingered only to die slowly from lack of food and water. Each morning the street-sweepers among the workers would clear the lumbering corpses from the threshhold of the hive, but by evening there were more of the giant bodies, until the last living drone had finally been killed.

The male population, a tiny percentage in any case of the whole hive, was now totally extinguished. No more of this masculine race would be made until the following spring. In the world of the honeybee, summer was over.

*   *   *

In the garden, summer lingered for longer. In Martha's white enclosure, the grey-leafed buddlejas bloomed along with the tall ghostly spires of the Virginian veronicas. Then, with the coming of autumn, the rosy and naked autumn crocuses unfurled in Elfie's old garden. There was only a quarter of the year that remained.

By now it was three months since she had stood in the archway at Mottisfont, wondering what would happen before June of the following year. The answer was already becoming apparent: that she had been right to expect nothing. She felt restless, having set in course a train of action which was slow to show fulfilment. She warned herself away from impatience. 'You think that action can solve everything,' she had told Philip as they sat sheltering from the rain in the summerhouse. She reminded herself that she had added: 'Well, it can't.' But she doubted whether she had accepted the wisdom she had so readily bestowed upon her companion.

That day at Mottisfont had been eclipsed by the weeks and months that had followed, but the images of its beauty still arose in her mind, faded, then came alive before fading again, and

137

she was grateful to Philip whom she had seen several times since. They had re-met among the guests at two of the summer's lunch parties. Since it was never permissible to sit next to one's husband on such occasions, what had happened was that Martha had been shunted next to Hugh at one end of the table and Elfie settled near Philip at the other. She now felt at ease with him. The afternoon spent among the roses had sunk into a mutual past and acted like a ballast: it had established that they shared a response to the same experience. It gave comfort, partly because it did not threaten any undue intimacy. She trusted him and sensed he treated her with increased gentleness.

As for Hugh, he found these new table-top pairings entirely satisfactory. It had given him the opportunity to re-cement relations with his customer.

'She's not so bad as you think,' he told Elfie after one of these occasions. 'I think she's a bit lonely actually. Dacre's away a lot and Tabitha's a full-time boarder.'

'Don't underestimate her,' said Elfie unsympathetically. 'She's poison and I doubt if she's ever done a day's work.'

'At least she doesn't sit around and mope.'

'Buying antiques at her rate is a form of moping.'

Elfie had replied glibly but thought after she had spoken that it was probably true. There was always a sizeable contingent of women like Martha at any good auction, and between these more sparkling occasions, they circled the antique dealers like satellites. They pointed at something and bought it. Old walnut bureaux were swapped for even better old walnut bureaux, which in turn were traded up for mulberry. The speed of exchange indicated the relative degree of unhappiness: the faster the greater.

How temporary Martha's satisfactions were compared with Philip's, thought Elfie. Hugh had called her lonely. She wondered if, rather, she was unstable. Beautiful, well-heeled women often conformed to a pattern of volatility. Their prosperity shielded them from the discipline of daily work and their beauty made them self-conscious. Self-consciousness lay at the heart of all neuroses. Until now, Elfie had only recognised why Philip had married Martha, not the other way round. It now began to yield a little to interrogation. She had needed his clear vision, his power of calm organisation, even simply his stability.

Thinking of Philip reminded Elfie that she had tried to arrange a belated thank-you for the trip to Mottisfont, but it had yet to arrive. She was seeking the old French rose he had described as elusive. 'I'll try to find it,' her friend, Melanie Hall, had promised, thinking she had enough on her hands running a one-woman nursery of period plants without combing the backyards of France. 'Gloire d'un Enfant d'Hiram', Elfie had repeated. 'A hybrid perpetual. 1899. Large, big and crimson. Very rich.' Mel had groaned. 'Sounds pretty gross. A man's fancy I should think.' She preferred the tender pinks. Elfie had not told Philip. It would be a happy surprise.

*   *   *

The hip of the rose mated by Philip had swollen quickly during the summer months, shading from green to yellow and then red. In September, he had slit it open and extracted its seeds. These he then bagged in moist peat for a few days before putting them in his refrigerator, a little one that he kept in his bee shed. There they would chill quietly for the next four weeks before being sown.

As it happened, the four weeks became six because he was holed up in Kiev. Here he had been stuck for days with an interpreter at $70 a day and a car at $40, unprepared for the large quantities of alcohol and food he was required to consume from early morning until late into the night. Weighed down by the heavy Ukrainian language and yet more ponderous hospitality of his business hosts, he found sleep eluding him in his uncomfortable little hotel bed. He lay awake feeling trapped. Thinking that a week was not a week here but a piece of elastic which had stretched to thirteen days. It had been difficult enough to arrive and was proving even harder to leave. Domestic flights had gone crazy. Baulked of departure on Tuesday and then on Wednesday, he had given his colleagues the slip and decided to console himself with a boat trip down the Dnieper. He had enjoyed this here one summer evening ten years ago when he had watched the moon float above the city, flooding it with lunar light. But now it was October and a decade later; the boat was berthed and the moon clouded, obeying the undeceiving laws of the rerun. He should have nourished his memories rather than testing them with reality.

So, instead, he was sitting in Tsian Deng, a Chinese restaurant on Gorky Street, some ten minutes away from the centre of the city. He thought about the comforts of his pretty house in the Cotswolds with its mansard roof and rows of curved-top windows. He thought of the 180lb of honey that he had extracted from the combs back in August. A good crop and a good honey. Bottled and sitting in neat rows in his bee house, it would already be crystallising into the ripe golden granules of maturity. He thought of the rose seeds in the refrigerator standing beside them and was reminded of Elfie. The memory of her face in the summerhouse arose, of the wet strands of hair plastered to her wax jacket. 'You think everything can be solved by action,' she had said. 'Well it can't.' He took a forkful of rice with some strange pink squiggles and more recognisable water chestnuts. Such a relief to have rice instead of wheat in what was once the bread basket of Europe. No, action couldn't solve everything, not Martha anyway. He had rung her the other night and he thought she'd been crying. 'You're always away when I need you,' she had said. He had been overwhelmed with the shock of being needed by her. 'Martha. Darling,' he had muttered, but a fuzz on the line made him doubt whether she had heard him. He had been gripped by a sudden fervour to return immediately, feeling a despairing need to bury himself within her, to have his wife lift herself against him to receive him. To want him. The sensation of being wanted. But he knew this time would be no different from other times when he had been delayed abroad. She only needed him when he was absent. He was without value when he returned.

At his lonely table, he now propped up a pretty hardback copy of *Evenings near the Village of Dikanka* by Gogol against his glass of fizzy lemonade. Amused by its subtitle which was *Stories published by Beekeeper Rudi Panko*, he had bought the book in a forward-looking mood on his icy journey through Moscow. He had been zestful then: one felt like a gold prospector at the beginning of a big new trip. Amidst the Oriental hubbub of diners and waiters, he now tried to concentrate on these tales of a Ukraine that had existed two hundred years ago. He read of devils and witches, and of beekeepers and blacksmiths. Of summers under the wild cherries and winters so cold and still that the crunch of snow under the boot could echo half a mile away. Recognising the stuff of magic, he tried to hear the jingle of tambourines and the whirr of the sabres. But the words of the lads and their lasses and their songs and *kolyadki* slithered into and out of his brain.

The dark image of Martha rose like a beckoning icon in their place. 'I need you,' she had said. She needs me, he reminded himself. More likely, she needs a light bulb changed, the other part of him thought wryly.

*   *   *

Two thousand miles away, the lights of the pretty house sparkled in the dark surface of the pool. Martha stood at the edge of the pond watching the upside-down reflections. The liquid stars of light swam together in the water when a breeze ruffled the smoothness and then drifted apart when the wind was stilled. She felt hypnotised by the alternate blurring and separation.

Awaiting the arrival of a writer and photographer who were researching an article on nice houses, she had turned all the lights on two hours ago in the early evening. The Dutch chandelier with its candles in the hall; the tall sconce-lights in the dark-panelled dining room; the long brass picture lamps over the paintings in the drawing room. The house was hushed and on hold, posing for the cameraman. She had laid a mahogany tray with three glasses and a bottle of white wine and added canapés of Feta cheese and spinach. A plateau of smoked salmon, lemon wedges and some thinly sliced brown bread and butter glistened beside them. She had put on cream corduroy trousers and a loose scoop-necked alpaca jumper to match.

On the walnut grandfather clock, the hands moved jerkily over the brass face to eight o'clock, then half-past. The tick was inexorable: an audible measurement of waiting. At nine o'clock, they rang to say they had been delayed and would therefore postpone a visit—no, they couldn't say when. She had looked furiously at the partyfied food which now nauseated her. It was non-food for non-people for a tinsel occasion. She recorked the wine and poured herself a vodka and then a second. The clock ticked on imperturbably in the progress of its eight-day movement. Its sound was called grandfather talk: a cosy term for what was simply nagging, an insistent reminder of her empty life, caused by a daughter who was away at boarding school, and a husband who was never there or locked into his own child-like world when he was. He had been beneath her when they had married; he was now above her and self-sufficient and she resented the reversal in their positions. He should remember he had been beneath her and that nothing had ever changed. She was angry with herself for telling him the other night she had needed him.

The clock reminded her to do something with her empty life other than the pretence of busyness. To escape its nagging, she had taken a third glass of vodka and walked out into the cold black air of late autumn and to the other side of the pool. The security lights flashed on, alerted to her movements, and she escaped into the shadows beyond their range until they had relapsed into darkness again. Now she stood beside the pool watching the inverted reflections. A beautiful topsy-turvy house with its glittering overturned lights, that made the shell for an upside-down marriage.

CHAPTER TWELVE

The telephone rang on and on. Both Judith and Giles kept their heads down, refusing to answer. It was nine o'clock on a Thursday evening. There was a time to live and a time to die and a time not to answer the telephone.

'It's not one of mine. It's for you,' said Judith, perusing a mail-order catalogue of country clothing. She was determined not to be deflected. She had just noted a jumper she had wanted to buy at the Agricultural Show last year but Giles had deterred her with his inhibiting husband act. Number 457, page 3, size 14 or is it 16, she wrote.

The rings continued.

'Judith.'

'It's yours.'

'Absolutely not.' Giles was uncompromising. He feared it might be an hysterical client who had traced his home number, as occasionally happened. There had been a weepie in the office that morning. He kept his head down, having reached the sole moment of action in a post-espionage novel.

The rings stopped. A moment's relaxation. Then they started again. Judith looked at Giles and made a nasty face.

'Whoever it is knows us, damn them. They know we're hiding from them.' She heaved herself up.

'You don't have to answer the telephone. We answer at *our* convenience, not theirs.' Giles had a highly refined notion of the pecking order which permeated every nook and cranny of his life.

Judith, however, had succumbed. She walked over to the dinky pie-crust table and lifted the receiver.

'Oh, it's you.' *It's Andy*, she mouthed at Giles. Then listened, puzzled. 'No I don't. We don't want a burglar alarm. We belong to a neighbourhood watch scheme. We are very helpful round here.' Well, quite, she thought

146

privately. They were neighbourly about property rather than people, adopting each other's houses rather than their owners. She had not actually seen their neighbours in weeks.

At the other end of the line, Andy was extolling the virtues of his alarm system.

'Andy,' said Judith, 'What's this about?'

There was a moment's silence. It sounded sheepish.

'I'm selling burglar alarms in my spare time. They've told me to ring up a hundred people I know and sell them one.'

'Andy.' Judith was shocked. 'A hundred people you know. We're your parents, not vacant spaces.'

Giles was hovering like thunder rolling round the room. It was the end of the week, it had been a long day and he wanted to make a roaring noise like Zeus in a temper. He kept trying to seize the receiver, but Judith made flapping motions to keep him at bay. At last he managed to wrench the telephone off her. 'What's this I hear Andy?' His voice reverberated like a machine revving up on its launch-pad. 'What's this about burglar alarms? What's happened to your seats?'

A moment's quiet ensued.

'They're in a pause situation,' said his son. 'Dad, actually, I was wondering whether I might ask you a favour.'

Giles exploded. 'If it's money, forget it.

You're twenty-six and should be standing on your own feet now. I warned you about the seats.'

'But Dad—'

Judith who had plastered her ear beside her husband's in an attempt to follow the conversation now managed to shove Giles away from the phone.

'Andy. Your father is naturally upset, but are you really in trouble?'

Andy sensed sympathy. He was silent for a moment, wondering how best to activate it. Instinct did not let him down.

'A bit of a hole actually.'

His voice went little and gruff as he sought a balance between manly understatement and child-like honesty. Judith, as she was meant to, received a picture of him as a small boy: brave but anxious and needy.

'Oh Andy.'

'Bloody hell,' shouted Giles, his ducts of sympathy long since run dry. 'He's twenty-six, not a kid of seven.'

'I'll come and see you in London,' she promised. 'We'll see what we can do.'

'He's probably living in a squat,' Giles interposed. 'Illegally.' It was always the worst adverb he could offer.

'He's our only son,' Judith put the phone down, 'and he's trying his very best.'

Gloom pervaded Giles. He thought of the thousands he had paid for his education—

148

money down the drain, and with a top-up now proposed. He punched a cushion in search of relief.

'Who'd want children?'

'Elfie.'

'Hmmm.' Giles had forgotten his sister in-law. 'Let's hope she doesn't have a son. They're neither decorative nor useful nowadays.'

The fracas had broken the novel's fragile hold on his attention. He walked disconsolately over to the television in search of diversion, to find that its social conscience was the only entertainment on offer. He ran through the channels encountering misery time in one form or another. Distressed single mothers, ethnic minorities and miscarriages of justice poured into his middle-class home, each one of them a drain on his taxes. 'As though I don't get enough of this at work,' he said unhappily. He was not an unkind man, but Andy had thoroughly upset him. No doubt some TV researcher was already enticing him to appear on the box and whinge about his father. Stick a microphone before someone's face and they felt compelled to complain.

Sitting on the edge of his flowery linen union chair, he zapped the first three of the offending channels, sending rockets of sound bites shooting across the room. 'We accuse ... Underprivileged ... Pregnant ... Rape ...' Despairing he switched to the fourth channel. It was a programme with two doctors and a

149

patient on camera. It looked short on fun, but *faute de mieux*, he was prepared to settle down to watch.

'Oh no,' said Judith. 'Not this again. There are wall-to-wall hospital programmes on the box. Anyone would think we all spent our entire lives being ill. Off with their heads.'

'Hmmm.' Giles's finger hesitated on the buzzer. It might be superstitious, but he feared that a thunderbolt of an illness would strike him if he zapped a hospital. He could not get pregnant or change the colour of his skin, but he might indeed become sick. He had been conscious of a twinge near his spine for the last two days which Andy had exacerbated. Whilst he dithered, Judith leant over him and zapped it herself. Giles waited until she had left the room before he turned it on for a two-minute squirt in her absence. He hoped that God had noticed and would spare him.

*   *   *

'Do come to bed.'

Elfie stood behind Hugh's chair and leaned over to kiss the top of his newly washed hair. He was wearing a navy-striped dressing-gown and navy pyjamas, having taken a shower before eating. He now lowered his book, turned round and peered at her over the top of his half-spectacles.

'It's awfully early. It's only a quarter-past

nine, isn't it?'

'Judith and Giles go to bed at nine o'clock.' Elfie looked at her watch. 'I expect they're cleaning their teeth right now. I expect Giles is complaining to Judith at this very moment about those nasty little circles of floss she leaves on the shelf in front of the bathroom mirror.'

'Judith and Giles. Pooh.' He gave a patronising little puff. 'Anyway, I've only just put another log on the fire.'

This was unfortunately true. The fire was a furnace on the floor of the big stone grate. It burnt with a good scarlet heart and small tongues of yellow flames had started to lick the fruit-scented oak log. In front, the two whippets were laid flat on the ground beside Baglady, a line of smoked kippers on the slab. Elfie could see the five of them would be here for another hour at least. Like all men, Hugh hated wasting a jot of fuel, especially when you could see it and feel it.

They both stared at the fire. Elfie watched little sparks meandering up the back of the chimney.

'When I was a child, I used to throw sugar on the fire to make it burn fiercely.'

Hugh looked scandalised. Even as a pre-war boy he had never indulged in such profligacy. He often thought it was the different worlds he and his wife had known as children, that gulf between the 1930s and the 50s, that made the age gap between them. Sharing their life together now, could never eliminate that twenty years of abyss between the pre- and the post-war experience.

'Would you still marry me, knowing what the last five, no, nearly six years have been like?' he asked suddenly.

'Yes.'

He felt reassured from which he deduced that he must have needed reassurance. Odd, since he hadn't thought he had felt insecure.

Elfie was now kneeling on the floor, rummaging about the base of the cupboard. He watched her, wondering idly what she was up to. He thought she looked lovely, dressed in a kaftan of slate-blue cotton with a garland of indigo butterflies round the neck and the hem. He wished he could see the expression on her face, but only the back of her head was visible. Her fair hair was caught in a loose elastic band at the nape of her neck. He thought he was lucky to have her and wished she had been his first wife; but then she would not of course have been Elfie, which was the usual conundrum posed by wishing things were other than they were. For the first time he wondered about a child. He had feared it, knowing the noise and disruption, and the sharing of her attentions with what he had until now visualised solely as a third and therefore alien party—and there was a deeper reason that he had not cared to examine which had lodged into a fixity. But, for the first time, he wondered whether he might one day, in the not too far distant future, change his mind. Next year perhaps?

Elfie shut the cupboard door with a bang at which Hugh winced.

'Elfie,' he exclaimed and his dark, rather bushy eyebrows met in a frown.

The piece was a big, seventeenth-century Spanish job, elaborately wrought, which he would probably sell in the spring. He wished she would realise their furniture was not always their own.

He had loved her a moment ago, but irritation now took command.

'Sorry,' she said, but she didn't look it. In fact, she was triumphant, clasping a bag of granulated sugar.

'Oh God. Do we have to recapture our childhood?', he groaned.

She knelt in front of the fire, sliding the whippets unceremoniously out of the way. It required a muscular effort. Though fragile in appearance, each dog could make himself as heavy as cast iron when he wanted and the pair weighed a ton. Tearing open the packet, Elfie flung a handful of sugar on the fire.

'Look.'

There was a spurt of white and gold, a shimmering of blends with a heart like the eyes of a peacock's tail.

She rose from her kneeling position and

153

walked round the room, turning the lights off.
Shadows flickered over the ceiling as the
flames glimmered and darted in the hearth.
Elfie returned to the fireside and knelt to throw
another handful, a bolder one this time. The
tongues leapt up. The hues were extraordinary,
a molten cream and yellow with a slate grey
centre.

Hugh watched mesmerised. 'You're mad.'

'I know. Shocking isn't it? But I paid for it.
It's my money.'

In their domestic arrangements, it was
agreed that she paid for the food.

'It's not that. It just seems so wanton.'
Demonic, too, he felt, but he was fascinated.

'Don't be an ass. You left a potato on your
plate tonight. Your waste, my waste, what's the
difference?'

She was rational, yet the act felt wrong. She
threw a third handful of sugar on the fire. He
placed his book on the little table beside his
wing chair and came to join her on the floor in
front of the fire. He took the bag of Tate &
Lyle gently out of her grasp. She lay back on
the old blue and red Hamadan rug and put her
arms around him as he bent down beside her.

Transported by the strangeness of the
moment, Hugh was tempted to make love to
her in front of the fire. Shall I, he wondered for
a moment as he held her. Normally he felt safer
in the bedroom, after she had been through all
the formalities, as he called it, of her

preparation. He hesitated. What if he changed his mind about a child now rather than next year? Elfie waited, outwardly relaxed and stroking his head, inwardly tense and listening to his reaction. If he does this, just once, she thought, it will be a turning point. She had hated deceiving him for the last three months, the need for stealth; if only he were a willing and loving collaborator. He drew back to look at her and she recognised with joy a yielding on his face. Happiness flooding her, she put her arms round his neck. At that same moment the telephone rang. The machine smashed the warm nest of flickering twilight.

'Ignore it,' she whispered. 'It's no one, nothing, forget it,' but it was too late.

Hugh sat up. The soft expression on his face had been replaced by the usual lines and tensions.

'Oh, I think we'd better answer it.'

Elfie lay back, paralysed by disappointment. She turned her face aside to feel the velvet comfort of the dog's muzzle.

It whimpered a little in protest.

'It's Judith.'

Elfie pushed her face against the silkiness of Bertie's ear. In return he placed a sleepy paw on her cheek.

'Come on,' Hugh mouthed at her.

'Tell her I'm in the bath.'

'She's right here,' said Hugh. The role of go-between took more patience than he could muster. He unlooped the flex so that he could carry the telephone to where his wife lay recumbent on the hearth.

'This is a bad moment, Judith,' said Elfie, taking hold of the receiver with poor grace.

'Then I won't go on.' What on earth, Judith wondered, had happened. Was a row in progress? Or was Hugh getting his oats in front of the fire? Really—and he sixty-four. She decided to say nothing of this to Giles.

'Just, I'm going up to London to see Andy this month. Do you want to come?'

'London?' Elfie blinked mentally at the thought, then literally as Hugh turned all the lights on. The rapid succession of emotions had left her dazed. This, amid the sudden brightness in the room, made her shade her eyes. She felt suddenly like crying, but it was somehow too deep for tears.

'I don't know. Perhaps we can talk about it another time.'

Judith agreed to call again the following evening and rang off.

Hugh, released for action, was picking up the evening's litter from around the fireside. The matter-of-fact tenor of a weekday evening had been agreeably restored and he was rescued to carry on just as before. He had been on the verge of wandering into dangerous territory.

'You know that mole?' he said. 'He's come back on the lawn. He's made a series of horrible little humps. I'll have to put my toy windmill out again.'

Hugh was trying to scare him with a plastic windmill which Elfie had bought from a local toyshop. It trembled and whirred in the wind. Its vibrations were supposed to act as a deterrent.

'Oh, let him be,' said Elfie furiously. 'The lawn's not so wonderful anyway.'

'*Acu rem tetegisti*,' said Hugh excitedly, using the last remaining scrap from his classical education. 'You have touched the matter with a bodkin.' He added as usual, 'Pliny'.

'Hit the nail on the head, you mean.' Elfie spoke sourly.

'The lawn isn't so wonderful because of the mole.' Hugh was in full pursuit of an explanation. '*Ergo*, it would be better without.'

'Oh, shut up,' said Elfie walking out of the room with the sugar bag. The conjuring show was over.

CHAPTER THIRTEEN

Lydia stood in the little conservatory and prepared to water the motley collection of potted flowers. It seemed superfluous when it was raining outside. How infuriating that she couldn't roll back the glass roof to let the heavens save her a chore. She looked wearily about her. At her last watering a week ago, she had counted up to forty pot plants, which was madness when they were tyrants, one and all. Lord, the years she had spent at their beck and call whilst she had fed, watered and potted them like puppies. Cleared the jasmine of scale, protected the pelargoniums from pests and freed the fuchsias from whiteflies. In the course of time, all had been threatened with the bonfire, but the cunning things had defied her and tottered on. She thought now that her love in return for their flowers—or one measly lemon in the case of the citrus tree—seemed a lop-sided equation by any standard, but she was bound to admit that it was unaccountable fun.

She took the watering can over to the tap and began to fill it. As she stood waiting, she heard the sound of the postman, then a door bang, then some shuffling, whereupon Ronnie and Ben appeared at the entrance, each as hairy and dishevelled as the other.

'Phostrogen in first', said Ronnie.

Lydia glared back. She was of the school that put the fertiliser in mid-way, which she now did with great ostentation.

'My Phostrogen. My watering can,' she said crossly.

'My conservatory.'

'My plants.' Lydia was unyielding.

The dispute could have been prolonged to infinity had they wished, but neither took it with the slightest seriousness. It was no more than enjoyable bickering. They both knew they were far too old and had been married far too long to lend either themselves or their property to disentanglement. It would have been like unpicking the most complicated patchwork quilt. In any case who owed what and to whom was no longer discernible.

'Anyway,' said Ronnie calling a truce, 'it all looks pretty nice.'

'Any letters?'

'At our age you mostly get junk.'

He bustled over to the wicker chaise-longue and subsided on its cushions. In the process he brushed against some leaves which fell sighing to the tiled floor. Lydia, not totally mollified, put down the can and made a great show of sweeping up the new debris.

'All right for some,' she said crisply. She was also keeping an eye on the dog in case he lifted a leg against a plant.

'Oh dear, are we a disgruntled keeper today?' Ronnie enquired from the comfort of his armchair.

He passed her the fallout from his mail. Lydia put down her dustpan and brush and leafed through the post, which contained two bills and a gift catalogue. Noting she had been distracted, the dog looked longingly at the lower foliage of a fuchsia which was at just the right height for a sprinkling. Why not? It was his territory too, but a sinister 'Ben' from his mistress warned him that a wallop would be

159

sure to ensue. He hawked with disgust.

'I've just had a look at my trees,' said Ronnie. 'They're very happy.'

'Good.' Lydia carried on flicking through the catalogue. She wondered whether there was anything to buy for Christmas presents. It was only six weeks away. A teddy-bear tea towel, an egg-cupboard, ceramic Wellington boots? Who could she inflict those on? A duck call or an owl hoot? For Heaven's sake.

'You don't want a lap-tray, by any chance, do you?' she asked Ronnie.

'No.'

'No what?' she said automatically.

'No thank you,' he answered in reflex.

'Wacky teapot?' She pointed her finger at it and showed him its picture in the catalogue.

'Absolutely not.'

Lydia sighed and leafed forwards. What a bore presents were at Christmas time. There was no help for it, she would have to give him an armchair tidy which from its photograph looked like a little dolly bag slung over the back of a seat. They had managed perfectly well for over eighty years without one, and could die equally happily without it, but it looked like its moment had come.

'I want a pair of new eyes, a hip, and a liver,' said Ronnie helpfully, 'but failing that, I'll settle for an armchair tidy if I must.'

Lydia stared at him anxiously. The cataracts and the osteoarthritis were old and familiar

160

friends, but the mention of a liver was new and therefore ominous.

'What do you mean, liver?'

She suddenly wondered if he seemed slightly yellow. She leaned over to examine the whites of his eyes.

'Nothing,' he reassured her. He had endured his wife's propensity for panic for over fifty years. 'I've got a touch of indigestion today, that's all.'

'Are you sure that's all?' She felt desperate to be soothed.

'Absolutely.'

'Not a portent?'

'NO. LYDIA.'

Honestly, she'd be no bloody use if it *were* anything, he thought to himself. All hot air and palaver.

Willing to let herself be sedated, she picked up some plans she had placed on the small wicker table and put them on his lap. He tried to decipher the arrows. The sketch was unfathomable, but he knew it would involve a rearrangement of the garden in some mysterious if tiny way. He looked more closely, trying to peer round the edge of his cataracts. As he managed to focus he realised it was his trees which were involved.

'Oh no,' protested Ronnie. '*They* are untouchable. One day in three hundred years we shall walk beneath them and thank ourselves for planting them.'

'We shan't be here.'

'Oh yes we will.'

'Well, in the meanwhile,' said his wife, 'I was only going to suggest that we planted some tulips beneath them.'

'No,' said Ronnie, no longer emollient. 'Ben if you like, or me, or even you, anything that is never dug up, but not tulips.'

A drip fell on the plan just beside the circle with a dot that marked the sweet chestnut. The conservatory was as leaky as a ship in wet weather and as noisy too. The wind was making it strain shakily at its supports.

He turned his head and looked out through the streaked glass at the pouring rain. It was true, he did feel a little liverish.

'How does it go?'

'What?'

'"When that I was and a little tiny boy . . ."'

'"With a hey, ho, the wind and the rain,"' said Lydia.

Ronnie smiled as the words reached out for him:

'"A foolish thing was but a toy,
For the rain it raineth every day."'

CHAPTER FOURTEEN

Elfie increased the speed of the windscreen wipers. In response, they jerked into hyperactivity, pushing the rain into waterfalls at the sides of the glass. The glistening motorway to London unfurled before her. She kept up a steady sixty miles an hour, letting the reps' cars swim past her in the middle lane, their presentation suits and personae hung up in the windows.

Judith prattled beside her in the passenger seat, airing her worries about Giles's job. She drummed the fingers of her left hand upon her knee, the gold of her worn wedding ring gleaming dully in the low light. A man in the prime of life had recently joined the solicitors, a go-getter of the silent and determined type. Giles was fifty-five which was old enough to be his father, and he was being faded out by the man who was young enough to be his son. She wished that Giles would object but knew he was doomed to play the Cheshire Cat and persist in smiling till the very end.

Judith had always been realistic about her husband whom she had met on the edge of a dazzling career at the bar. But the hoped-for QC, indeed future judge, had become a young solicitor, then a middle-aged one confined to a drab country practice, none of which had mattered as the process of inching downwards had long been disguised by moving sidewards. In any case, Judith contented herself with the thought that a mediocrity made a better husband than a genius. However, the latest development distressed her. Giles might soon be an ex-solicitor and no peace of mind could be extracted from job-loss.

'I suppose,' said Judith, her eyes tactfully on the road whilst she extended an active feeler from the passenger seat, 'I suppose, if he does get eased out, that Hugh doesn't need any help with the business, does he? Giles would be terribly useful with, uh-huh, tax and so forth.'

It had occurred to her that a reminder of Hugh's excess earnings would not go amiss.

'Well,' said Elfie thoughtfully, 'I don't think Hugh has either the spare room or the cash.'

Hugh's spare capacity was strictly limited as far as Giles was concerned: it stopped short at three occasions a year.

'Oh.' said Judith, 'Just thought I'd ask.' Her loud voice, bright and braying, boomed boisterously in the car.

She now turned round and ferreted for a tissue in the pocket of her green wax coat which she had flung into the back seat. She had a new Paddington bear sou'wester to match, both lined with a red tartan. She had done a series of bunny jumps to show them off to her sister when she had arrived at Rooke House that morning.

'What's this?' Judith now asked as her fingers encountered a paper bundle of odd size and shape that was lying beneath her coat.

'A rose,' replied Elfie after a second's hesitation.

'Nice?' Judith was apparently untroubled by the fact that a rose should be travelling with them to London on a wet day in November. Her mind was still grappling with Giles.

'Yes.'

Elfie hunched over the wheel lost in thought. It was the rose she had ordered for Philip. When the plant had arrived yesterday, barerooted and paper-bagged, it had posed the problem of how best to send it to its destination. A deterrent lurked in every avenue. If it was impossible to send it to his country home because of the scenario that could ensue, it was equally inappropriate to post it to his London home. 'What's this?' Martha would say. Philip: 'I don't know.' Martha: 'A rose?' Philip: 'Where did it come from?'

Oh God, thought Elfie, this is ridiculous. Even more absurd when it becomes apparent to Martha that it's a single red rose. She cringed with embarrassment. The implications were awful and misleading. One red rose says, 'I love you'; one red rose was only one degree less intense than a diamond is forever. At the time of its order she had been aslosh with goodwill; now, five months later, it had ebbed to a level, cordial certainly and even fond, but which nonetheless exposed the rose as inappropriate. Tempted at first to bin it or, better, to plant it in her own garden, she had finally decided to drop it into his office with a short note of explanation. If he were there, she would avoid seeing him. If he were away, the rose could sit in its bureaucratic surroundings for a week or so without suffering.

She was interrupted in her flow of thought by Judith trumpeting into a tissue.

'No luck I take it with getting preggers,' said her sister, turning from her own problems with Giles to those of Elfie with Hugh.

'None.' Elfie was irritated by her attempt at schoolgirl banter, but underneath she was worried. The months had rushed past with no result. Her latest anxiety was Hugh's repeated absences. Even now, he was away for a two-day fair at a time which was crucial.

'None,' she repeated. She flinched as a lorry flooded them with spray, sending the wipers into frantic overdrive. *Torschlusspanik*, Judith thought again to herself.

'You're OK, I suppose?'

'What the hell's that meant to mean?'

'You've had yourself checked out?'

'Yes.' Elfie thought back over the tests she had organised on the quiet. '*I'm* fine.'

Her emphasis left Judith in no doubt where her finger pointed.

'It's poor old Hugh, I suppose. Not a Charlie Chaplin obviously.'

'Leave Hugh out of this,' warned Elfie. She abhorred the thought that Hugh's sperm count could be batted from one female member of the family to another.

Judith, feeling the rebuff, reached over to fetch her Paddington bear hat which she now donned for solace. Sitting, scrunched up like a small dumpy animal in the front seat, she pretended she was in a burrow instead of going off to see poor Andy to deny him a loan. She envisaged a future wedged between a welfare son and a workless husband. Thank God, her daughter, Lucinda, with whom she would spend the night, had proved self-reliant as well as reliable.

* * *

Philip sat alone in his office. He had instructed Ellen not to disturb him for the next two hours but now longed for an interruption. Any diversion would do. A report sat before him which he had pledged to complete by the end of the afternoon, but instead he had caught himself counting the cracks on the ceiling. The office had been redecorated a year ago and the cracks should not be apparent.

As he stared around him now, he thought that the decor was a positive affliction. Embracing both the antique and the modern, it had been designed to appeal across the spectrum of taste. Large oil paintings, on hire and therefore exchanged at regular intervals, floated on wood veneered walls. Two ergonomic chairs were drawn up either side of a Knowle sofa upholstered in sepia velvet. A minimalist table floated to his right and two computer terminals sat before him. According to Mrs Korowski, its interior designer, this was the school of happy and confident contrasts. Rather, the school of sham, thought Philip as he looked at it in its pool of artificial light, though no less suited to his way of life.

Philip wished now, yearned actually, that he had not joined the persuasion industry. He should have been a maker and a doer, laying roads and making pipes, instead of an influencer with a gilded tongue and shiny theories. Even his hands—large and strong like a craftsman's—had destined him to be a worker, but he had been doomed to be otherwise. The little boy from 9a Kershaw Road, the bright son of the railway worker, had fixed his heart on being a member of the *haute bourgeoisie*. From 9a to Cambridge and Harvard, and then to Martha and now to his current eminence, the pilgrim had moved onwards and upwards, spoilt at all stages for choice.

He pulled open the top left-hand drawer of his desk and withdrew three photographs of his wife. The first, a snapshot taken the year after they were married, during a brief holiday in Kenya—Martha in a safari shirt and jeans, her dark hair falling across the left side of her face, laughing. How long since he had seen her laugh? Next, Martha in a rowing boat off the coast of Mombasa. Then, Martha beside him, together at the camp at Tsavo. The model Veruschka had only just preceded their arrival.

Veruschka, Martha, Philip, the little boy from 9a Kershaw Road. Oh yes, he was an insider, a member of the élite for the last thirty years, and every one of these he had relished and his current bout of disenchantment could not persuade him otherwise.

Scrabbling around in the drawer, he now took out another photo. Tabitha as a baby, those dark liquid tilted eyes even then, Martha's eyes, not his, a child not made in his form or substance. His fair, strong sturdiness, inherited from his father, his eminent fitness for survival, would die with him. He had wished many times that Martha would have another child, but she had always refused. Another, he thought now, might have kept the bond between them, mutual sympathy locked by a common interest. Who knows? Perhaps he was wrong. Children had complicated the relationships of most of his contemporaries, not simplified them, which was odd given the routines they imposed. But then his spoilt generation was ill-adjusted to routines, especially the persuaders and manipulators like him.

In an attempt to dispel this malaise which he had not truly shaken off since his return from Kiev, he took hold of the draft report that lay before him and made a strenuous attempt to discipline his mind. But, too clever and slippery to be caught, it darted away before him. Distracted by the sound of music from outside, he rose to look out of the window. Four floors down, at the street level, he could see a curly-haired boy of perhaps twenty, who was sheltering from the rain. A latterday tramp, he was leaning against the stucco of the building and playing a flute. The clear pure notes floated like single bubbles upwards to reach Philip as he watched. He listened for a moment, conscious of reaching out from his place within the system to borrow from without. The notes entered his head, cleaning it with their musical oxygen, momentarily clearing his mental pathways. He sighed, closed his eyes and strove to relax.

*   *   *

Judith plodded down the road in search of Andy's flat. A basement flat, he had told her. Which meant damp and cockroaches and the tube train so close you could feel it. She was in Wandsworth, or was it Lambeth? She was startled at the number of black people around. No aspect of the multicultural or multiracial world had entered her share of Wiltshire village life. There were no yams, no mosques and few bagels, and most of the latter eaten in private. Unaccustomed to form a minority, she splashed on in the pouring rain. Wax-coated and Barbour-booted, a pasty foreigner from feudal England. A magnificent black couple swept past, supple of voice and loose in joint, six feet tall with a new-born baby clothed in snowy white. Stately chieftains, they were members of a master race.

Waiting outside the flat for Andy to let her in, Judith looked around and sniffed fastidiously. The ground by her feet was green with generations of damp.

'Andy,' she exclaimed anxiously as the door opened.

She scanned his good looks for signs of starvation, assessing his rib-cage as he allowed himself to be hugged.

'Mother.' He was beaming, but his smile faded as she stumbled and stepped back. 'You're treading on my moss-bed,' he said crossly.

'Oh dear.' Judith hastened to remove her Wellington boot from a patch of green liverwort. How remiss of her to mistake it for neglect.

She took off her coat, then followed him through the narrow hall, dipping her head left and right like an investigatory hen. Such a relief that the flat was clean and empty with no trace of the squat or the souk which she had anticipated. No dirt, no fleas, not even a mouse-dropping. A blitz of mortal proportions must have preceded her arrival. She peered around her, boring down on nooks and crannies, trying to avoid appearing like a health and safety inspector.

Radiant with benevolence, Andy chatted on

171

regardless, keen to indulge the aged parent.

'By the way, I am Andi now,' he said, 'with an i.' He walked to the gas stove and flourished a wooden spoon. 'As in Gandhi.'

'Gandhi?'

Wasn't there an h somewhere, wondered Judith, scrutinising the newly scrubbed sink.

'A-N-D-I.' He had never been able to spell.

Judith noted some herbs struggling to grow on the shelf by the kitchen window. Also a little tray of—what?—could it be cannabis? Better not to know. With luck, the low light levels would see it off.

'Where is everyone?' She could only grasp the presence of other people by a couple of futons in the rooms she had passed.

'We're all busy people, Mother. Out.'

He sniffed, then tasted the careful and decorative cous-cous he had prepared for his mother who would be his saviour and the bank. He had feted her accordingly as though she were the King of Morocco. He pulled out a chair for her beside the table and began dishing up the banquet: vegetables, ginger, coriander, semolina grains as fluffy as angora, a rich harissa sauce with raisins, and a slice of salted lemon for the side of her plate.

Judith watched, bewildered. She could not remember him ever cooking at home. She felt disorientated. A hundred questions thronged her brain. Where were the signs of trouble implied on the telephone? What was he doing?

Who paid for the electric light bill which must be huge in a basement flat? Who, indeed, paid for the flat. (How did social security fraud actually work? which she quickly suppressed.)

'Oh Andy, there's only one of me,' she protested, looking at the size of the portion he was placing before her.

It was three o'clock, an abnormal time for her to eat cous-cous. In the Citizen's Advice Bureau where her sense of civic responsibility induced her to work two days a week, they would be opening the old tin of McVitie's Digestive biscuits and dipping them in stewed tea. Disgusting, but sitting in the basement flat, she would have preferred to be with them. She thought uneasily there was a lot to be said for clinging like a barnacle on one's own territory, when one's confidence ebbed so quickly on other's.

Andy—no, Andi, she corrected herself—was on a high. She had never known him so garrulous.

'What we're planning is to start a nursery of exotic plants.' He waved his fork in the air, the prongs perilously close to catching in his one hoop ear-ring. 'Ginger plants and crotons, bananas, crazy bamboos, giant Bolivian fuchsias, angels' trumpets and—'

Judith recalled his plans for his seats and remembered their demise. She grew even more nervous.

'Who's we?'

173

'Wadi, Jinja and Mark. We all live here.'

Mark, bearing the warrant of the New Testament, sounded pretty safe, but Wadi? Jinja?

How things had changed. She remembered her parents' catechism a lifetime ago when she had mentioned her friends. 'What school, dear?' 'And their fathers?' And later still: 'Any degree, darling?' Such questions were no longer permissable. And in any case, did they apply to a Wadi or a Jinja. What age, dear; what gender, darling and what origin seemed more pressing, but these simplicities had become industries of offence.

'What do they do?' she ventured.

'Wadi's at Kew, Mark's a broker, Jinja's a model.'

'Not of course a supermodel?'

'Not of course that kind of model.'

That left only two other kinds in Judith's rural experience. Either topless or knitting patterns, she inferred, with the latter distinctly unlikely. Some business partner. She swallowed and stared hard at her food.

'Your father and I—'

'Leave Dad out of this. He's never understood.'

'He cares about what happens to you, Andy.'

'He just wants me to plod on in life. The world's changed since he was young.'

'Not that much. Take this nursery—'

'Mother, we're breaking the matrix.'

174

'You did that with your seats.' It seemed a low blow.

'The seats were different. This is for real. Exotic landscapes for churches. For weddings, christenings, funerals—'

'Bananas at a funeral. You can't be serious. Your father will—'

'Forget Dad. Wreaths and posies are out.'

'Andy, can I ask if your friends are going to pay for the start-up of the nursery?'

Andi put down his fork and gazed at his mother speechless. Didn't she understand? He frowned in perplexity. For the first time his confidence had taken a dent.

Dear God, thought Judith miserably. She feared that the moment of confession was imminent.

'Mother. That's why you're here, isn't it? To arrange a little loan?'

'Oh Andy,' said Judith, gazing at him across the gulf of incomprehension. 'It just isn't possible,' and her eyes filled with tears.

*   *   *

Philip folded the pages and closed the file. His report lay before him in his neat, measured handwriting, its words equidistant and its lines evenly spaced. The considered product of a controlled man, it summarised all he knew on trading in the Ukraine and Ellen would type it up tomorrow. He rose and went to fetch his coat from the dusky corner of the room, outside the pools of light cast by the two standard lamps. He glanced at his watch, noting it was five o'clock, and opened the door to tell Ellen he would leave earlier than intended. On the point of switching off the light, he remarked that the pamphlets on his desk were strewn in random disorder instead of precisely arranged in right-angled formation. Leaving the door ajar, he returned to align them, thinking this was a bad sign as he did so. The release afforded by the flautist had not lasted very long.

There were noises in the reception and he heard the low tones of a woman's voice. Half-hiding in the dusk, he peered cautiously around the door, wary of being trapped. He could see the rear of a black redingote bending over the desk, then as the visitor straightened, the back of a sort of Renaissance hood, black filleted with gold and ruby, lined with a dark fur trim. Intrigued but still careful, he dared to advance a fraction further.

Ellen registered the furtive movements on the edge of her arena and signalled in his direction with her eyebrows. Encouraged by the desire on the part of the caller to keep a privacy that was more than equal to his own, Philip walked boldly into the light. He paused, but meeting no response, now stepped forward, far enough to allow his presence to be felt. The visitor turned half-profile to him, then apparently overcoming some reluctance, full-face. From the depths of the black-furred hood, he was surprised to recognise Elfie Lyle. For a second they stood in silence, reviewing one another without much evident welcome. Ellen observed the little interlude.

'I didn't want to disturb you,' said Elfie, holding out the paper bag. 'I've simply dropped this in.'

'Elfie. Such a surprise. What is it?' Philip was mystified.

There was a long pause. Elfie's mind sprinted through the answers—a plant, a rose, 'Gloire etc'—and froze po-faced at each. Not one of them bore scrutiny.

'Tennis balls,' he offered helpfully, beginning to smile.

She suddenly laughed, pushing her hood back.

'No, no apology goes with this.'

'Elfie, this is really all rather intriguing.'

Ellen, riveted, was furious to be interrupted by the telephone.

'It's a rose—"Gloire" himself,' whispered Elfie, suddenly released by the distraction of the audience.

Philip spread his hands in amazement. A rose in his office. It felt surreal.

'I must go,' she muttered in embarrassment. 'Really, I've arranged to meet my sister. This was just a belated thank-you for that day in June.'

'No. Wait.'

He was suddenly touched. Like the flute player, she had brought a strange otherworldliness into the pressure-cabin of his existence. How awful to think that only a few minutes ago, he had been arranging the top of his desk in rectilinear squadrons.

'Wait,' he repeated. 'Please wait. We'll have a quick drink, then I too will have to leave.'

* * *

'Of course,' said Lucinda, 'the fact is that you always spoilt him.' The fact is, she thought, you loved him more and what a mess that made me.

Resentment, never very far away, engulfed her. She stood in her Kensington flat, toasting her roly-poly rump by the gas fire. Her mother, who had arrived an hour earlier, was slumped in an armchair nearby.

'We were fair and firm with both of you,' protested Judith. Quite odious, the pair of them. Intolerable to be the butt of both children's recriminations in a single afternoon. She had yet to recover from Andy's.

Lucinda was relentless. 'He was the baby and the boy. You never blamed him for anything. It was always me who took the rap.'

She was thirty-one, five years older than her brother and far plainer too. Goddy in his heaven, as she used to call him when young, had divided the assets most unfairly between

them. A beautiful boy and a drab older sister—
so broad of beam and thick-ankled that she
always wore trousers, a solution to the second
problem but detrimental to the first. If the eye
travelled upwards it met with scant physical
improvement. No portion of Lucinda, whether
seen independently or together, was actually
pretty. If only, she had often prayed, a
transplant could have been effected which
would have evened out the differences between
her brother and herself. A couple of
millimetres from her face, grafted onto his. Oh
the cruelty of it, she had once thought, that
millimetres should be so crucial in the axis that
ran from ugliness to beauty.

Remembering the old torments, Lucinda
now turned round to warm her tummy instead,
She stared in the gilt mirror above the wall-
mounted fire.

'The trouble with Andy is that he's got no
grasp of reality.'

'He's full of ideas.'

'Ideas. We can all have *ideas*.'

'He might just pull this one off.'

'There you go again. Giving him the benefit
of the doubt.' Why couldn't the scales crash for
ever from her mother's eyes?

'Exotics for offices are frightfully old hat.'

'Not offices. For churches. Funerals,
christenings, weddings and things.'

'WEDDINGS.'

Lucinda looked stricken. Not effing well

mine for a start, she thought. Shall I tell her or hug the secret for a little longer? She hummed a silly little jingle that accompanied a commercial for a cocktail.

'You sound very happy,' said Judith morosely.

'I have something to confess.' Lucinda left a dramatic pause for effect.

'Only if it's nice.'

Probably pregnant, thought Judith, and certainly unwed. Oh God. How much better, she considered gloomily, if the emancipation of women had never happened. All it had meant was more cars on the road, more divorce, more illegitimate children, jelly babies for men, and put-upon grandparents. Pregnant for sure. Oh God, Giles would go berserk. She looked at Lucinda in despair and awaited the pronouncement.

'Martin and I are getting married.'

'Oh, Lucy,' exclaimed Judith. She struggled out of her chair and hugged her with relief.

Martin, a greying military historian, was boring and blissfully respectable. She envisaged a nice sober, registry office wedding, not expensive for Giles, a house near, say, Sandhurst, and, oh heaven, the deep deep peace of the British bourgeoisie. It was amazing, she thought, how pretty Lucinda now looked. Freedom from debt gave one's child a positive glow.

'It will be in about three months time.'

180

Lucinda leaned forward. 'Actually, we were wondering about a really nice white wedding. Something special, though let's keep poor old Andy away. Worth a celebration, don't you think, Mummy? Shall we go out when Elfie gets here? Where is she, by the way?'

*   *   *

'This is terribly unsatisfactory,' said Philip.

He looked at his watch and rose to his feet, putting his whisky glass down on the table. Elfie stood up also. Delayed by the rain and the traffic, they had arrived at the little mews house only fifteen minutes before. Neither had bothered to take off their damp coats.

'No,' he said, 'please sit down.' He put a restraining hand on her arm for a second, then removed it, sliding the documents he had needed to fetch into his briefcase. 'Do wait. I'll only be away for an hour or so, then we'll go round the corner for a bite to eat.'

He named a restaurant, a sober place that was strong on fish. His stomach had felt delicate ever since his return from Kiev.

'I've arranged to eat with my sister and niece.' She thought that a family excuse always sounded feeble.

'Ring them.'

In a rush so therefore impatient, he indicated the telephone, pale grey like the rest of the calm, Gustavian drawing room. 'I shall expect you here when I get back at half-past seven,' he announced.

It was trade dogma that confidence was self-fulfilling, but watching her face, he feared he had produced an unwanted effect.

'Make yourself at home. Please,' he added more gently, as he walked out of the room.

She heard the front door bang and then silence apart from the hum of the radiators. A very quiet house, not lived in too much, not as comfortable as a dear old shoe, certainly not a place to make yourself at home, no cat, no dog, no plants; more like a salon, with a large eighteenth-century Swedish-style glass chandelier in the drawing room where she stood. Poised, exquisite and barren, Martha's magnetic field enclosed her. Only the rose, much travelled and still paper-bagged, lay outside it; propped up against the leg of the drinks table, it was thorny and resistant, teeming with the life contained within its twigs. Poor old thing, she thought, I should have kept you for my garden.

Her legs were aching but she walked round the perimeter of the room, coldly admiring the elegant arrangement of its spaces. A billow of silk enfolded the curtain pole. She parted the drapes and looked over the narrow Knightsbridge mews. The cobbles were shining blackly in the blowing rain. The golden light from a Victorian street lamp fell on a woman, tall and slim, who was walking with quick,

182

echoed steps to the house opposite. Elfie watched her look up at her, turn back, unlock the door and disappear. All these manifold self-contained lives behind their secret-keeping, closed doors. She left the curtains parted and walked away from the window. Glancing at her watch, she noticed it was nearly half-past six. She decided she would drink her whisky quickly and leave to find Judith who was noisy and clumsy but had the redeeming gift of life which was missing here in Philip's absence.

*   *   *

It was not until Pont Street that Philip found a vacant taxi. He clambered in, shouting his destination to the driver, clutching his briefcase and brooding about Elfie. As the cab waited at the crossroads for the lights to turn green, he realised she would not be there for his return. Caged, she would refuse to wait. He sat in the taxi, perched tensely forward on the edge of the back seat, the rain from his umbrella forming a spherical pool on the floor. He remembered the expression on her face when he had exclaimed at the rose. He remembered that when they had entered the house half-an-hour ago, she had kept her coat on but changed her wet boots in the hall for some shoes she had bought that day. A pair of pumps. Cut so low at the front that he glimpsed the cleavage between her toes. The intimacy of the little perception had startled him.

She will not wait, he thought in some despair. He leaned forward to the driver.

'Turn round,' he ordered, directing him back to the house. 'Hurry. I've forgotten something,' he added.

He thought it was ludicrous that shame at his emotions should force him to give an excuse to the other faceless man.

'Bloody hell,' said the driver. 'All this song and dance and it's only a couple of hundred yards back to the road,' but he made a lumbering U-turn between a flow of traffic.

Philip was unaccustomed to U-turns; the volatility of his feelings shocked him. He was aware he was not allowing himself to think or to control.

Paying the driver double, he hurried, almost ran over the cobbles, slipping once on the wet surface but righting his balance before he fell. He glanced up to see if the light was still on in the drawing room and felt a flood of relief that the window was lit. She was undoubtedly there, too conscientious a person to leave without switching the lamp off.

As he let himself into the hall, he called out: 'Elfie.' Then feeling a little panicky at the lack of response, 'Elfie' again. He yanked open the drawing room door: it was empty, her glass empty too beside his. As he burst back into the hall, he saw her coming out of the cloakroom, re-booted, dressed for departure with her redingote buttoned to the neck, her bag on her shoulder, two parcels in her right hand. For a moment they faced one another without speaking. She was logical enough to assume at first that he had forgotten a document, but it was immediately apparent that this was not the case.

'You were leaving,' he said. 'I knew it.'

'What about your meeting?'

He shook his head slowly. He felt deeply ashamed. To flout the habits of a lifetime was unthinkable, and for a woman. He was not a teenager. He would doubtless regret it, but he had done it and there it was.

'Stupid thing,' he said. 'I didn't think you'd stay.'

He went straight to the telephone in the drawing room and she heard him speaking.

She followed him and stood by the window, tempted to protest. He ignored her, turned his back massively on her. His words reached her as though from a distance. He was detained; it was unavoidable and there was nothing he could do; could they rearrange it for tomorrow?

She stood rooted, wrapped in her damp coat and boots, still clutching her possessions. Part of her was stirred by the rawness of his need to which she responded. Another part remained sufficiently aloof to realise that to stay now was to acquiesce and embrace a complication. Or was it? Unacknowledged and buried fathoms deep was the hope that he could be a solution. How does one start another life? The huge desire filled her breast. She had a sudden image of standing beside him in the close air of the glasshouse last summer, watching him brush one rose against another, crimson on lilac. His quiet voice returned: 'The pollen adheres.' She remembered the soft velvety potpourri of the fallen rose petals on the bench. She recalled the two words: 'controlled chance'. In the still point of recognition, she now accepted what she would do.

She slipped the bag slowly off her shoulder, put the parcels on the floor and came towards him.

'You will be discreet, won't you?' she whispered. Foolish question. It was in his interest as well as hers.

Still swaddled in their thick wet coats, they put their arms round one another. For a moment they rested one against the other for consolation, not passion, their heads side by side, his turned towards hers, a strand of her damp fair hair catching in his mouth. He withdrew briefly to look at her and traced the edge of her high forehead lightly with his finger, then bent to kiss her, enfolding first her wide full upper lip and then her lower. He recognised in her face the mingling of desire and gratitude that he felt on his own. Years ago, before he had married Martha, he had made love to a girl of seventeen, a beautiful

186

creature, who had lain back on the grass, her long straight hair fanning out in a million rays. 'I love this more than anything,' she had whispered. An abandon, total yet savoured, that he had not experienced since.

Like dancers, in slow movements they unbuttoned each other. Their bodies felt strange, years of marriage and all its fidelities habituating them to familiar shapes and to other rituals.

'We're not comfortable here,' he murmured.

'Do you mind?' he asked as he took her into the bedroom. Do you mind that it is Martha's too? he meant, though he could not bring himself to say it. He minded himself. Habits were as hard as rock. They ran like coal fissures through his life since time immemorial. He had by habit been faithful to Martha and, even now, it tore to turn aside.

As he entered her, he thought again of the girl spread out on the grass. Nakedness, secrets laid open, but now in a mature woman. Her lips were parted against his face, and arching upwards, she pulled him voluptuously against her, burying him in her hot wet depths, swarming around him. The violence of their coming made him groan. They lay for a few moments exhausted and unmoving, her long thighs holding him, her knees tented.

'Don't go, please.'

He just caught her words as he tried to pull out. He braced himself on his arms and looked down at her with utmost tenderness. Hair fanned out. The glistening sweat on her breasts. She smiled back, smoothing his hair away from his face. He thought of the strangeness of this day, each part extraordinary and unlooked for. The floating notes of the flute, the crimson velvet rose, the ardour of her body.

CHAPTER FIFTEEN

It was an old maxim, thought Philip with some bitterness, that if you intended to play around, you should choose a married woman. Even a mere MP knew that and, God knows, they had more at stake than others. And probably more opportunity too, he imagined, recalling a group of them who had been jocularly known as the four o'clock fuckers.

However, this maxim was scarcely one that applied to him. He wasn't playing around and the seriousness of his involvement alarmed him. He knew this was no case of simple lust. Indeed, he feared his dependency would be greater than hers. Part of him was frightened that she was the one who might be indulging in a dalliance and had earmarked him, a married man, for convenience. Yet he could not believe this. Her personality defied it. All her demeanour and actions so far had marked her as warm, principled and sensitive. Neither tricky like Martha, nor a foolish romantic, nor the classic bored wanderer.

After she had left him early the following morning, he had lain there thinking, a prey to doubt and answerable to all the boll-weevils that lie in wait for the loneliness of the morning after. The strangeness of it still surprised him. How had it happened? And on her part, why? Or was he silly to seek out an explanation. Women were so often foreign territory—not the old simple opposites to men now, but speakers of a different language. Was she at loggerheads with Hugh? She had given no sign, but then loyalty could be a possible reason.

'What do you want of me?' he had asked her in the middle of the night.

There had been silence.

'Nothing. I have no claims on you.'

That was not quite what he had meant. And the odd thing was that though he should have been entirely relieved, part of him felt slightly rebuffed.

She was lying folded around the back of his body. Her breasts against the hollows of his spine, her hand shallowly laid over the fur on his chest.

He had no wish to make comparisons but he felt the difference from Martha who slept curled in upon herself except for their brief occasional couplings.

He had turned round to face her in the dark. He could not see her properly, but traced her features as though he was brushing a relief sculpture.

Doesn't Hugh make you happy? he had wanted to ask. But he shrank from introducing her spouse, or his, into their nocturnal duet. Unpractised though he was at this sort of situation, he sensed that two could so easily become four. Indeed, had already become four, in that both brought their marriages as baggage which could not easily be left outside the room. Doubts flickered and darted around him. He realised how little one knew of anyone's life. Did Hugh have a secret world, and for that matter, did Martha? Was this why she had scarcely used their London house this autumn, whereas in previous years she had been desperate to spend most of the winter in town.

Even after he had got out of bed, the confusion within him persisted. I am over fifty, he had thought, shaving in front of the bathroom mirror, surrounded by Martha's decor: maize-coloured walls, sea-grass carpeting, big white bath with limed oak panelling, glasses of sea-shells and apothecary sundries and doodahs on the shelf above. Over fifty, no beauty now, crumpled, five feet nine and half inches, a bit paunchy, well past my first flush and even my second, an ex-squash player, ex a lot of things actually, but still striving and quite powerful in my own horrible persuasion industry way, and not unattractive I suppose—

well I must be given that plenty of women have hung themselves out on the line though like an idiot I've always held back. Even so, none of this actually explains why she of all people in her position should want me.

He nicked himself with the razor and winced, in self-disgust rather than pain. A cut on the chin always looked at odds with a spruce navy suit. Like a convict, escaped from the chain gang, dressed in borrowed clothing. Staunching the tiny trickle of blood with his finger, he licked the tip and the salt taste suddenly brought back to him her rich womanly flavour and he screwed up his eyes at the intensity of the memory which was still scarlet and alive within him. The strength of the feeling warned him he mustn't make a fool of himself. Too easy for an old faithful by habit like him. Such a conservative emotional life he had led, his male vagrancies entirely contained by the to-ing and fro-ing required by his work.

In any case, did he really want what had happened? He brooded as he climbed into his underwear and slipped on his pale blue shirt. Beforehand, he would have said no, that it ran counter to all the cool regulations of commonsense that he set his faith in. Indeed, he still said no, but felt he had now moved into a region where the climate was so different that he risked saying yes. 'It may be difficult,' she had warned, 'but I usually come to London once a month or oftener. Last minute perhaps but I'll try and see you if I can. And if you want.'

And if I have time, thought Philip, feeling brisker now that he was fully dressed, briefcased and about to bang the front door on his private life. He looked down at the rose package which he had left by the entrance before taking it home to his garden later in the week. It had been responsible for rather a lot.

*　　*　　*

'You could have rung a bit earlier,' said Judith, taking her turn at the wheel on the drive back.

'I know but it was awfully difficult, bumping into an old friend like that. Was Lucy upset?'

'Too engrossed in the wedding.' Judith gave a grunt. 'You know what that will mean? Marquee, oodles of guests, a jamboree, in fact a positive durbah, Giles will die at the cost, we can't afford it, oh God, and Andy will be in a corner adding up and saying it's terribly unfair not to spend the same on him. And his only a loan and not gone forever.' Judith's face buckled in despair.

'He'll understand surely.'

'He won't. Children never understand unfairness.'

Nor will they, dear Judith, thought Elfie, as long as you treat them as children.

'Then don't do the wedding for Lucy,' she said out loud. 'She'll understand that, won't

192

she?'

Judith treated her to a glance of pitying contempt. How little Elfie understood the demands of a family. Nor would she, even if she had a sprog of her own. Real motherhood didn't exist unless you had two or more children to juggle. With only a single child, it was more like alter-egohood.

'So difficult.' said Judith. 'I admit I had the full works at my wedding, but you didn't, did you? A very sensible little registry office affair to which I wasn't invited if I remember correctly.'

They both knew her accuracy wasn't in question. She had yet to forgive Elfie for the absent invitation and reminders were issued at frequent intervals.

'Elfie? Are you listening to me?'

'Yes,' she replied, whilst preferring to be deaf. She had no wish to be reminded of her wedding. The guilt suddenly rose up in her throat and struck her forcibly. Even a registry office ceremony was not without meaning. *Let no man put asunder.*

She twisted her head aside as though to escape from the thought and looked out of the window. To avoid a traffic jam, they had turned off the motorway and had just passed the familiar and evocative sign to Christmas Common on the left that marked they were halfway to Oxford. The rain had stopped but the sky was banked with horizontal layers of

193

silver and mackerel grey. The leaves had mostly fallen and the ploughed earth had turned much of the landscape to brown. Have a little accident, her sister had said earlier this year, six months ago, when those leaves were still new on the trees.

'Judith,' she said.

'What?'

'Oh nothing.'

She felt terribly alone and frightened. The brave part of her character had jumped into deep water last night, forcing the fearful remainder to follow and it was now shivering on the brink.

CHAPTER SIXTEEN

For the last three years Susan had enjoyed a free Saturday. She had always been glad to escape. It was normally a nasty day in the showroom with a high percentage of browsers and people who never said thank you. All these she was happy to bequeath to her replacement, Mrs Sarabanda, a woman with a fortune-teller's name, though she was actually a local doctor's wife and grateful to avoid the weekend clamour of the quick, sick and the dead.

This Saturday afternoon, as for the last three months, Susan had taken her daughter riding. Funded in part by a small commission on the sale of the Chippendale-type chairs, it was the first plank in the Cultivation of Jessica, as she called it at home. People, and especially children, became the company they kept and Susan prayed that nice little girls on cobs were the answer. Kitted out in a second-hand boy's hacking jacket (£10), a pair of old jodhpurs (£8), Nicola Paine's riding boots (free in return for Susan's tape recorder) and a huge helmet (brand-new in case of risks), Jessica had made good progress.

From a nervous beginning, she had mastered the bridle, the saddle and ultimately Spotty, who was grumpy as well as mottled. Cross and hairy, he ambled round the ring, his flanks resistent from years of kicks. Toes up, heels down and knees in, whispered Jessica to herself. Child and pony plodded onwards. 'Watch that fatal triangle,' yelled the instructor, referring to the gap between knee and saddle. Jessica quaked and gripped more tightly.

By the second lesson, she and Spotty had done a little trot, both bumping around like sacks of coals. By the third she was rising to the rhythm, up-down, one-two, Spot-ty, Jess-ie. By the fourth, they were cantering and by the fifth she was flying. All Susan's maternal love was kindled when she watched her daughter set off in an Indian file of eight ponies, her position always last but one, her pockets bulging with carrots, her peaky little face dwarfed by the bug-sized helmet on top of her head. Jessica was still fearful and there would be a nervous exchange before every session. 'I won't be sick, will I?' she would ask anxiously. 'No. You won't be sick,' was Susan's ritual reply. But this Saturday, Jessica had forgotten to ask.

When Susan picked her up, she was as usual ecstatic.

'Cloud nine?' asked Susan.

'Heaven numéro sept.' It was her mother, not her school, who had taught her to count to ten in French.

Smelling hotly of hay and dung, she sat in the passenger seat of the car practising the trot within the confines of her seat belt. Her cheeks were scarlet.

'I looked at Spotty's teeth today.' She glanced expectantly at Susan and maintained a steady up-down rhythm. Her light brown pudding-basin hairstyle, trimmed every month by Susan in the kitchen, bounced in time.

'Oh?'

'He's twelve.'

'Oh, yes?' said Susan absent-mindedly, pulling out of the muddy stable drive and into the lane.

'That's two years older than me. In—,' Jessica counted her fingers, 'six years we'll be able to marry.' She wound an elastic band round the fourth finger of her left hand. She twanged it.

Susan glanced at her and laughed. There was no doubt that the pony culture had swallowed Jessica wholesale.

'You'll want to marry someone else by then.'

'No.' Jessica lifted her chin and averted her head. 'I gave him my troth.' She joggled up and down excitedly. The trot had quickened.

My troth, thought Susan. This mode was certainly different from the old disco babble. It must be in imitation of Emily, a pretentious child with plaits and a pointed nose who preceded Jessica in the Indian file on the hack. How quickly the change of allegiance had been effected. It was alarming, this plasticity of children. They could go north or south at the turn of a handle.

She stopped at the T-junction and then pulled out on the main road to Witney.

'Where are we going?' They usually went straight home.

'To see the end of Nick's game.'

It was a big one, quite serious rugby. He'd made the grade of the first fifteen.

He won't want us to watch. He can't bear us to watch,' but she quite wanted to. Nick was her hero.

'He will if they win. We cheer if they do and hide if they don't.'

Susan yawned with tiredness. She slumped in the car seat. Hugh, Elfie, Nick, Jessica, even Madame Sarabanda wore her threadbare by the end of each week.

'You're lolling,' said Jessica. She had become very bossy about posture since riding.

'Right.' Susan sat up straight. With one hand

she ferreted in the glove pocket and was surprised to make some discoveries. 'Want a nose-picker or a carrot?' She extended her palm to her daughter.

'Really,' said Jessica. 'Nose-pickers are made for babies.'

*   *   *

It was a sunny early November afternoon and the car park was full. Susan managed to find a space at the far end of the field. Walking back over the grass with Jessica cantering at her side, she was surprised to see Walter's old yellow Fiesta with Maisie sleeping in the back. How sweet of him, she thought; she had a pang at the idea of the old man's loyalty to his young colleague. She knocked on the door to offer a welcome. Maisie had been dozing but was now jolted upright by the intruder. Patting her felt hat to rights, she made a token bob and smile at her husband's boss, then relapsed into fury. The purple colour rose to her powdered cheeks.

'I'm locked in,' she protested. 'That stupid man.'

Susan tried the door. It was true.

'Oh dear,' she said. 'We'll try and find him,' though it would be wiser, she knew, to consider Walter's marriage as tamper-free as his car. It was the more likely of the two to burst open if you tugged at its doors.

The rugby game was in the full swing of its

198

second half. Susan and Jessica walked round the perimeter of the pitch. They peered through the gaps in the little knots of spectators. It was the usual gathering of meaty boys destined to be future prop-forwards, old Oxford blues and the odd sprinkling of groupie blondes. After five minutes she found Walter on the far side of the pitch. Jessica rushed towards him.

'She's locked in,' she yelled.

'Yes, Walter,' said Susan, her progress more sedate. 'Maisie's stuck in the car.'

Walter beamed, his thin wizened face shining. He pulled his flat cap forward and sucked on his pipe for a moment. Susan had never seen him in such a good mood.

'Her's stuck, is she?' His accent was at its thickest.

Susan frowned suspiciously.

'I locked 'er in,' he said suddenly. 'She locks me out so I locks 'er in.'

The laughter bubbled out of him. He was breathless, hiccuping with pipe smoke and glee.

Man locks wife in box, thought Susan. Surely she had read that line on page 3 of the *Telegraph* back in the early summer. Marriages took all shapes and forms: tit-for-tat probably kept feelings alive over the years quite as well as service and solicitude. An eye for an eye no doubt instilled passion.

'But Walter, what if she needs to get out?'

Walter wasn't listening, distracted by shouts

from the crowd.

'It's even,' he said. '9—9.'

Susan saw Nick on the pitch. From a distance, she tried to examine whether he was bloodied, bruised or just muddy. The last certainly, though it was a dry day.

A roar went up from the spectators at a surprise drop goal. Walter gesticulated with his pipe. Its end was pointed in the direction of a beautiful dark girl with slanting eyes and a floor-length grey and white scarf. Susan recognised Tabitha with some interest, though she had only seen her once.

'What's she doing here?'

'Nick thinks she's—,' Jessica hesitated. The battle between the language of the pony world and the playground left her increasingly speechless.

'Her dad has asked me quite a bit about Elfie,' said Walter, pulling on his pipe reflectively and wheezing a little. 'And about his bees,' he added proudly.

'What do you mean?' She was keeping an eye open for her son. He was a courageous runner and she loved physical bravery. It was a rare quality now that the late twentieth century had bred a race of wimps.

'And *she* has asked me about *him*.' This had happened once or twice when they had worked together in the vegetable garden.

Susan did not care for the change in his tone. He spoke with the sly insinuation of the peasant, that oblique cunning, so ancient and child-like.

'What are you implying, Walter?' She hoped she had struck a balance between reproval and a question mark which encouraged more. There was a below-stairs quality to this gossip that she felt was beneath her, but curiosity impelled her to invite more.

'Watch,' said Walter.

At first she thought he meant she should keep an eye on Philip and Elfie, but his attention had switched to the pitch.

'Nick, Nick, Nicky.' Jessica was leaping up and down.

There was a howl from the crowd. Susan stopped breathing as she saw him pounding over the pitch. He had intercepted a clumsy pass halfway down the field, sold a skilful dummy and was racing for the line. He was tackled as he ran. She gasped and winced as the two men collided, but he pulled free. A few yards more. She was shouting without realising as he hurled himself on the ground and scored a try.

'He did it. He did it. Nicky,' called Jessica.

Tears of pride stung in Susan's eyes.

Nick lay on the ground, clasping the ball, gasping and glorious. He looked up laughing to the place where Tabitha had been standing. Empty. He could not believe it. It was empty. She had left. She had not stayed and witnessed his triumph.

CHAPTER SEVENTEEN

Snow fell in early December, only a few inches but for a week it was reluctant to melt in the countryside. A sudden Arctic plunge in temperature kept it packed at the side of the lanes, capping the branches of the trees from which powdery drifts sprayed to the ground in spite of the lack of wind. The sky seemed drained of strength, never fully awake in the daytime, dormant like the land and like the beehives in Philip's garden which were also furred with snow. Within these wax palaces, the massed honeybees were drowsy with winter though their dwelling had the balmy warmth of a spring afternoon. Guarding their queen, they clustered in a dark sphere in the sheltered centre of the hive, fanning their wings for heat, passing the honey from one to the other, the sap of the hive sustaining them through the long nights and dead months.

Other animals were killed by the sudden cold, the aged and injured succumbing swiftly. A buck rabbit with scaly eyes and manged fur sought shelter under the eaves of the Lyles's house. For three days he pressed shivering against the cold stone walls, too blind to see and too weak to care about his mortal enemies. On the Wednesday morning, Elfie found him dead. She slid his frozen corpse onto a shovel and trudged over the crunching snow to the crest of their land where she would give him a

Valhalla burial. The whippets barked and whimpered behind her, plunging around in circles of exultation over the virgin surface. The ground, so soft to look at with its white velvet nap, was almost too hard to be pierced by a spade. It was heavy work. In the middle of digging the grave, she stopped to ease her aching arms and rested a moment on the shaft of the tool.

The intense stillness of a midwinter day. In the distant sky there was a hum from an aircraft, invisible but doubtless shining with pink and gold in its world of light. Riding above the clouds, it drummed its route north to south, leaving her behind in a pillow of white scarred by black trees and branches like a Chinese painting on silk. The only colour came from the red berries that still hung on the guelder rose. The birds had not plucked them, though one which was pecked bared its pulpy seed through the gaping wound. The gash of crimson reminded her that she had bled as usual in November. In the next twenty-four hours she must decide whether to go to London again. She recognised the self-deception that lay in the impersonal phrase. To London. Such weasel words. To London meant Philip who had rung her in her studio a week ago. She thought it was probably her only chance and it was a narrow opportunity anyway, as Hugh would be back the day after. Another occasion would not be easy, even impossible as Hugh would be regularly at home after Christmas. Should she go? Last time, the decision had been taken on its own momentum and she was its passenger. This time her amorousness would be tainted by severe guilt. To do this twice would not be covered by that convenient term 'a little accident'. Twice was sinning, a compulsive flame in the mind. And yet, when she looked down at the dead rabbit, she wondered whether she was so dreadfully wrong. She was following the law of nature; why resist?

She began to dig again with a renewed vigour, her breath steaming in the icy air. The clods of earth, sticky but soft beneath the crust, stacked up beside the little grave. In any case, she thought, could the ethics of deceit really be invoked by just two occasions, seen in the context of many years? She, Elfie, was an insignificant speck in a huge white world, spinning in the eternal cosmos. Absurd to be so self-important when one thought of things this way. Just one more time, she decided. Her spade flew in and out, inspired by fresh conviction. She rolled the stiff rabbit bumpily towards his little grave and he fell with a thud on its floor. The whippets stood peering over the edge of the chamber, a pair of sentries prepared to guard him all afternoon if need be, but one by one the hard thin rectangles of earth concealed him from their view. Within a few moments the ceremony was complete. The displaced clods of earth rose proud above the surface of the snow.

*   *   *

'Are you still in bed or something?' asked Rupert with one eye on the dealing screen.

There was a delicious groan from Kristina on the other end of the line. He could picture her lying across the sheets. There was something sumptuous about her, yet she had never sated him.

'Where have all the flowers gone?' he enquired smiling. It was a silly reference to the fact that she was using her fatigued Marlene Dietrich voice.

'Are you going to come, then, at Christmas? A nice English family Christmas? In Oxfordshire.' He transferred the phone to his left ear and leaned back in his chair whilst a dealer muttered in his right. He listened with perfect efficiency but it was Kristina's voice that suffused him.

'I don't see the need to take me to the bosom of your family. Are you broody again, Rupert?'

The clipped German cadence was always at odds with the sprawling metaphors and loose syntax of the English language. It was one of her many contrasts that fascinated him.

'You'll be a lonely foreigner if you have nowhere to go at Christmas.'

'But out of town, oof.'

205

'OK, come for the day. We'll go down on the 27th to Meredith's if you prefer. That's sporty, not family.'

He put the phone down, promising to ring her at a later stage. It was mid-morning but a feeling of exhaustion overcame him. He was a fool and a masochist to keep seeing her. Dealing with her on even simple issues meant pushing a boulder uphill and he had enough of that each day. Running a futures fund was stressful enough, high risk, potentially huge losses and breakdowns were not uncommon. It had happened to a friend of his, Daniel, who had taken a loss and had concealed it in the books. 'Bottled and cracked' was the way they had summed it up. It was an epitaph to be dreaded, a term of dismissal for soldiers who had run from the fire of battle.

They were all under strain, from those like him in the upper echelons to the futures floor dealers in the trading pits, the *Untermenschen* who during their short life screamed bids and offers at one another with their complex rituals of hand signals. This 'open outcry' system, as it was known, might be antiquated compared with the electronic dealing in newer exchanges like the *Deutsche Terminbörse* in Frankfurt, but there was a sweaty thrill to it. The smell of the pits, vast sums of money pressed, as it were, by flesh, rather than the anonymous posting of bids and offers on a screen. It was exciting, maybe too much so. He knew he would have an easier and more peaceful life if he could turn his back on derivatives, as the futures and options sector was termed, and become a normal fund manager, a prudent soul of sober habits, a long-term investor who had no need to deal every day. But he was warped by adrenalin, by the speed with which his own market responded to events, by the dangers inherent in the gearing which caused the prices to magnify, by the power of his arena, by the way it towed the equity market, a plodding dobbin, in its wake. At good times he felt the master of the market not its slave, the star not the satellite.

Besides, there had been occasions when, in a bizarre limited way, he had felt he was beating life itself at its own game. A future was merely a binding contract to buy or sell a commodity or a financial instrument at an agreed price at a specific time. Prosaic and material it might be, but when he got it right he felt like a god.

*   *   *

In the immediate aftermath of her visit, Philip had not intended to telephone Elfie. Once out of her orbit, he had assured himself that it had been a moment's anarchy in the tenor of his daily life. Just as the body was accustomed to return to its norm after illness, so too was the mind with its quaint agues. In colder retrospect, he could even see the pattern of events as though on a graph. The level flow broken by a sudden giddy voltage due to an odd conjunction of events. In his case, feeling had temporarily trounced reason. Absurd to think it serious.

In any case, he had plenty to occupy him including a three-day return trip to Russia, though this time he stayed in snow-drenched Moscow. A brave new world indeed for consumers with its *businesmeyni*, stretch limousines and corner kiosks for Absolut vodka. On his return Martha had proved eager to see him and a reconciliation of sorts seemed in prospect. It was a domesticated weekend, visiting her old father in Suffolk and then on Sunday evening, Tabitha's school for a concert. The feeling of the clan returned. The little family kingdom which had started to unravel now had the promise of remaining intact. He thought he had been in peril of neglecting his real treasures, familiar and consolidated, for a trophy of more recent acquaintance. It occurred to him that if Elfie rang, he would demur. But she did not ring.

The following weekend, there seemed a slippage in his relations with Martha. She had wanted to go to a December party which he had resisted. He suddenly felt he had spent enough of his life standing around with a drink in his hand. He refused. It was a trivial difference of opinion but a ridiculous row had developed, quicksilver, from nowhere, sucking her into her usual accusations. The image of a graph came to him again with its withering setbacks and deceptive rallies. He listened to her long list of complaints: her boredom at home, his absences, the empty mews house in London, his work, her lack of it, he owed his success to her. I don't need this, he said to himself. Immediately afterwards, he realised that this thought had sprung to life because he knew now that he had an alternative. This option no longer seemed chaotic and threatening, but tranquil. The following day he had rung Elfie. Her prevarication had left him dismayed.

On the Monday night, he had just clambered into his pyjamas when the telephone rang. Thinking it was Martha, he picked it up without hesitation and froze.

'You shouldn't ring me here', he said, not meaning to start with a reprimand but venting the tetchy uncertainties she had caused him. He remembered her saying, 'You will be discreet.' The obligation cut both ways. Such an egoist to forget. A little fool too.

'Can I talk?'

'As it happens, yes.' He knew he sounded grudging, though underneath he was also relieved. 'Where are you?'

'At home.'

He waited. She had made the call, so let her begin but she didn't. She was in no hurry.

'Are you coming to see me?' he prompted.

'I don't know. What about your wife?'

He had a sudden and inappropriate recollection of a married friend of his who, many years ago, had been asked the same question whilst he begged like a randy dog, waiting on an entry phone for the girl's permission to climb the stairs to her flat. 'What about your wife?' 'My dear, a wife is a wife,' his friend had hissed into the phone in reply.

The memory of the little comedy almost made Philip laugh out loud at first, but part of him winced at the squalid parallel. The recollection sobered him. To what extent could one ever say: this is different; though he knew that it was. He could have paid her back by asking 'What about Hugh?', but instead he said 'Please come. Will you?'

CHAPTER EIGHTEEN

Meredith had invited Hugh and Elfie on the 27th to the country cottage in Oxfordshire. It was a ritual, as also the choice of an off-centre date, since the bull's eye of Christmas Day was reserved for George's parents, or so she always claimed. Rupert would bring Kristina, she had added. The prospect of another outsider, a foreigner to boot, was especially pleasing to Elfie who had rarely taken comfort from the occasion.

This year she was more nervous than usual.

The curse was two days late. Surely meaningless, two days, but it was often early, scarcely ever delayed. On the morning of the 27th she had driven into Burford under the pretext of buying some flowers and wine for Meredith, but she had also bought a pregnancy kit from the chemist. It was incautious on her part and it terrified her. She yearned to try the oracle but feared she could not trust it at this stage. She resolved to resist uncorking it for a few days at least and thrust it to the back of her dressing-chest in its brown paper wrapper. Though out of sight it dominated all thoughts with its power to sit in judgement. She doubted whether she would be able to wait more than a day or so, though she knew that this was too brief an interval for a totally true diagnosis. Absolute certainty could not be guaranteed until a fortnight after the last missed period.

They arrived at Meredith's for lunch. George opened the door. He looked like a pink piggy-bank, which in effect he was, with a satiny face, blue eyes, fair hair brushed straight back and spectacles for gravitas. He exuded a porky satisfaction. His children hurled themselves at Hugh's legs though not Elfie's, vying with each other to capture admiration for their presents.

'Look what I've got,' said Mona and she took her round arms from her grandfather's knee to point to a glossy leather saddle.

'It's for the Shetland pony,' added Florence. She was not in fact suitably dressed for riding but was wearing a white Madame-de-Pompadour wig with ringlets, one of the myriad toys and distractions of Christmas which in this case had arbitrarily transported her two hundred years into the past. It made her look more grown-up and even more dangerous than if she had been wearing her mother's high-heeled shoes.

'She won't take it off,' explained George. 'She went to bed in it last night.'

His presence, substantial for a man in his late thirties, had waxed a little. Elfie felt he had been tucking into one of those gargantuan meals so favoured by one's omnivorous ancestors to warm the blood in winter: carp, a fat capon, venison and a couple of blackbird pies.

She went off to find Meredith in the kitchen. Dressed in designer jodhpurs, she was piling cold goose leftovers on a large pale blue-flowered meat dish.

'Hello, ducky,' said Meredith, which was a bit cheeky for a stepdaughter.

Elfie bent to pick up Albert who was in his tiny cloth chair below the level of the golden retriever, Amos. Meredith flickered her knowing blue gaze over the pair of them.

'How he has grown,' exclaimed Elfie. His powdered intimate baby smell filled her nostrils. He was less pliant than before, less boneless, already a chunky boy in fact in his Paisley boiler suit. She thought of the brown

212

paper-wrapped kit in her chest of drawers. She saw it as a gate to an Albert, but was it open or shut?

There was a fresh wave of greetings in the hall. Rupert and Kristina must have arrived. Still carrying Albert flopped over her left shoulder, patting his satisfyingly resistant small back, she wandered along the corridor over the jute matting into the hall. Amos followed at her heels, his feathery wheat-yellow tail whisking left and right, a dog prepared to like anything he encountered, his DNA programmed for amiability.

As she entered the large room, she could see the little knot of people, each displaying the frantic animation that goes with all arrivals and exits. Even Hugh was affected, his bushy eyebrows working up and down in reaction to the sight of his son and a girlfriend. By now, the children had transferred their attention from him to Rupert as the new bearer of gifts. Both Mona and Florence were transfixed by two large gaudy packages festooned with satin ribbons. Rupert's presents, doubtless purchased through some intermediary or other, were always a marvel of shop-wrapping. Every year Elfie contrasted them with Judith's and Giles's which wore last year's wrapping-paper freshly ironed for this year's Christmas. Rupert did not know that she now passed his paper automatically to Judith. Three years later it would return to her again around some

213

festive offering. She was thinking of its busy itinerary when Rupert bent forward to kiss her. She was struck as always by his similarity to Hugh: the dark grainy skin, the chiselled nose and chin, the speed of gesture. He was only eight years younger than herself. It was always disturbing to recognise she was his generation rather than Hugh's—a match for the son rather than the father. He patted Albert's well-wadded bottom and then turned to the tall blonde woman by his left shoulder who until this moment had been dazzling George.

'Kristina,' said Rupert, 'meet my stepmother.'

'Oh Rupert. Really. What an awful introduction.' Elfie winced at the pantomime description.

The woman turned towards her. Elfie remarked the fair hair groomed to flow in a single movement and the very good sueded skin of the pure Aryan. She was wearing a crimson mohair top and ruby moleskin jeans and was clothed in an adamantine gloss that even the softness of the fabric could not dissolve. The two women measured each other instantly and expertly. There was not actual rivalry in their glance, nor any need for it, but each took account of another attractive blonde on her stamping ground. It occurred to Elfie that the woman was familiar; or was she merely responding to an alertness in the gaze.

'We have seen each other before, I think,'

said Kristina.

'I'd remember.' Elfie shook her head, though uncertainly. She did not recognise her voice, swaying and a little stagey in its use of English.

She could feel Albert give a tiny yawn on his perch beside her neck. She half-turned so that the new visitor could greet him also. Perhaps something appropriate would slip out like '*Mein Schatz*' or an endearment with -*chen* or -*lein* at the end of it, but nothing was forthcoming.

'How are you doing, Albert?' asked Rupert, but he turned back to shepherd Kristina through the hall, leaving a lustrous sexual trail in her wake. He wanted to avoid looking too baby-prone in her presence, after her crack about his broodiness. Elfie thought that all his urbanity could not conceal the fact that he was obsessed with her. Even George was responsive. He had taken off his horn-rimmed spectacles in order to display a little more conspicuously. She wondered whether she had indeed seen her before. She had not met her, she was sure of that, yet her form was familiar but different, like a person caught in monochrome rather than colour.

Without its centrepiece the knot had broken up. The men meandered out of the hall. The two children scuttled after them, uttering little cries, each bearing a huge shiny parcel, like ants manoeuvring outsize eggs to their nest.

Elfie, left alone, bent to pick up the present she had given Mona. A knitted wool doll, Rumpelstiltskin one way up with a crochet skirt hemmed with ruched roses, and a gipsy the other way when you inverted her and folded the skirt down to its patchwork reverse. An enchanting doll, made with love and painstaking attention to detail, but it had not enchanted Mona. I shall give it to my own, decided Elfie, and immediately erased the thought.

Part of her wished desperately she had never bought the dreadful pregnancy kit this morning, that she had never met Philip, that she could obliterate the recent deviance, that she might peel back the months to that cool still time before complications. She stood alone in the hall with Albert, their heads resting together, his heart beating its butterfly wings below her collarbone, his chit-chat of coos and gurgles fluttering against her left ear. She felt possessed by a strange sense of enclosure, burdened by the knowledge that whatever might happen, she would always be walled up with the weight of a secret within her. She looked round the hall, at its deep gold-painted walls, the two upright padouk chairs provided by Hugh, a pot of white poinsettia on the oak chest, at the large logs smouldering in the hearth to which George had administered his hearty squire's kick before departure, at the whole carefully constructed country scene of

216

plenty and pleasure. In the distance she could hear the whoops and murmurs of the family gathering: banter, belly-laughs, the tearing of paper, the pouring of grog, all the high-grade noise of the party season. Albert stirred in her arms at the sounds and scents of his first Christmas. Dear God, thought Elfie, let me not be pregnant.

There was a rustle at her side and she looked down to find Florence, bewigged and wearing navy corduroys and a navy Guernsey.

'Mummy says are you going to be a ghost or do you want to come and eat something. Even if you don't, Albert does.'

Florence was clearly not only word- but also tone-perfect. Hers was a flawless performance. Force-fed, she had captured and re-enacted her mother's voice without fault. She exhaled a miniature version of her lack of respect for her step-parent.

You bitch, Meredith, thought Elfie. It'll be one in the eye for you if I bloody well am pregnant. The idea was invigorating.

About to say 'Lead on' to Florence, she switched at the last moment to 'Follow me', then added 'I think you should take that wig off. Tell Mummy there's a time and place for everything.' Florence, alert to a change of role, looked up at her, cherry mouth slightly open so that her large white teeth glistened. Startled into submission she yanked at one of the white ringlets. The wig slid off and her long straight

217

hair slithered to her shoulders. She turned round and charged off down the corridor. Doomed to shuttle between two opposing forces, she had been kitted out with a new message. In the distance Elfie could hear her yelling, 'Mummy, I've taken off my wig. Elfie says there's a time and place for everything.'

*   *   *

'Did you enjoy yourself, darling?' Elfie asked Hugh as they drove home in the dark. A sense of shame had driven her to be extra solicitous all day. She now took his hand and kissed it.

'I've got indigestion.' He rubbed his upper chest and tried to burp. The airlock remained unmoved.

'Oh Hugh. Not that goose, I hope.'

'Those children on my stomach. They pulverised it.'

'You were laughing.'

'Was I? It seemed fun at the time.'

She had a moment's fear. He had been removed from the orbit of normal boisterousness for so long. Was he really too worn to endure what might be inflicted? She envisaged years pandering to his tetchiness. It was likely that the bill she would have to pay would be considerable, hugely inflated no doubt by an element of hidden revenge.

'What did you think of Kristina?' she asked as they swung left into the drive.

218

'Quite a banquet. Element of indigestion there too.'

'Rupert's happy to tuck in. He's mad about her.'

'Poor Rupert,' said Hugh, sitting in the dark for a moment before opening the car door. 'I just hope she doesn't marry him.' Like father, like son, he thought.

*   *   *

They walked across the cobbles of the mews, the echo of their steps ricocheting from one side to the other. It was deserted at ten o'clock at night, most of the residents choosing to spend the entire Christmas holiday in the country or abroad.

It is a long time, thought Rupert, since I have been as happy. He felt at peace. The day had proved a surprising success, sealed by the mutual admiration between Kristina and Meredith and George. The club, clannish and exclusive, had claimed a new member. He reflected that, having spat Elfie out, they would the more enthusiastically digest Kristina, since all comparisons invoked greater contrast. He whirled the car keys around his index finger, watching Kristina walk slightly ahead of him. I think it will be all right, he thought, feeling a little woozy from tiredness and contentment.

'Rupert.'

'Sweetheart?'

'It was here.' She stopped abruptly near the door of her little terraced house.

'What was?'

He went up to her and ran his hand down her right side. Her lips were blackberry in the light from the Victorian lamp.

'I knew I had seen her before.'

He stopped, puzzled.

'Elfie.' She had been emphatic about this on the drive back to London. 'Twice.'

He dropped his hand from her flank.

'And so?'

She stood against her front door, her back resting against it, in no haste to enter, indeed in no haste to continue talking.

'Well?' he prompted again.

'I don't know whether to tell you. It's not my business. Nor yours.' She paused to correct herself which she often did, being perfectionist in her use of a foreign language. 'Yours neither? Which should it be?'

'For God's sake, Kristina, it doesn't matter.'

'Nor yours, I think.' She looked up at the opposite house.

'Tell me.' He felt suddenly anxious that there should be no secrets between them. He wanted to share, to be joined.

'It was in November. I was coming back here early in the evening. Rain, wind, I was in a hurry. I looked up at the window of the opposite house. See?' She pointed.

Rupert followed her direction. It was dark

and closed. A white façade like the others, a balcony on the first floor. It looked serene and untroubled, not a party to any complications.

'I saw a woman looking out of that upper floor. Half an hour later a man embraced her. When you're on your own you see these things. They had not pulled the curtain. The following morning, early, about seven, she left. I did not see her face, she tucked it down, but her hair, its form is very distinctive. About a fortnight ago, perhaps a bit longer, the same thing happened again. I saw the same woman leave early in the morning. It is your Elfie. I have no doubt. I would not say this if I had any doubt.'

He felt shaken, terribly flaky in the face of her emphasis, but aversion made him protest. He needed to deflect the blow against his father.

'You could be mistaken. A face at a window, poor light in the early morning.'

'Does she have a black fitted coat? A redingote you call it?'

Rupert thought back. She had been wearing a full-length sheepskin today. But last winter? He groaned inwardly. They had met him the previous March for a drink before the opera. He had handed her the coat.

'It's still meaningless,' he said.

'A kiss? Of that kind?'

He felt a spurt of anger. 'You've been compiling a fucking dossier on my father's wife.'

She compressed her lips, a thin black line, and swung round to put the key in the lock.

'As if I should care about your family. I told you I did not want an involvement.'

'I'm sorry.' He caught her shoulder. 'It's not your fault.' He was appalled at the speed with which the wind could change direction.

They entered the hall and she pressed the light switch.

'Who's the guy?' He submitted, because he didn't want to fight her, to imperil their love-making

'He is called Philip Dacre. He spends the week here and has a second home in Oxfordshire, not far from where we went today, I believe. I know the wife by sight. She has scarcely been here this winter.'

The exactitude of her description left him infinitely depressed. The name, the place, the figures at the window began to take on a bleak form. A cloud of misogyny affected his spirits. He told himself that maybe the two incidents she had recounted meant nothing, but he had that awful bone-marrow conviction of their truth.

'Well,' he said as they climbed the stairs. 'As you say, it's not your business, nor mine. Forget it, it's probably nothing.'

And if it is, he decided, what the hell, human beings are no better than you expect them to be. But this impersonal approach had only a brief life. The man-of-the-world pose capsized as a sense of blood betrayal engulfed him, a tiny bolt of the vendetta. That too passed but it left him with a real heartache for his father and a painful desire to protect him.

CHAPTER NINETEEN

I shall do something very hopeful, thought Lydia, but her hand was trembling as she stretched it out for the seed catalogue. Hope is in the seeds, she instructed herself, remembering how Ronnie had told her that hope was in his trees, but the sleight of phrase failed to deceive her. If hope wasn't vested in the person, she knew it was nowhere.

It was seed catalogues that had hooked her irrevocably onto gardening as soon as Judith and Elfie had grown up. Inhaling dust, surrounded by rubble in the old house they had moved into, she would fall asleep at night in a haze of flower pictures and promises. Until recently the magic had continued to work even though she had learnt better than to subscribe to St Paul's 'Whatsoever a man soweth, that also shall he reap' which was no more true of gardening than of life. Yet she persisted, even after passing the milestone of her eighty-second birthday. When a special plant thrived which she had grown from seed, there was nothing to equal the puff of self-congratulation.

Which shall it be this year?, she asked herself briskly, though it was hard to think of seeds rather than Ronnie, or of the future not the past. She started to flick through the catalogue and strove to concentrate. In previous years, she had usually sown one plant for the conservatory that looked like a challenge. Sometimes its defiance proved no more than bluff. The plumbago had produced its milky blue showers in its first season from sowing, so too had a passion flower with great pink crystalline stars. Others in contrast had turned out a disaster. The first year she had tried to sow a crimson banksia. It had germinated, put out two thrilling leaves, then damped off in agonisingly slow motion. The second year it didn't get quite so far. Last year she had refused to try it, fearing it would become one of those obsessional obstacles that sap one's best energies. Now, once again, as she leafed through the contents, she noticed it lurking on page sixty-two of the catalogue, a contemptibly flashy piece trying to catch her eye. We shall snub it, she murmured to Ben, the spaniel, who was muttering and groaning at her feet in the depths of ancient sleep. He gave an epileptic shudder through his coma. 'Oh no, not you too, don't you leave me,' said Lydia, putting the catalogue aside to place a hand on his lumpy flank.

The little gilt carriage clock chimed half-past three on the stone mantel, a prissy ding-dong that always irritated her. Ronnie had received it as a retirement present twenty years ago from the firm. She heaved herself out of her green velvet chair and walked over to his photograph by the clock. He should have seen the doctor by now and be on his way home. He had refused to let her accompany him, stoic as ever in the face of adversity. She stared at his picture taken fifty years ago, youthful, the way one's kernel always felt no matter how old the cells or how hard the crust. He was fit then and full of life, one of his feet planted in a confident, colonising sort of way on the wide flat running board of the old Rover. The nauseous smell of its mingled petrol and leather swamped her memory now.

The telephone rang and she walked stiffly towards it. Could he have been detained, rushed at once into hospital, a victim in one of those plangent, clamorous episodes, a top-gear car chase with klaxon whooping and blue light flashing? But it was only Judith, dear Judith, lumpen but genuine.

'No,' said Lydia, 'he's not back. I'll ring you as soon as he comes.'

She put the receiver carefully back on its perch, unable to talk, indeed to invent anything to say, because paralysis in the face of the unknown held her brain in suspense.

It was cold because she had forgotten to stoke up the fire in the grate. Her hands hung like stones. As she crossed the room, she heard

225

a tapping and fluttering against the window. She turned and saw that a blue tit had flown in through the upper casement and was trying to peck its way out. It was ominous, she thought: a bird in the house meant death. The superstition gripped her. She went to open the large window to release it. The little terrified morsel of feathers was hiding behind a stack of magazines on the shelf. He fluttered within her cupped palms, shitting in panic. She could feel his heart pounding up into his blue and white head, down into the tips of his scaly toes. A fighter, he pecked heroically at her thumb. Such life-force, she thought, as she released him like a bullet from the window.

So much life around, though how much in Ronnie? She remembered a manuscript painting Elfie had shown her from a book on those terrorising mouth-of-hell visions of the fifteenth century: Death with his hook seizes his prey. Had Death with his hook grabbed Ronnie? She turned back to the seed catalogue, her only defiance in the face of the Grim Reaper. 'Whatsoever a man soweth, that also shall he reap,' she murmured mechanically with her usual contempt. She turned the pages again but the flowers passed before her unseeing gaze. The seed, the burst into life, the cutting down of the hay, renewal, resurrection with a small 'r', so much more consoling and convincing than the myths and implausibilities of the big 'R'. A snatch from a childhood poem floated into her head. 'Little brown seed, oh little brown brother, Are you awake in the dark? Here we lie cosily, close to each other, Hark to the song of the lark.' I am mad, she thought, quite mad, to cling on to these sentiments.

She heard the noise of his horn before the drum of the motor. He would always sound a double toot at the bend in the road. She jumped up, thinking it a good sign that he should still be careful about his licence: it suggested continuity. When the spaniel had been younger, he would bark with joy at the hoot, his hosanna that his master was returning. Now he was too far gone to notice. Watching from the window, she saw the flash of silver metal through the leafless trees as the Ford puttered gently into the garage. There was a familiar crunch of gravel as Ronnie got out, deceptively familiar perhaps, the same sound whether he was returning to the house with a bag of groceries from Sainsbury or with a note pronouncing a death sentence. Who could tell the difference? She was about to open the door and rush towards him but some instinct restrained her. She noticed he was returning to the house with no more and no less than he possessed when he had left it an hour and a half ago. The observation chilled her. A happy heart buys a packet of biscuits, a newspaper, anything, on its way home because it is reassured that it will carry on. It will eat, it will read, it will live. The doomed travel light. Possessions are already a burden.

She saw him close the driver's door carefully with a precision-made clunk. Had she been present, it would have been done by way of instruction. He was always annoyed that she shut it intemperately, with insufficient force so that it teetered on its catch, or with an excess that caused metal fatigue. She expected him to climb the three paved steps to the terrace and she held herself in readiness to put her arms around him. But he didn't. Instead he walked slowly towards the back of the garden. It was muddy from the recent melt of a light snowfall two days ago, but he was undeterred. She watched him go first to one sweet chestnut and then the other. He tried to bend down but straightened swiftly as though there were some impediment within. Then he walked over to the small greenhouse on the way back to the house.

Oh dear God, she thought. She knew, she simply knew that she was watching him going through the process of withdrawal. She knew she was witness to his first step on a solitary journey. He had sought consolation amongst his tools, his plant labels, his John Innes composts, rather than face another human being, rather than see his wife. Dust to dust. Compost to compost. She left the front door open and went out into the garden without a coat. It was very cold and spitting slightly, a fine sleet or rain, but she didn't notice. Clouds of

228

mist from her quick breathing preceded her. She stepped with care down the slippery terrace slabs and over the grass which was knobbly with wormcasts. Her shoes sucked a little at the squelchy ground. As she opened the greenhouse door, she saw him standing there, not doing anything. He lifted his head at the noise of the sliding glass. For a moment they gazed at one another in silence.

'Oh my darling boy,' she said, 'is it?'

'Yes it is,' he replied simply. 'Sorry to be a nuisance.'

CHAPTER TWENTY

It had not been difficult after all to postpone using the pregnancy kit. In fact Elfie had made a great success of obliterating it. Every time she opened the chest of drawers she refused to meet the eye of the brown paper bag which was snuggling in wait at the back. When January came, she thought of its two-faced god, Janus, looking backwards and forwards, and decided she wanted to do neither. All desire had veered to fear of the consequences of what she had done.

She knew she was both irrational and pathetic, but half the trouble was that she had not been alone. Hugh, who had been suffering the effects of a heavy cold in the new year, was a constant and noisy presence in the house.

'Christ,' he kept saying at every sneeze, putting his hand to his head. If this was his reaction to the drama of a sneeze, thought Elfie, feeding him hot whisky and lemon, what pray would a baby elicit?

On 5 January he returned to the showroom. It would have been normal for them to drive in together. She was working in the studio on a canvas, a protracted and arduous job, and the date of delivery was threatened with delay. Instead, she pleaded the onset of his cold and stayed at home. Her period was now eleven days late. There was no shred of doubt that if she took the test it would be 99 per cent correct, not 95, nor 96, nor any other per cent but virtually the absolute truth. There would be no hiding place.

She walked out of the kitchen, through the flag-stoned hall and up the stairs, leaning briefly on the bannisters for support as she fell prey to a second's weakness. She crossed the bedroom floor, walking straight over the aging Shiraz rug which she usually avoided in deference to its worn pile. She pulled open the mahogany chest of drawers, seized the kit and wrenched off its wrapping. The brown paper floated to the floor. The cellophane, shrink-wrapped, proved harder to penetrate. Cursing, she tore at it with her teeth. The telephone rang.

'Shit,' she said, spitting out a sliver of plastic. She wondered whether to answer it, then duty compelled her since it might be Hugh. It was.

'Where have you put the invoice for those shipping goods to New York?'

'In the desk drawer,' she said tersely, hoping that was it and that she could put the telephone down.

'You know,' he went on, 'this cold hasn't really gone.' He wanted to talk about it.

'Is it so very awful?' she asked, knowing that in the long run, this was the quickest way to get rid of him.

'The worst I can remember for years.'

'Headache?'

'Headache, catarrh, coughing all morning—'

'It's just a cold, Hughie. Better soon.'

She remembered Judith complaining how much fuss men made when they were ill. Not true of my darling father, she thought sadly. The confusing, painful cross-sections of all their different lives struck her. So much simultaneous departure and arrival. Death, birth and marriage. She had only managed the last so far. She waited at the rim of the second, her father at the mouth of the first.

'Elfie?' said Hugh plaintively. 'Are you there? I think I might come home at lunch if I don't feel any better.' He gave a bellowing cough like an elephant. 'Christ,' he added to convey agony.

'Oh darling,' she said, 'I might not be here. I've let the heating go out.'

It was a damned lie and the pipes gave an

231

ardent rumble of protest at that very moment. But she felt desperate not to see him immediately. She would need a day's practice at composing herself. She looked down at the kit, reading the instructions. It promised it would take only five minutes to pronounce.

'Well,' he said, 'perhaps I won't come back just yet.' He had envisaged a nice nest, well-lined with fluff and feathers, his brown leather slippers, a good autobiography or some Cabinet reminiscences say, beside a wife-stoked log fire. Since the prospect had faded, he rang off.

The call had a sobering effect on Elfie. The temperature of the room seemed to have dropped in sympathy. She picked up the cardboard package and went into the bathroom to open it. The instruction leaflet looked complicated with its diagrams of urine collection tray, small window (the control), large window (the result) and the sample window. She frowned in anxiety. She belonged to a generation that was one of the last to be reared on words rather than pictures. As a result, diagrams always panicked her. She felt those that were now before her had all the air of an aptitude rather than a pregnancy test. She could feel her heartbeats in her fingertips and her hands trembled slightly. For a moment the text and pictures blurred before the severity of her gaze. Then her sense of purpose returned and with it her usual lucidity.

It seemed there were seven steps to the test. The culmination was the development of a thin blue line in the large window of the slide, or not as the case might be. No blue line meant failure. She peed half a tea-cupful into the little white tray, then took hold of the plastic dropper: she counted as she plopped one, two, three, four, five precious beads of the clear golden liquid into the slide. She waited a second hesitantly. I could go away, she thought, and return in five minutes or even an hour, but she sat mesmerised, watching the liquid, now blue by some chemical trickery that she had never bothered to learn, seeping slowly across the little windows of the slide. She felt alone and remote and paid no attention to Bertie who had wormed his way upstairs and was making snuffling noises at the foot of the bathroom door. The cobalt blue tide seeped on. As it neared the crucial stage, she rose to stare out of the window, unable to sit passively and watch the slow-motion progress. A squirrel was digging in characteristically jerky fashion for nuts in Hugh's precious lawn. It was undeterred by two plastic windmills, relics from his last mole campaign. I shall turn back as soon as it stops, she thought. She felt like a puppet acting, not like a real, breathing person. The animal, startled by a noise, scuttled off. As if programmed, yet dazed that the moment had come, she turned and peered down at the slide. It was a phenomenon, remember? A test-tube which would change nothing. As she gazed, she saw as though from a distance that a blue line had formed in its large window. She stared at it incredulously. It must be the wrong window, surely it was the wrong window, but no, it was the right window. For a second she was afflicted by self-doubt. This was some frenzy of the mind, some defect in her sight, both fallen victim to some inner conjuring trick. Yet as she stared, she also knew. It would seem, and indeed there was no doubt, the word 'seem' was inadequate to the occasion, that she was going to have a baby. For a moment she felt tongueless, then she repeated the words out loud. I am going to have a baby. 'Oh my God,' she said to Bertie, who had at last managed to nose his way through the bathroom door, 'it's worked, oh my God, I am going to have a baby.'

As she spoke the words, the feeling of remoteness that had gripped her for the last half-hour fell away and the vacuum was replaced by euphoria. An extraordinary sensation like being airborne elated her. The sense of achievement was overwhelming. It had actually worked. She had made it work. She had taken a fragment and made it whole, from nothing she had created a universe. Her senses were charged with an incandescent energy. She could smell the burnt peppery scent of the bronze chrysanthemums on the bathroom window-sill, hear the tiny whiffle of the compressed wind through the join in the sash.

Happiness engulfed her, so huge that it was physical, so complete that it was self-justifying, so exultant that it brought in its wake a perfectly clear conscience. It had worked.

*   *   *

'Judith.'

'You. What a funny time to call. It isn't Daddy is it? He's not worse?'

'I haven't rung about that.'

'Well, it's a very expensive time to ring,' said Judith reprovingly. Only serious illness justified phoning a member of the family before six-o'clock cheap rates.

'It's important.'

'Cough up then.'

'Do you recall what you said to me in the spring?'

Judith scratched about in the soft earth of her brain. Like most people who talk a lot, she was unselfconscious about what she said and it went consequently unremembered.

'Umm. What? Give me a clue.' She was happy to play guessing-games on someone else's paysheet.

'You said have a little accident.'

Judith's mind, befogged and one-dimensional with the onset of family illness, immediately focussed on some catastrophe or other.

'Not an accident,' she said groaning. 'Oh no,

235

what's happened now.'

'Judith, I'm pregnant.' Elfie had practised saying this to the dog but had not entirely managed to make it her own as yet.

'Pregnant. You. Oh Elfiekins darling.' Judith had not called her this since childhood. She was genuinely stirred. 'How simply amazing. When is it due?'

'September.'

'Not for ages. You've only just found out. I bet Hugh's pleased after all. I told you they always adjust.'

'He doesn't quite know yet.'

There was a pause. The elation, previously at boiling point, settled to a simmer.

'Not quite, or not at all?'

Silence.

'Ah,' said Judith. 'When are you going to tell him?'

'I'm practising on you.'

'I don't think a rehearsal is much use in this case.'

'No,' agreed Elfie, slightly stung to be reminded of what she already knew. 'No point in bowling over rabbits, is there, when there's a lion in the sights.'

There was another silence. Both women reviewed the difficulties of lion-taming. The prospect daunted.

'Just make sure he's well fed and cossetted, then he'll love the idea.'

'Hugh's not Giles you know,' said Elfie

236

dismissively.

'Of course not, Hugh's precious isn't he?'

Elfie shut up.

'By the way,' prodded Judith. 'I've not asked you how you did it. It really was an accident on purpose, wasn't it? You left the thing out?'

'Sort of.' Elfie felt in serious need of vagueness. She glanced in the mirror. Her face had flushed pink.

'Goodness.'

Judith was awed by the starring role she had played in the whole affair. She imagined herself saying to Giles in the evening, 'It was actually my idea, you know'. She could swear him to secrecy. Giles was terribly discreet after all, well practised at containing his clients' confidences. He only leaked them to her.

'Judith,' said Elfie. 'You are not under any circumstances whatsoever to tell Giles or anybody else about the nature of this event. It was an extraordinary accident.'

'Crap,' said her sister. 'I said "let there be light" and there was.'

*   *   *

Lydia put the telephone down and went over to Ronnie. She sat carefully on the crochet bedcover avoiding his legs. Little sticks, they would splinter if she leaned against them. How much weight he had lost in the space of a few weeks. Once he had looked like a snowman,

237

round of head and round of body, but his snow had quite melted away. From the chair beside the bedroom window, the day nurse looked on. Lydia had vowed to keep Ronnie at home as long as possible but his deterioration had been so rapid that a nursing home would soon be inevitable.

'He's such a good patient,' said Nurse Williams brightly. Her knitting needles clicked rhythmically as she pearled and plained her way along the ribbed neck of a pink jumper. Lydia wished she wouldn't knit. Many a patient's head must have fallen from the tumbril in front of this particular tricoteuse.

'Can you hear me darling?' she asked. She took his hand which was plucking at the sheet in a way that she did not like. Mortality was in his fingers.

He was heavily drugged and his hearing as well as his sight could be fitful. However, he now focussed on her and something of the old alert Ronnie flickered behind his eyes.

'We are going to have a grandchild.'

Lydia had felt a tug of joy at the news, even in the pit of her depression. She hoped desperately that he would be pleased. He asked every day about his infant trees.

'Judith?' He looked puzzled. He associated all things fecund with his Judith, but wasn't she a bit old? It must be these damned fertility drugs with their humiliating effects.

'Not Judith. Elfie. She's got a baby coming.'

238

'Little Elfiekins? She's a bit young for this isn't she?'

'She's going to come and see us at the weekend.'

'Oh isn't that a fine thing,' said Nurse Williams. 'There, you'll be a grandad and all.'

Ronnie murmured something. Lydia bent down to catch it.

'One comes in as I go out,' he repeated. 'I like that.'

It would not be simultaneous, thought Lydia, gazing at him. She knew there would be a long gap before he was replaced.

'You must hang on to greet it,' she said however.

'You must say hello to it for me,' he replied.

He shut his eyes again. It was indeed nice news but it was awfully irrelevant. He was caged by the near horizons of illness and death. In any case he found it hard to sift real life from the miasmas of the mind. Last night he had dreamed he was drowning in Marks & Spencer. 'Can I help you?' a salesgirl had said.

'He's gone again,' said Nurse Williams. 'My last patient would come and go like that.'

Lydia went to the window. In the foreground she could see her neighbour putting fat out for the birds. As it was a clear morning she could also see the peaks of the grape-purple hills in the distance. Ten years ago she had tried to force Ronnie into making a pact that they would push each other off the nearest Eiger

239

when their days were numbered. Ronnie, who was less than convinced, had made her totter up a foothill for a recce. 'No good,' he had announced peering down at the run of green ledges and slopes. 'You would just roll over and over to the bottom.' And at the bottom, thought Lydia, there was always a florid Nurse Williams who went clickety-click in wait.

*   *   *

Do I greet him with sackcloth and ashes, fretted Elfie, or a magnum of champagne? Neither extreme seemed right. She had the harrowing thought that Hugh might prefer her to down a pint of gin instead. One must be sanguine, she advised herself. In the end she took Judith's advice and settled for a good solid nursery meal.

The oxtail casserole and steamed treacle pudding worked their usual miracle. The result was that Hugh seemed a new man by the end of dinner.

'I feel heaps better with all that marrow inside me,' he said happily. The treacle had oozed into his veins which were already lightly pickled with red wine. The strength of John Bull had started to pulse through him.

'A bit more?'

'Well perhaps the scrapings.'

He helped himself to the archipelago of syrup that remained on the plate. His spoon made a series of furrows, leaving the ridges of golden juice behind.

'Can't waste that,' he murmured and gave one or two surreptitious licks off the plate.

Elfie considered letting him have a cigarette but that would be one bribe too many.

She turned the main kitchen light out and they sat in the warm glow of the lamp swinging over the kitchen table. She had knocked it as she passed him the coffee and the light rocked gently back and forth, illuminating first his side then hers. Shadows swung rhythmically over the sand-coloured walls. Replete with the food of olde England and mellowed by half a bottle of wine, Hugh watched the rhythm of sun and shade play over his wife's face. He thought again how lucky he was.

'I'm a selfish pig,' he said suddenly. 'You know you're everything to me.'

'Oh Hugh.' Tears pricked in Elfie's eyes. Her confession, looking for an opportunity, faltered on the brink. She dreaded her power to destroy. She took a deep breath for her launch but felt despairing.

'I've got something to tell you.' She plucked at a crusty crumb of bread that had fallen onto the table and started shredding it into bits. 'Something extraordinary has happened. It's awful but wonderful.'

Hugh recoiled and frowned. This sounded downright unsettling.

'Nothing to do with your father?'

'It's to do with us.'

'Oh no, not me and you, not tonight. Sweetie, my cold, I really think I'm not—'

'Yes. Us.'

'Uzz. Must we?'

'Hugh—'

'Do put that piece of bread down. You're making me feel jittery.'

She dropped it as though scalded.

'Hugh. We're going to have a baby.' She stared at the crumb lying on the table and rushed on. She could not look at him, dreading his arctic ability to freeze. 'I don't know how it happened but when I went to see that gynae a few months ago, I wonder if she gave me a dud. I've only just found out. It must have happened in December.'

A nervous salesman, she was talking too much. She picked up the piece of bread once more and began rolling it into little white moist worms. Remembering his warning, she dropped it again. The dogs who had anticipated some bite-sized pieces falling their way, fell back into the shadows.

Silence still. She glanced up. He was twirling an empty glass round and round in his hands. It chinked rhythmically as it hit his signet ring at regular intervals. His eyelids were down which made his expression unreadable. She recognised that telling Judith and her mother had been poor preparation for this. They had not inclined her to expect silence.

242

'Hugh. Please say something.'

She felt desperate. She was doomed to knock endlessly against the door of an empty house. He was still rolling the damn glass round and round. Chink, one, two, three. Chink, one, two, three. Its monotony was driving her crazy. The little knot with which she caught up her hair pinched suddenly and she put up her hand to release the elastic and her tension. The tress swished and rustled to her shoulders.

In the distance there was the muffled roar of a train. Probably three miles away but on quiet winter nights the sound would be carried through the freezing air. Other people and other lives and other problems, but this, this here, was the centre of the universe, where she sat and he sat and the faint shape stirred between them.

'When is it due?' It was the first time he had spoken. At his most reserved, he talked without separating his teeth.

'September.'

This morning she had been ecstatic, in love with the fruitfulness of the month, its endorsement of her ripeness. Now, looking back from the perspective of a single day, she thought how quickly the discovery had evolved from a thin blue line to a real month on a real calendar and from there to this awful moment, pushing against Hugh's door.

The restless sound of the twirling glass

stopped. Alerted by its absence, she glanced up, first at his motionless hands, then higher. His head was still bowed.

'Hugh,' she said again, but his face was shrouded in its own shadow.

The silence was intolerable.

'Please understand, Hugh, that these things sometimes happen. It's nobody's fault.' She loathed herself for saying that. Only the weak tried to deflect blame, but she was impelled to continue. 'I know we agreed we wouldn't have a child but,' she shrugged, 'it's happened.'

She shut up immediately, terrified of going down the road that led to debate, argument, questions, insinuation. Even silence, frightening because it was open to too many interpretations, was better than that.

'Hugh,' she said again, more loudly. She wondered if he was even listening to her or just lost in his own catatonic trance. She felt like shaking him, so fiercely did she hate him for being able to do this to her. The anger was restorative. She rose from her chair. As he lifted his head in response, she was amazed to see tears on his cheeks. She had never seen him cry before. For a moment the diffuse anxiety that had squeezed her in its giant grip shrivelled to a worry the size of a nut about the meaning of his tears.

She walked round the table, impelled to put her arms round him yet half fearful of her welcome. He too stretched out a blind hand, not looking, a sort of fumbling forgiveness. She stumbled towards him and stood beside his chair, folding herself around him, pushing his head against her breasts.

'So rigid,' she said. Dry-eyed for months, she was aware her own tears had brimmed in response.

'I am old and fixed in my ways.'

'Oh God, Hugh, are you not at all a little pleased?'

'Shocked I think.'

'Not displeased?'

She separated herself from his grasp, bent down and cupped his face in both her hands, tilting it towards her. She had never seen it so vulnerable, distinctly ashamed of its own nakedness. She felt a gush of infinite tenderness that the shyness his vanity kept always at bay should reveal itself at this moment.

'It is ours,' she said, and realised she believed it passionately. 'For both of us.'

'It will change everything,' he said, and the old anxiety returned to his face.

'I swear to you it will be the same as before but better, closer.'

Unwilling any longer to sit at a lower level submissively looking up at her, he pushed away his chair and stood, putting his hands on her shoulders. He scanned her face intently. For the first time he noticed that the fair hair had slithered down to her shoulders. There were lines around her eyes and mouth. She would be an old mother, just as he would be an old father.

'Tell me,' he said searchingly. 'It wasn't an accident was it?'

'Yes,' she replied stoutly.

'I wish you'd be honest.'

'I am.'

'Never mind.' He realised that, since it was not within him to believe her, it was better for it not to matter. No one's motives or actions bore investigation, and probably least of all his.

He was stroking her hair, his fingers smoothing down the tress that had tumbled to her shoulders. He remembered his feelings after she had thrown the sugar that night on the fire. When was it? November. He had at that moment wondered about giving her a child. What kind of love was it to deny her? Instead it was she who had given him one, a cell, a fragment of himself.

'You are happy aren't you?' he asked her.

'Yes but only truly if you are.'

'It takes some getting used to.'

'It's newer to me than to you.'

'It's new to me too.'

'I was terrified of telling you.'

'Oh Elfie.'

'That you might think such a gift could be a curse.'

He felt suffused with shame that he should belong to the ungrateful. That category of human beings who were sated, jaded or warped.

'It's hard to explain,' he said helplessly.

'Tell me.' She took his hand and kissed it, then each finger one by one. 'Explain to me, I terribly want to understand.'

'I don't think there's anything to understand.'

'Isn't there? But you cried.'

She saw that his face had become strained again. He sat down at the table and put his head in his hands.

'Please explain to me. Why did you cry?'

'Because I think I was relieved you had made a decision.'

'It was an accident,' she said again, thinking how like a mynah bird she sounded.

'Well, whatever.'

She had a feeling she was not getting the complete truth but a submerged voice reminded her that neither was he.

'Come here.'

She noticed that his eyes were wet again. He put his right arm round her and drew her back against him.

'Such a strong heart,' he murmured, listening to its drumbeat rocking within her ribcage. 'You are programmed to live forever.' He paused then began to speak slowly. 'I have never told you, in fact I've never told anybody, but my first wife returned to her mother's family near Malmo about nine months before

247

Meredith was born. She had been going to marry a distant cousin, Arne, an architect, before I met her. I think, I've never stopped thinking that Meredith is his daughter. It was why I didn't want another ever again. I couldn't change. Even when I married you, even when I could start all over again, I was a pillar of salt. You were willing to give but I was too fixed to receive. I can't explain it? Who can explain these things?'

He looked up at her frowning. 'I'm sorry. I've caused you a lot of unhappiness. You do understand now, don't you?'

'Yes,' said Elfie, though it was too late for understanding or for anything actually. The 'yes' arrived from a far distance. It sounded polite and strangled, the 'yes' that is produced under stress. She felt a central lurch and assumed for a moment that she was about to faint. A fluttering had started within her, some nerve or other protesting against being shafted. She wondered whether Hugh could feel the trembling along the pathways inside her. She was engulfed with sympathy for him and at the same time terrified for herself too.

She rested her chin on the top of his head. Unable to think she gazed at an old print on the wall, a pretty piece called '*Noces de Village*'. A boy in a dark frock coat and cockaded hat was marrying a milkmaid in a cream apron. All very natural and French and rustic. What would that lot do about this situation? They

248

seemed to manage these big events better in the eighteenth century and perhaps in France. No bother, no fuss. She wished they were French. They handled these disruptions with perfect dexterity. Just an eighteenth-century Gallic shrug. This situation was alien to Anglo-Saxons. She put her lips against the top of his head and rested them there, feeling awful. His hair, still dark grey, was thinning. She ached for him, so fragile within his privacy, in need of all her protection. The grim thought crossed her mind that it was a bit late for sentiment, but then her brain went stiff. I shall think about this another time, she thought.

She thought about it in the night. She lay awake from one in the morning and heard the clock chime in the hall, two, three, four, though the distance between the intervals seemed telescoped. Hugh was lying against her in the big dark bed, his breathing deep and regular though interrupted by the odd catarrhal snort. He had thrown the top blanket off his side as he was a hot sleeper. She folded her hand lightly over his hip. It was a clear night and in the first stage of her watch the curtains were suffused with moonlight. We are both the products of our past, she thought, him and me, all of us. We take each other on in later life: so much that no one ever knows. How could she know when he had kept his silence for thirty years? Later still in the night, it occurred to her to wonder whether he was right or wrong and

249

for a moment, this seemed a means of escape. Though deep down she knew the truth of his conviction scarcely mattered. Either way, real or fantastic, it had rendered her action a terrible mistake. As she lay there brooding, the self-blame she had felt earlier in the day rose up and struck her but she set it aside. She was not sinless, but it was also true that she had sinned in ignorance. All that mattered now was to make it work.

CHAPTER TWENTY-ONE

It was a warm wet spring, though the honeybees had exploded to life long before the first breath of a soft wind from the south. Even in the hostile blizzards of late January and February the queen had started to lay eggs in the dark scented sanctum of each hive. Passing from cell to cell, ceaseless and methodical, she was peopling it with her own substance which would replace the old bees who were dying. From just twenty a day she could increase her eggs to two or three thousand. The huge multitude of brood was destined to include a handful of princesses, a few hundred males and the vast throng of female workers.

The tiny worker grubs lay folded in their six-sided cells like swaddled infants in cots. Fed on pap and weaned on honey and pollen, they awaited the stupendous changes that would

250

take place to their bodies. Within the shelter of their cocoons, they grew into curled white nymphs, their heads bent forward, whilst their soft pale skin developed its horny armour, they sprouted eyes and a tongue, then a sting, their antennae and finally wings. By the end of twenty-one days, it was a perfect honeybee that teased the cap aside from her cradle and climbed out. A few more days and she was able to shoulder her duty in the hive, as a nurse or a janitor, a mason or a street-sweeper, a hunter and a gatherer.

Whenever the wind blew softly from Africa or the Atlantic, the foraging workers cascaded from the hives, each threading its own mysterious compulsive route to the first blossom of the year. By noon of any mild day the lengthening ice-green catkins of the willows were clustered with workers. The dark violets and the milky anemones, the nut trees and the gorse were also yielding a feast of pollen and honey. The pouches of the bees bulged on their hind legs with the precious dust in all the colours of the rainbow, gold and orange, dusky red, black, indigo and violet. Their melodious humming mingled with the other sounds of spring: the fuss of small birds, the stirring of sap, the rushing rivulets of water. Although from time to time winter tried to reassert its grip with a Siberian flutter of snow, it was clear that spring was at last unstoppable. Hibernation was over.

It is over, Philip reminded himself; there is nothing to feel low about and everything to anticipate. He was annoyed at the defeat of his spirits. The month of March was usually a time of great satisfaction and relief and this year was proceeding better than usual. To mollify Martha he had moved the hives of bees over winter and could now attend them in peace. It would be one less area of dispute. Protected against winter rains, all the colonies had survived, even the weakest whose roof he was now lifting in order to give them a store of food. The light solution of syrup would help to sustain it until the start of the full honey flow. Normally he loved the feeling of contributing to a renewal, but this spring he had the sense that he had been left far behind. It was as if the numbness of hibernation persisted within him, as though the nights were still early and the mornings late and dark.

It was, he supposed, the aftermath of the loss of Elfie, but it surprised him that he should at this stage mind. He had a troubling memento of her every time that he walked past her red rose. He had planted it at the back of one of the borders and already its shoots were growing fat. He had developed mixed feelings about the rose. Until three months ago, he had liked it but the plant now undoubtedly irked him. His favourite had fallen from favour. Though blameless, he had invested it with an unfair share of his irritation. This had swollen during

252

the winter.

Back in January, he had tried several times to contact Elfie but had been told by Susan that she was out. This pattern had repeated itself in February. Then late one evening, she had telephoned him at his London home. 'As usual,' he had thought, though there was of course no as usual since only one precedent had been established. He had assumed, again based on the previous occasion, that she was proposing to see him as she had before Christmas, but in this he had been wrong. It turned out that she had simply rung to give him a dear John. It was confused and apologetic but still a dear John. Though it rankled a little at the time, it had seemed to him in retrospect a sensible decision to put a stop to something that had scarcely begun. In fact, even on the telephone he had argued against his own desires by pointing out that now was better than later, before either had invested capital, whether time, feeling or lies, in an affair that might not be so readily unwound. Since he believed this to be genuinely true, such disappointment that he felt was mingled with relief.

Alas, his reason and his feelings had since started to diverge. The result was that his sadness lacked the solace of any compensations. It was not simply his regret for Elfie that weighed on him now, but his awareness that she had wedged open a gap in his marriage which had lost its chance to be filled.

It was a brilliant Saturday morning in March. Watching the bees swoop around him, the bright pollen ferried on their flanks, he felt annoyed that he should fail to rejoice. Yet as he walked back along the path through his trial bed of roses, he received another awkward reminder. He noticed that the seedlings of the cross he had made last summer were already sprouting. 'If you like, we'll call it Elfie,' he remembered saying at the time. In the circumstances he now felt rather a fool.

*   *   *

Digging the compost heap in Elfie's garden, Walter found a nest of baby hedgehogs. He summoned her to look. She knelt down enchanted. Folded serenely against each other, they were pink-bellied and soft-spined. She thought of her own child in its nest with its eyes tightly shut and its webbed fingers and toes; it would be about the same size as each infant hedgehog.

'I'll give them a new nest,' promised Walter.

'No.' Elfie pierced him with a look. 'We can't use the heap.'

'Not use it? Course we do. No reason why not.'

'Walter, we cannot use it.'

Walter was aghast. It was his compost not

hers and he took his pile seriously. It was not one of your get-rich-quick composts, usable after six months, but a brew which had used all of his patience. Vintage 1994: just leaves, bracken tops, wood ash, tea, grass and straw. He had stirred it, sniffed it and sat on it with the tortoiseshell cat last June, when it was nice and hot under his bottom. It had smelt then of earth, smoke and summer. He had pulled slowly on his pipe and had looked forward to crumbling it around the plants the following spring. But now it was ripe, it was to be squandered on hedgehogs.

'It's a good compost,' he said plaintively.

'We can't use it,' repeated Elfie, guarding it with her body.

'I'll give 'em a nicer nest,' he wheedled.

'No.'

'Walter, I know this may seem a bit non compost-mentis,' said Hugh coming up behind.

As he spoke he knew he was wasting a corker. Half his audience was brain-dead and the other half never laughed at his jokes anyway. Bloody hell, it would be years before he could have another crack at a compost joke, and in Latin too. He wondered whether to have a second go now. He doubted whether his wife or Walter had heard him first time round. Neither had reacted. Both were staring round the little sanctuary garden. Hugh had to admit it looked rather nice. Even without the bonus of compost, the plants had grown fat and happy. There were carpets of sky-blue hepaticas and anemones, and clusters of cool lemon primroses. One Jack-in the-Green had survived from last year and two hose-in-hose primulas. The setterworts, showered with lime green waxy bells, spread their dark fringed leaves like canopies over the black ground.

'Could do with a bit of compost,' said Walter cunningly. 'Why don't I just skim the cream off the heap?'

'No,' said Elfie.

Walter spat tobacco in disgust.

'Women are full of prohibitions,' Hugh consoled him. 'But in this case, it's a bit different.'

He glanced at Elfie who had turned round. He raised his eyebrows meaning, shall I tell him? She rolled her eyes and nodded faintly to convey rather you than me.

'You see,' said Hugh bravely, 'my wife's going to have a baby.'

It was terribly tempting to use some remote euphemism. My wife's in a delicate condition flashed across his mind.

Walter froze. He looked incredulous.

'A baby?'

'In the autumn.'

Elfie decided against coming to Hugh's rescue. With maddening airiness, she drifted off instead to examine a primrose. Walter continued to stand, wheezing a little. Slowly his incredulity faded to be replaced by a locker-

256

room slyness. Hugh chose not to receive it. He had set his face in rock, of the non-porous variety. Rain, sun, wind, rudeness, it was not going to be reactive. But behind the scenes he remembered that Walter hadn't enjoyed a leg-over for thirty years. In this as in all things life was decidedly unfair.

*   *   *

Spring was indeed unstoppable and Nick was still desperate over Tabitha. Since Christmas he had tried and failed several times to get her. She was now at a crammers and was proving elusive. His goal was made harder by the fact that they had no friends in common. Casual meetings and even sightings were no longer likely, which put him at a disadvantage. However his self-confidence had recently received a boost when he had been given the eye by several of Hugh's married clients: women, moreover, contrary to his mother's fears. He had not dared to dabble because his job went with the injunction not to fuck the customers up, a warning he took literally in this case. Nevertheless, the episodes had served to put a shine on his self-esteem.

He stood in front of the mirror to assess his charms. He felt teeming with animal power, a lion not an ox.

'The pale pink proud peacock pompously preened its pretty plumage,' intoned Jessica,

257

entering his room. She had attended two elocution lessons. She prodded him in the kidneys and drew a heart in the air with a dagger through it and drops of blood.

'Who is it?'

'Not going to tell you.'

'Boring.'

'You're just a kid.'

'It's Tabitha, isn't it?'

'What would you know about these things? You're sweet on a four-legged donkey with spots.'

'I know lots. Honest. I can help. I won't josh.'

'Dipstick.'

'Just go for it. Don't be a wimp.'

'It takes a wimp to know a wimp,' snapped Nick.

Jessica skipped out of his reach, then out of the room. She banged the door. 'Wanker,' she trilled through the keyhole.

'Oh piss off.'

At the time Nick was scowling. Later, however, he wondered about his sister's advice in the light of a friend's twenty-first birthday party that loomed promisingly ahead. Just go for it? But what would a girl like Tabitha expect?

He decided to send her a note beforehand. He kept it brief but reeking with confidence. Here's the place, here's the time, look forward to picking you up. It did not elicit a reply, which was disconcerting but, primed to carry it through unilaterally, Nick turned up at the crammers at eight o'clock on Friday night.

Dressed in full tuxedo, he signed in with the porter and, following directions to her room, walked up the cream-painted corridor, turned right, left, up another corridor, along a cross-axis, reversed through a passage, zig-zagged left, right and left again to 13d. It had taken him seven minutes to walk the three sides of a rectangle. He was about to knock when the door opened and she emerged. She was wearing a long silver coat and dress with a deeply scooped front. Her breasts, tightly bound, burst upward. He kept his eyes propped well away from her chest but was awed by the scenic view on the periphery of his gaze.

'You look terrific.'

'Oh Nick, I tried to ring you but you were out. I can't come tonight. I was already fixed.'

As she turned the door opened a little further and a man appeared. Nick recognised, oh Jesus, one of the boys who had been working in Martha's garden last year when he had delivered the sphinx. He was wearing a black tie and burgundy velvet waistcoat, his blond hair slicked back with some poncey gel. Was it Felix or Adam? They were interchangeable; either would flee if he met a prop-forward.

The two males sized each other up for the second time. It was the rutting season. Nick's feet itched to paw at the ground. Inaudible but somehow felt, a roar of several thousand decibels reverberated outside the range of human hearing. Invisible in the air over their heads the pair of antlers locked and disentangled. Adam/Felix won. He had the arrogance of squatter's rights.

'We'll all walk back together, shall we? Yah?' he said smoothly.

The trio set off down the corridors. No one spoke. Nick winced at the thought of the three sides of the rectangle to be traversed in slow motion. Back down the long cream-walled corridor, zigzag right, left, right again, down the passage. The smack of three pairs of feet echoed from floor to ceiling. The pace was measured: Adam had no need to hurry and Nick could not afford to. At the cross-axis he thought of stopping to do up a perfectly tied shoe-lace but carried on. Down the fourth corridor, right, left and at last to the entrance of the college. Nick glanced at his watch. The return trip had taken ten minutes. His rival had dragged out his fun.

On his solitary journey to the party, Nick remembered too late as usual what he should have called him. In a blind fury of swearing he repeated it again and again. In his imagination he said to Tabitha: 'But everyone calls him that.' He heard Tabitha: 'Oh Nick, I didn't realise he was a bumblepuppy.' At the party later, he dedicated the night to getting drunk.

CHAPTER TWENTY-TWO

'Who giveth this Woman to be married to this Man?' asked the vicar.

'I Giles Bertram Coles, father of Lucinda Jennifer Coles,' announced Giles creatively and quite unnecessarily.

The service did not require him to respond in such detail but he resented the fact that the father of the bride did not normally have a speaking part in the wedding ceremony. Like a child he was expected to be seen and not heard, which was tough when he was footing the divine bill, indeed the whole flaming caboodle. Every single person present and not only the vicar had been paid for by him, Giles Bertram Coles.

This bill, or rather bills, had surpassed all his expectations since Lucinda had pleaded for and been granted the full works. A marquee, a sit-down lunch, a three-tier cake, a vintage car, photographers, the list had proved to be inventive and endless. 'But Daddy, we shall get it back on the presents,' she had urged. 'You will but I won't,' protested Giles, appalled at the costs. He looked at the lunch price and groaned. 'What's the point of being a cookery book editor if you can't make your own food?' he had ventured, but his daughter had only retreated in tears.

In the end the only person with whom Giles could forge a contract to economise was himself. In consequence, he was now standing at the altar in his dead father's sixty-year-old morning suit that was reputed to have belonged to Edward VIII. Beside him stood Lucinda in a cream shot-silk dress burdened with superfluous material. She was large, he admitted but surely she had no need for twenty yards of cloth to cover herself. It had cost Giles £2000 from a superior dress hire shop but on its immaculate return he would be reimbursed by seventeen hundred. Walking up the aisle he had avoided touching his daughter in case he should soil her sleeve. 'Hold my arm,' she had whispered but he had affected not to hear. He had begun to fret about the rocks ahead. Would she have to kneel on a grubby hassock? He feared so.

Beyond Lucinda he could see the grey beaky profile of her husband. He suspected Martin had been unlucky in love. A late marriage, there would have been plenty of false starts on the way, probably one unmitigated avalanche and a fair number of cautious retreats. An only son and a military historian, he would be wary, nay terrified of women. He was speaking now, his stiff upper lip motionless, his chin working like a bearded snapdragon: 'I Martin Jacques, take thee Lucinda Jennifer Coles, to my wedded wife, to have and to hold . . .'

Over to you chum, thought Giles, yours to have and to hold, though he would have preferred to be divesting himself of Andy. Out of the corner of his eye he could see two of the banana trees with which his son decorated the church. This had caused a serious row.

To his rear Giles could sense the two flanks of the dear little grey stone Wiltshire church stretching to the western horizon behind him. It was a full house though not equally or even fairly divided, as there were ten in the bridegroom's party and no less than seventy in theirs. It was a classic wedding, reflected Giles. Each family, sundered by the aisle and cloistered in its own separate half of the church, had hated the other on sight. Like all minority parties, the smaller contingent was a pit of resentment. 'Very vulgar,' the bridegroom's mother had been heard to pronounce over the selection of church florals. In contrast his own lot brimmed with enjoyment, forming for once a most unsilent majority. He could hear them rehearsing the words of the service, reliving their own marriages in a mixture of tears, hopes and cynicism.

From the front row to his rear left there came a sniff which he recognised as Judith's. It came once and then a second time, more softly, like an echo. Unseen to Giles, tears stood in Judith's eyes. It is the first proper wedding in the family for more than a quarter of a century, she thought, and it may be expensive but it's worth it. She looked appreciatively around the church. Ginger plants in the alcoves and banana trees on the window-sills had made it a marriage to remember. 'I want freesias and lilies,' Lucinda had exclaimed furiously, but Judith and Andy prevailed. 'We shall have everything,' she had declared, reluctant to be divisive.

She sat now, fiddling with her long muslin fichu. As befitted the bride's mother, she was sporting a brand new outfit, poppyred with cream diagonal swirls and a huge crimson hat. Giles had looked at its ticket before assessing the dress and said it had all the bezazz of a barber's pole but that was just Giles. She now stared at his back and thought he looked no better. She prayed that the morning-suit would not split. An hour ago, she had shoehorned him into the jacket and it was bursting across the shoulder blades. Edward VIII must have been thinner. Watching him now, she remembered her own wedding thirty-five years ago: to love, honour and obey. Hers must have been the last generation that promised to obey. And had she obeyed? Most certainly not. She had promised but he had obeyed, which showed what ritual tomfoolery this was.

And yet she had no doubt that it was necessary, convinced that it was vital to do things in the old rigorous way. The ancients had made no concessions and look how it had paid off. Nowadays everyone was in such a muddle that their marriages were in permanent chaos. They needed a ceremony that

264

reaffirmed the rules, a group of vows made in public, the Solemnisation of Matrimony that said this is how it should be done. Without it, there was no doubt that people just drifted, especially in Lucinda's world. Judith had seen her float from one relationship to another, each easily redeemable when one of them had decided to swim off. Rich man, poor man, beggarman and, who knew nowadays, perhaps even a thief. A fluid, moving life without dropping anchor, here today but not tomorrow, drifting and not building. It was this that she feared for Andy.

On the pew beside her, she felt her mother shift. She was crying and Judith took her hand.

'All right Mummy dear.'

Lydia nodded. She had been frightened of coming in case she made an exhibition of herself, but Judith had insisted. Lydia was staying with them and she had not wanted to leave her at home. Judith now assumed her mother was crying in desolation, hugged her and began to indulge in a little weep herself.

She does not understand, thought Lydia who was crying in anger. She felt angry that no one could share the stoicism required to endure life, the pilgrim's progress that beset its victims. The wedding service put it into words: 'for better for worse, for richer for poorer, in sickness and in health, to love, cherish and (she had noticed its absence and mentally included it) to obey, till death us do part.' What a see-saw of turbulence it promised.

She wished now she had not come, but fate had blown her helplessly to one ceremony after another. The last had been Ronnie's funeral, here was a marriage, the next would be her own death which she had once dreaded but would now welcome. She would tell them to scatter her ashes at the foot of his chestnut trees as she had scattered his on that sleety day in February. She had released them slowly and at intervals, seeing them drift in the wind and mingle with snowflakes before coming to rest beneath the matchstick trunks. Ronnie had hoped to provide a bit of nourishment. The spaniel had watched beside her. Let him rest in peace, she had said to doddery old Ben.

She now leaned over to Judith.

'You will remember to put my ashes under his chestnut trees, won't you?'

She spoke strongly. The row behind could probably hear, for there came a responsive shuffling.

Judith looked round at her sharply. 'This is a wedding, ducky. Let's take it one at a time, shall we? Don't worry about your funeral now.'

To Lydia's left, Elfie whispered. 'Ssssh. Anyway, there'll be a christening before you drop off the perch.'

Maddening, thought Lydia, how they tried to steer her away from thinking about Ronnie. Horrid that they should force-feed her with the future and not the past. What could the future mean to her now? Tears of anger spouted afresh. Stop it, she instructed herself, I shall have a panic attack and then shan't be able to breathe. This had happened once or twice in the night, but an unruly demon within her had now moved her beyond caring.

Elfie and Judith exchanged glances over her head.

Lydia knew what they meant. What to do about Mummy? Good, thought Lydia, I am going to be a bad-mannered old woman who enjoys throwing away decades of good behaviour. Just watch how awful I can be.

Oh God, thought Judith, I do hope she isn't going to become senile.

'Take her out, can't you,' whispered Hugh.

Elfie closed her eyes but kept her fingers clasped over her mother's in a controlling kind of way.

Handcuffs, thought Lydia, and now a muzzle too, when Judith whispered 'Hush'.

Elfie tried to concentrate on the service. The last marriage ceremony in the family had been her own but it had not felt remotely like a wedding. Indeed she was doubtful afterwards whether she had been married at all. It had started at half-past three and was finished by twenty-to-four. The registrar, though kind and well-meaning, had performed his functions like a speaking-clock. 'Are we wed?' she had asked Hugh later, but all he had answered was 'As much as my previous time,' a deflating

267

reminder that his last dearly beloved had run aground and that serial shipwreck might be here to stay.

The recollection of her wedding made Elfie glance down at her ring. It was no longer the conventional hoop with which they had married, but a wide flat eternity ring with five small diamonds which he had given her the Christmas before last. Wedding rings are just for a day, he had said, but this is for keeps. At the time she had ascribed it to his funny old-fashioned streak of sentiment; though now she recognised it as need. An eternity ring was not only a pledge and a symbol, but also a plea to defy change and time. For richer for poorer, in sickness and in health, in life and in death, now and forever, amen. Hugh was more vulnerable than she had once thought. It occurred to her that she had become the strong one; she would one day be his rock. She stretched out her left hand wearing the eternity ring and placed it above Hugh's, interwining their fingers to impart reassurance.

'Do you remember?' he whispered.

Remember what? Their wedding? The eternity ring? But she nodded. To her right, she noticed that Lydia had stopped weeping. She sat upright between them so as not to squash the infant inside her. Husband to her left, mother to her right, child within her, all dependent. She was the strong one. At the altar the ceremony was drawing to its close and the audience was united in an expectant hush. The ancient warning was upon her before she noticed. She had been waiting for it, alert and on hold. 'Those whom God hath joined let no man put asunder.' *Let no man put asunder*, but she need not have worried. It lapped harmlessly around her feet. She felt closer to Hugh than at any time before.

CHAPTER TWENTY-THREE

'Lot seventy-eight. May I have £15,000 to start this?'

It was Wednesday, the first day of a huge country house sale in Devon. The auctioneer, a seasoned showman and well into his florid act, looked professionally around the packed room. It was bristling with hands but Hugh kept his still. The price made him wince. He usually set a ceiling of £25,000 for his showroom stock. By the time this piece, a pretty walnut bureau, was bid up, adorned with a buyer's premium, partly taxed, then worked on, his margin would collapse.

He wriggled with impatience in his seat and stared frowning at his fellow bidders. They were the usual lot, tiered from the jet setters all the way down to the married couples who ran the shop on the corner. The mix was familiar: agents, dealers in person, decoys to deflect attention, and a salty sprinkling of amateurs.

Lord, these amateurs who went potty at auctions. He knew from experience that the prices would shoot to three times the estimates. No need for Peter Ropey to pick bids off the chandelier today. They would fly at him like arrows, and continue until Saturday. This last day which was earmarked for knick-knacks—fans, footwear, firescreens, fol de rols—was usually the ghetto for amateurs but a number had clearly strayed into the limelight of the launch.

It was a serious international sale though Hugh didn't feel terribly serious at the moment. Still, the catalogue was as usual brimful of impressive warnings. UN embargo on trade with Iraq; embargo on importation of Persian/Iranian works of arts and carpets to the States; American buyers of ivory would have to contact the shipping department before the auction. Here was a sale guaranteed to lure all the blue-chip bunnies from their burrows. Hugh stared at the fat rear of old van Harlem, whose helicopter had unaccountably landed in the wrong field. He was happy to see his crocodile shoes plastered in mud. Beside him sat Mr Okama and Reza Shirin and a host of others whose faces were familiar though their names were unknown. Bet there aren't many who are fathers at my age, it occurred to Hugh smugly. Four months down and five to go. The thought filled him with happiness and a love of life. It was a joyful spring day and he planned to

270

wander out at lunchtime and feed the mallards and downy ducklings on the lake. 'Speaking as a new father, one takes an interest in ducklings, Mr Okama,' he longed to say.

How astonishing it is, he thought. The passion of his involvement amazed him. Every detail was of interest from the decoration in the room they had chosen for the nursery, to Elfie's maternity clothes, the trousseau for the baby, even relaxation exercises. 'This is jam-making all over again,' Elfie had said to him in alarm. I shall attend the birth even if all those junior doctors do patronise me, he thought. Who cares if I do look a fool to the midwife? Bet they don't have many fathers of—he paused, he would have a birthday before his child was born and welcomed the boost it would lend to his age—sixty-five.

These thoughts were proving distracting and with some effort he pushed them far away. He screwed up his eyes and concentrated on watching the bureau being snaffled by a London dealer whose clients were in a position to pay more than his own.

'Now,' said Ropey, 'what many of us have been waiting for.'

And I one of them, thought Hugh.

The objects were in truth glorious. Two mahogany globes, the one terrestrial, the other celestial, made by Newton who was one of the best globe-makers in the nineteenth century. Hugh wagered these beautiful spheres would be bid up very quickly. This kind of erudite item was guaranteed to flatter its owner. Snapshots of lost and changed dominions, he craved the pair of them himself. This morning, with his left hand on India and his right clasping the stars in their Heaven, he had spun them full circle and marvelled at their silken feel.

'I shall start the bidding at £8,000. £8,500, madam? You, sir, £9,000. £9,500, thank you, sir.'

Two seats along from him, Mrs Bannerman, his rival down the road, waved the paddle clasped in her lizard-skin hand.

'£10,500, thank you madam.'

Mass hysteria, thought Hugh.

'£11,000,' indicated his neighbour.

'Ah, Arnold,' said his American wife.

Right, thought Hugh, forgetting his resistance to auctionitis. To his horror he raised his arm.

'Thank you, sir.' Ropey's glance mopped up his £11,500.

'£12,000' waved Mrs Bannerman upping the stakes.

She was unworthy of them. '£12,500,' indicated Hugh.

'£14,000' mouthed an interloper.

Hugh and Mrs Bannerman both dropped out, neither looking at one another, like two chastised little toddlers.

Ape, thought Hugh, knowing that local
272

buyers hated moving above ten. He felt slightly sulky as he watched out the sequence.

'For the last time, then, £18,500,' said Ropey and the hammer blow dropped.

In truth Hugh was somewhat relieved because the next lot had also captured his personal interest. He had loved it as soon as he saw it. It was a little eighteenth-century canvas of three children playing with a red ball in the green and sunlit clearing of a woodland. Its beauty was concealed beneath a thick and syrupy varnish which he hoped might allow it to slip ignominiously by. He was sure that Elfie could clean and rekindle it to life. If so, he also knew that he could not fail to keep it, which was the ultimate luxury, even crime. He sighed at the thought of his unsupportive bank manager.

Yet he felt entranced by the smiling children, a young girl and two brothers. All three looked so natural. The eighteenth century, that age of grace and translucent reason, had freed them from the stiffness of the previous hundred years, and not yet encumbered them with the sentimentalities of the century that would follow. The girl, perhaps six years old, in a long pink silk petticoated dress; her brothers, a year or so older in russet and teal blue breeches, each sporting lace collars. The sunlight falling golden on their faces, the red ball juggling between them. Elves in the woodland, freedom and mischief, a family at play before they grew

273

up to the burdens of age.

Looking at it that morning, Hugh felt how much he had missed a brother or a sister. His had been a lonely childhood and he knew it had made him self-centered, self-contained, self-sufficient, self-everything. It might be the hopelessly romantic view of the outsider, but he regretted the teasing and the laughter, the shared roots, that loose warm feeling of belonging to the same litter and the same free-wheeling clan.

Staring at the canvas, he had realised not only that it showed him his missed childhood but that he could not have fully appreciated how much it was missed until now that the child was on its way. It was like seeing an angle on a view that had been previously concealed. It was only in maturity, too late indeed, that you discovered the secret of youth. The time when you lived life in the present tense, the horizons pressed against your nose. Perhaps we should have a second child as well, he wondered. He felt desperate to rediscover or create his own childhood through his children. To think he had left it nearly too late. He felt as though he had been buried in a peat bog for the last thirty years and had just come creaking to life.

*   *   *

'We have treacle tart, cherry and almond trifle or Earl Grey sorbet,' said the waitress. It was her boast that even with a blindfold she could manage to match pudding to guest. Two men, dining alone, look alikes, father and son probably, would go for the treacle tart.

'Treacle tart,' said Hugh. 'Cream?'

'Lots of cream,' promised Sally, in a swipe against their absent wives.

'Rupert? What do you fancy?'

'Treacle tart. Cream and ice-cream too?'

'I remember you always wanted more,' said Hugh, feeling as though he had taken his son out of school for a treat.

'We all want more. Oliver Twist wanted more.'

Men did indeed want more, thought Sally, scribbling treacle, cream AND ice-cream in her big round-vowelled handwriting. Pigs the lot of them, but they were so satisfying to feed.

'It's on me,' said Hugh, referring to the meal.

'No, Dad.'

Rupert was on a presentation tour around the country for his fund and could stick it on his bill. He was spending the night at this country house hotel near Hugh's auction.

'It's a celebration,' explained Hugh.

Of what, wondered Rupert, though he was glad to note his father's good spirits. It confirmed Kristina's reassurance that Elfie had not been glimpsed again. Rupert now hoped the whole incident, or two to be precise, were phantasmal.

'Look,' said Hugh, 'do you like it?'

275

He pulled the painting out of the cloth wrapping;

'What is it? A bit dark isn't it?'

'Wait till you see what Elfie can do.'

'It doesn't quite seem your usual line. Mind you the beef is coming back into the art market,' offered Rupert encouragingly.

'You can't guess why I got it?'

Rupert paused. 'It's worth a lot is it?'

'That's not why. Try again.'

Rupert gazed at it, perplexed. Three children, two boys and a girl. He knew about the art index but not much about art. He realised he knew even less about his father.

The bonny waitress reappeared. As she leaned forward, a bunch of fair hair drooped over her right shoulder. It occurred to Hugh that two hundred and fifty years ago at the time of the painting, she would have been a reaper, stooking sheaves in a local meadow.

'I bought it,' said Hugh when the girl was out of earshot, 'because Elfie and I are going to have a child.'

Rupert stopped eating. How wonderful, he thought mechanically, but it seemed more complicated than that. There seemed a crack in the middle.

'Terrific, Dad. We must celebrate. What a dark horse. You said you never wanted one.' Was that the crack?

'Did I say that? I was wrong.'

'You changed your mind.'

276

'Let's say Elfie changed it for me.'

'Great. We must celebrate.'

If his father was happy then he was, but something seemed wrong. Not only wrong for himself, leap-frogged by his dad, wifeless, childless, and therefore metaphorically homeless at thirty-four, everyone would soon think he was queer, but was it quite right for his father?

'It's simply wonderful, Dad. When's it due?'

'September.'

September, August, July but he did not need to work back through the preceding months. Used to quartiles of three months duration in the City, and three times three equalled nine, he landed immediately on the neon baseline of December. He felt breathless. He had thought he had forgotten the bleak image of the two figures embracing in the mews house window that Kristina had evoked, but the cells that contained it were not lost. It rose again in perfectly imagined detail. The kiss, the dawn departure, once, twice, November, December, then never again.

'Champagne, Dad?' he said kindly, because in the City a bonanza was rarely toasted with anything else.

Glad to take action, he beckoned Sally and ordered a small bottle of Bollinger.

'She's had a test,' said Hugh, toying shyly with his spoon, 'you know, an amniocentesis, and it's fine. We don't know the sex. The labs

277

don't report it as a rule now.'

'Great.' A baby step-brother or -sister? Or was it? Rupert felt he must sound a bit rigid. He seemed unable to move out of his groove of superlatives.

'I know,' Hugh leaned forward but did not actually look at him,

'I do know that you didn't see much of me when you were a child. Then there was all that difficulty with your mother.'

'We survived. Don't worry about it. It happens to everybody.'

'I feel a bit to blame about all that. Anyway I'd like you to know that it'll be different this time round.'

'I'm sure it will be perfect.' It should indeed be just dandy.

'Here it is, Mr Lyle,' said Sally, reappearing. It was clear she believed that Bollinger deserved proper monogrammed service.

'It's a celebration, I hope.'

'Yes,' said Hugh. 'A new baby.'

'Oh how wonderful.' She spun round beaming to Rupert. 'Fancy that, a new baby. That is something to celebrate.'

'Don't look at me. It's my father's.' He spoke jovially but felt the pinch of failure.

'Well now,' said Sally. 'Whoever's. It's a baby.'

Whoever's, thought Rupert, it's a baby.

*   *   *

'I've been away for three weeks. You can hardly accuse me of coming on heavy because I want to see you as soon as I get back.' Rupert was perched on Kristina's little cream sofa which was uncomfortable even when a visitor felt relaxed.

'Well, I wasn't in.'

'I know you weren't in. I rang you until midnight yesterday evening. Where were you by the way?'

'At the opera.'

'At the opera?'

'*Ariadne auf Naxos.*'

'Where did you sit?'

'What a funny question, Rupert. Some normal person might ask who sang. Did she have a big voice? Or what did you think of the music? Which is not my favourite by the way. But where did you sit is a very funny kind of question.'

She is toying with me, he thought, a cat with a mouse, she knows bloody well what this is about.

'If you must know,' said Kristina, drifting towards the mirror, 'I sat in a box.'

'A corporate box?' he was distressed to hear himself say.

'A corporate box. No. Not, I think, a corporate box.'

The bitch with her sly triumph, thought Rupert. He knew and she knew that a private box meant a rival. He despised her for confirming his worst fears. He wanted to change the subject but the infidelities of women preyed upon his mind. He thought of his dear father's ignorance and paralleled the possibilities of his own.

'You haven't seen my step-mother again, have you?'

'No.'

She began to brush her hair. She was wearing a red dress, sleeveless, her arms were brown as always, and she had two thick gold bracelets which slid up her forearm as she lifted the tortoiseshell brush. A golden blonde in a red dress. He could not look at her. He went to the window and stared out into the cobbled courtyard. The house opposite was dark, silent and closed; it kept its secrets. The window boxes were empty and looked unloved.

'I think, Rupert, that perhaps you have become a little bit excited. Maybe we don't see each other for a while, yes?'

'You are seeing someone else, aren't you?'

She shrugged. It was so obvious. We don't discuss the obvious.

'I have never deceived you. Come on, Rupert. Drink up. Cheer up.'

She leaned over him and he smelt her foreignness. It was palpable and he was addicted to it. He feared he was hooked on the exotic. At work, he prided himself on the strange financial fancies designed by the rocket scientists: the straddles and butterflies and naked dog baskets of the derivatives world. Hooked at work and now at home. He ached in advance with the loss of Kristina. He would have to adjust to a lumpen native successor, a female of predictable quantity. Don't invest in anything you don't understand was a wise motto and it had just been confirmed by Kristina.

CHAPTER TWENTY-FOUR

On the last Saturday in April, Philip returned to his home in Oxfordshire. The garden was at its most beautiful with weeping cherry blossom and white daffodils but this was not his main preoccupation. Instead he walked straight to the boundary where he checked the hives and groaned. It was obvious that the strongest had swarmed. Sitting in his sunlit office yesterday after a week of rain, it had occurred to him that there might be a mass departure in such unseasonable heat. Maddening to be caught out so early in the year. He hated to lose a swarm just at the time that foragers were needed to gather nectar and pollen. A swarm meant a depleted hive, which meant a depleted crop of honey.

He sat down on the grass and grimaced. There would be no honey at all if he did not take immediate action to prevent further swarms. The hive would contain a number of queen cells and it was quite possible that a succession of swarms would emerge if he failed to remove them. He fetched a knife, then paused and decided to call Walter. The hive now had a new, virgin queen: she was larger than the workers, slimmer than the drones, but one amongst thirty thousand and terribly elusive. If he could only find her and mark her, he could always locate her and know her age in future. Walter was magician enough to do so.

He rang him, moved a seat to the side of the hive and waited. It was warm and tranquil in the sun which made him feel drowsy. From a distance the word agapanthus reached his ears which must come from Martha exhorting Felix to move the Ali Baba pots into the white garden. Nearer to hand the grey cat lay in the cowslips and watched him. Swishing the tip of his tail, he pondered the risks of approaching.

Lulled by the scent of flowers and the stillness, Philip also sat quietly, noting the aerial comings and goings of the colony. The drones were much in evidence. Had he been aware of them earlier in the month he would have been forewarned that the hive had swarming on its mind. Poor, hapless, stupid drones. Drunk with honey and crazed with lust, there was only one purpose for which these males were produced and it was due to be enacted at any moment. The mating of the virgin queen. Was there a chance he would see it? Highly unlikely. Would he even recognise what was going on? Probably not, but the simple truth was still awesome.

This new young queen had been raised only when the hive was confident there was a battalion of drone suitors to mate her. It was her birth that had signalled to the old queen that her reign was now over and that she and her huge retinue that formed the swarm must take their chance in the world outside, leaving their wax palace to her successor.

Soon this virgin queen must embark on her life's unceasing toil of laying eggs, but first she must take the nuptial flight for her mating. Such a gruesome Gothic mating. The soaring queen, the mad, pursuing drones, the fatal winner, paying his prodigious price for a moment of ecstasy, death to him though life to her. He with his sexual organs ripped out and a burst abdomen hurtling earthwards. And she, fertilised and entire, returning triumphally to her hive with the trophy of his remnants trailing from within her, able at last to fulfil the maternal duties that were her destiny. Cruel that the natural world should be so full of such examples.

Mulling these sobering facts, Philip was disturbed by the cat which against its better judgment had plucked up courage to advance. It undulated against his ankles.

'Be grateful you're castrated,' he said. It had the moon-face of the feline eunuch.

'What's that, Mr Dacre?' asked Walter from

283

behind. 'You speaking to me?'

'Nothing personal. Just thinking about the bees.'

The two men applied themselves to the hives. Philip was fully netted and protected, Walter bare-headed and -armed but smelling resinously of wintergreen to pacify the colony. One by one, they lifted each wax frame and peered at the scattering of pendulous cone-shaped queen cells in which the selection of royal nymphs were immured.

'She's out,' said Walter. 'Look.' He pointed at an empty cone whose hinged lid had been tipped backwards. It was the birthing-chamber of the hive's new queen.

Philip stared at the open cradle. He noticed that the other vessels were unviolated. This meant she had not yet killed her sister princesses to ensure her supremacy. As in all things, raw Nature was both barbarous and practical. He watched Walter revolve the frames slowly and calmly in his hands. He was humming, perhaps unconsciously, perhaps at one with the bees. It drummed like a mantra. His smoker stood on the hive, exhaling its tarry scent. The bees clustered in fear on the combs, seeking the darkness of the underside as the frame turned over. Both men were alert for the queen.

'There she is,' said Walter softly.

He picked her up with infinite gentleness and, so as not to crush the wonderful creature,

284

put her between his lips. Philip watched in fascination. More golden than her workers, possessed of a curved sting, she lay there unstruggling. He took a little pot of quick-drying marker paint from his pocket and put a speck on her thorax. A virgin, not yet mated and less than a month old, she could live for four or five years. The humble workers for as little as six weeks. She was a miracle, capable of laying up to three times her own weight in eggs within the space of a single day. She was a mystery: mated in the dazzling empyrean, yet a seeker of darkness, terrified of light. Philip gazed in awe at this marvel and enigma.

Walter took her from his lips and put her back with her consorts on the wax comb and replaced the frame in the hive.

'Might as well check the others whilst we're about it,' he suggested.

It would be slow time-consuming work and they both knew it would be pointless unless it was repeated every seven days. As fast as they mutilated the queen cells, the bees would repair them. The swarming impulse could never be mastered, just imperfectly contained. This required continuous care and it would have to fall upon Walter. Philip regretted as so often his own erratic absences. He frequently wished now he could turn his back on his work or slow down. When I retire I shall be free to do this and everything else I might want, he told himself.

The job took an hour. It was hot for late April and both men grew thirsty. After, Philip fetched two bottles of Guinness from the kitchen and they sat in the thick grass with creamy suds on their upper lips.

'How's Maisie?'

'Chirpy as a cricket. Her's been to two funerals this week. Her loves a proper funeral.'

'She likes a good death, does she?'

'Only one thing her likes better and that's a good operation.'

Philip grinned but put Maisie aside. She had only been a decoy anyway.

'And how are the Lyles?' he asked casually.

He watched a tree-creeper sliding as smoothly as a mouse up the ivied wall of the potting shed.

'In the pink.' Walter gulped the beer and brushed his hand across the beige foam on his mouth.

'Hugh OK?'

'A dog with two tails, isn't he?'

'Why? Business booming?'

'Doan know about that. They doan pay me more, do they? Skinflints. No, it's the baby, see?'

'What baby?'

'You doan know about the baby? They're having a baby. Sly old dog at his age. The cat's got the cream.'

Philip took another swig at his Guinness. The tree-creeper had reached the roof. What would he do now?

'What terrific news. When's it due?'

'September, his missus says.'

The tree-creeper had disappeared amongst the ivy clustering the eaves. He would have to check that the plant hadn't choked the guttering. There seemed an arrow that led back from September to last December.

'How extraordinary. I imagine he's celebrating.'

'A dog with two tails,' repeated Walter, this time with a suggestive swoop of his hand. He pushed his flat cap backwards and shot a sideways peasant's glance at Philip.

'You haven't asked about his missus.'

'Is she well? She's not young for all this, is she?'

'She's blooming.'

From behind there came the neat rhythmic rustle of small feet in the grass.

'Have you two finished? You look very comfortable.' It was Martha. 'Oh no, I don't think Gowrie should be with you. He'll get stung.' She gathered up the cat, its fur cuffing her arm.

'Not a stinging day,' said Walter.

'The Lyles are having a child, darling,' announced Philip, using the endearment as a demonstrator for Walter alone.

'How extraordinary.'

'Yes,' said Walter, muscled up with the news. 'In September.'

'He's very youthful of course. But what an unusual gap between his first and second family. It must be all of thirty years. Well, we must congratulate him.'

'Yes,' said Philip. 'Be sure to give both of them our congratulations.'

Walter inclined his head. It had been a satisfying morning to show his paces as a master of bees and the bearer of gossip. He gathered up his jacket and pipe.

'I'll be buzzing off then,' he said as always after working on the bees. 'I'll check them in seven days' time.'

They watched him walk, his gait rolling, to the path between the hedges.

'Buzz off indeed,' said Martha. 'How very droll.'

'I think it's unconscious and genuinely funny,' said Philip irritably.

Her lips moved a fraction as though she intended to say something but she simply raised her eyebrows and turned away, carrying the cat. They too disappeared down the path between the beech hedges. It was white with snow from the falling cherry blossom.

He was left alone in the grass. He was outside the flight path of the hives, but a bee—they were all upset by this morning's disturbance—bumped into the top of his head. Trapped in his hair, its wings vibrated with a furious panicky whine. He slapped his skull to crush it, then tried to winnow it out of the strands of hair. Too late: it had stung him. A welcome distraction which should stop him from thinking but it didn't; he couldn't stop thinking. Knowing the thought process had been dammed for the last half an hour, he awaited with dread the tumbling effect of release. His child? The old Ukrainian word for father came into his head: *Batko*. Then, *Batko* and *Mamo*, mother. He stood up to distract the chemical messages of the brain into his limbs, but sat down again because of a weakness in his legs. His head hurt too: it was the poison from the bee sting which he should have extracted to prevent its pump injecting more of its toxins. He could feel it forming a poisonous thought. It was dreadful, worse than any bee poison. He did not want to think this thought but it was upon him, swamping the realisation that it might be his child she was bearing. It came on the coat-tails of that thought and dwarfed it. The thought came to him that she had used him like a stud, no, not like a stud, like a fucking drone, a poor, stupid, hapless drone. Like the bee in his hair, once in, the thought was trapped, he could not eject it. Once in, it vibrated. Once in, it pumped in reinforcement poison. He remembered sitting in the summerhouse of the rose garden. 'Do you have children?' the abrupt No. He recalled the distance between her first and second visit to him: a month. He remembered her lying in the dark against him, her gentle hand folded around his chest. 'What do you want of me?' Her pause. Silence. 'Nothing. I have no claims on you.' He thought of her confused refusal to see him. The five months of absence. But of course. He was a drone, fooled on honey and lust, mated by the queen, then flung out, a cavity, disembowelled, de-sexed for all she cared, to be thrown away in the trash can. All that mattered were her eggs. No weakness in his legs now, he was a vat of fury and anger. He remembered seeing the light in his drawing room as he crossed the cobbles of the mews to his house on that first occasion. He had thought at the time that she would be too conscientious a person to leave without turning off the light. Jesus Christ, such a fool, what a misreading. Too conscientious not to turn out the light but without the ghost of a conscience in using him. Stop, this is crazy, he told himself, but sensible control was beyond him.

*　　　*　　　*

The painting was propped on an easel. Normally she stood when working but now she sat as much as possible to rest her legs. She had a slight headache. Perhaps the smell of solvent: diacetone alcohol, though it was very dilute. Perhaps the goggles which pressed her forehead like a visor. Perhaps peering through their lens which magnified x five. The photographic lights were also harsh to her eyes but necessary. She took up to sixty transparencies in the course of a restoration to confirm its different stages. You never knew when an argument mightn't ensue with the client.

As always it was painstaking work. She cleaned the picture by rolling the solvent-soaked swab on a little stick down the painting, sometimes across, a small patch at a time. A delicate application for by the time one saw colour on the swab one had removed too much—a slight grubbiness on the swab was the goal to aim for. She worked in silence, intensely focussed. It was a significant moment. With each stroke of her swab a little more was revealed. A little more of the fifteenth century, of the high Renaissance, of the Venetians, for she was working on an old master though you would not know it. The painting on the surface was entirely different from the art beneath. She had some idea of the life lurking below because X-rays had disclosed it. But the detail and the colour were as always a matter for wonder.

She rolled the swab gently down for a couple of inches, a little bit more, then again. Ah, no risk of dismantling the pigment beneath: it was stable as it was easy to bind. The loveliest pigment, the deep blue of heaven, its intense singing azure, the colour of the *quattrocento*, real lapis lazuli on the canvas. This first shift of the veil, the revelation, always entranced her. Five hundred years old and made manifest by her craft. As often she had the sensation of releasing a thing of great beauty from a tomb. Obliterated and silent for centuries, it could now begin to speak. She too started to sing as she worked, a rhythmic snatch, melodious and full from a Mozart opera. The *Seraglio*. She stopped for a moment to put on the tape, searching to find the song outside the Pasha's palace. There it was, the beginning of Act III. A run of *pizzicato* to establish the plucking of strings, then the lilting, plaintive tune of the mandolin serenade.

She was singing in full flood and did not hear a knock at the door. Even when repeated, she was deaf to any interruption, even the turning of the handle or the opening of the door or the sound of her name. He had to clasp her forearm before she registered his arrival. She stopped singing though the tape played on. It was a boring bit of recitative. Elfie and Philip stared at each other. They did not speak immediately, but in the background the operative dialogue pattered onwards, like a third-party interpreting their silence.

'Turn that thing off,' said Philip quietly.

She put down the swab and pressed the switch of the machine. Its sound swerved to a halt.

'What a surprise,' she said blandly, covering the fact that his visit was both shocking yet not unexpected.

'Don't give me that hostess treatment.'

Her face flinched as though hit. Keep calm, think of the baby. She went to her wooden chair and sank down.

'What is this?'

'You lied to me.'

'I have never lied to you.'

'You didn't tell me you were going to have a baby.'

She gasped then began to speak slowly. 'I wasn't sure. I suspected. What, for God's sake, could I say.'

'For a start, you could have told me what I had to learn from Walter. That it was due in September.' He was watching her closely.

She said nothing.

'September, *Delphine*. It's my child, isn't it?'

'No.' She was not looking at him.

'Do I need to go through chapter and verse with you. Do you suppose I'm a cretin? It's my child isn't it?'

'No. It's Hugh's.'

'I don't believe you.'

'You must believe me.'

Her face was alabaster, perhaps from shock, perhaps from the harsh studio lights which were still on. He felt pity seeping in. It was unwelcome so he pushed it away. He would not relent. A sudden access of fury protected him and made him shout.

'Do you know what I think? I think you used me. You used me like a stud.'

'No.' She cried out and then froze. They

293

both fell silent, hearing the sound of receding steps. Oh God, she thought, Susan. She would normally bring her coffee at this time. Had she heard anything?

The thought of an audience sobered Philip too.

'Does Susan know you're here?' she whispered.

He nodded, frowning. She had been with a customer in the shop when he had passed, explaining he had a photo of a picture to give Elfie in her studio.

'Christ.' Elfie cradled her head in her hands. A wave of raw alcohol nauseated her from the swab she had picked up unawares after turning the tape off. She put it down again and stood up.

'Please, just please remember what happened. You began it. I responded. Be reasonable. You wouldn't be saying this if we were still seeing each other. I couldn't go on as soon as I knew I might be pregnant. Do you imagine it wasn't a shock to me too?'

He stared at her in despair. How to argue with a woman? The only one who held the truth and therefore the trump. He could not dent her. He began to doubt himself. He thought of presenting her with each of the arguments behind his conviction, but confronted with the complexity of a real human being rather than the mathematical simplicities of ideas, the clarity of his beliefs had begun to crumble. In any case, what would be the point? He would be faced with complete denial. He threw up his hands, enraged afresh at the impotence of his position. Yet was she more to blame than he for the predicament? He sank down in the one armchair in the musty room, bereft of the energy that had propelled him there. They looked at each other with the understanding of a shared mess. She came to him and put her hands around his head and drew it to her stomach.

'Don't,' he said, in sudden distress, 'I can feel it moving.'

Batko, he thought again. Ridiculous and inappropriate that this Ukrainian word for father should be lodged in his brain. Another thought came to him. How foolish it had not occurred to him before: he had been too inflamed by the parallel with his bees.

'That morning with the roses started this, didn't it? The breeding of the roses.'

He looked up at her intently and caught the second's recognition in her eyes, then it was gone.

He shook his head. He knew for sure now and he knew that she knew too. She did not accept complicity but it was there.

'What do we do?' he asked but realised that there was no we. That second of understanding, the touch of her hands, the stirring of his child, had all conspired to give him the illusion that this was a shared experience but it wasn't.

'You'd better go now. It's for the best.' She drew back to look at him again.

'For the best? For your best.'

'Both our bests. All our bests.'

In one's best interest; he recognised this was as always the final line. There was no room for illusion whether the domain was work or feeling.

He searched her face to which the colour had begun to return. The full mouth, the folded hair. She was wearing a blue smock, an artist's shirt or perhaps a maternity top. She bloomed, a madonna.

'I am truly sorry you were snarled up in all this.'

He might have believed her, but for the chill thought about the rose and the drone. Too bad he got caught up in the machinery. She now needed him to die quietly.

She went to kiss him goodbye, but he stepped back, unable to be passive. It was for the best that he should retire quietly, for all their sakes, his too, but it was too much for her to expect a loving reconciliation.

'Don't worry,' he said. 'I wish you well.'

He turned and opened the door, walked down the stone steps and crossed the courtyard. He stared grimly ahead, stubbing his toe on a terracotta pot of blue pansies.

As he entered the back door of the showroom, Susan watched him pass. He did not acknowledge her, doubtless did not see her. The two cups of coffee she had carried to the studio only a short while ago had cooled; a scum had formed on their surface. I must throw them away, she thought mechanically. She expected Elfie to appear at any moment and awaited her charade of normality.

CHAPTER TWENTY-FIVE

'"In the High and Far-Off Times the Elephant, O Best Beloved, had no trunk. He had only a blackish, bulgy nose, as big as a—".'

'What a yawn,' said Florence.

'We don't want that one,' agreed Mona. 'Not really.'

Rupert and Camilla, his fiancée, exchanged glances. It was nine o'clock in the evening and Mona in particular should have reached that twilight stage before sleep. Instead she was over-excited as always by a new person and was alert to showing-off.

'How about . . .' said Rupert in his most soothing manner.

'No. Not Mrs Tiggywinkle either,' added Mona.

'Augustus who wouldn't eat up his soup?'

'No.'

'I know quite a nice story,' suggested Camilla.

The girls ignored her. She was an unknown

297

intruder with an untried story. She could watch and applaud them but was not allowed to take part.

'It's actually a rather good story. My mother made it up. We used to listen to it for hours.'

'We want your man-eating lion story,' said Mona. She had climbed on Rupert's lap and was trying to prise open his mouth.

He sighed. This one involved amateur dramatics. He looked at his watch. Five minutes were all that had passed. Five past nine on 30 June. He resigned himself to the full ritual.

'A hundred years ago, there was a fierce lion in Africa that ate men.'

'How did he do it?' asked Mona.

Rupert opened his mouth wide and roared. Mona peered into the glistening strawberry-pink cavern.

'I hope I don't see your willie,' she said.

'It's the other end, stupid,' Florence said witheringly.

'Go on,' said Mona.

'A hundred years ago there was this lion in Africa who ate men.'

'Did he say anything before he ate them?' Mona wriggled as she prepared for the forthcoming lines.

'He certainly did.'

'What did he say?'

'The l-i-o-n s-a-i-d—' Rupert knew how to string it out. Mona gave a tiny whimper.

'The l-i-o-n s-a-i-d "I'-m—"' He paused deliberately.

'Say it,' begged Mona.

'The l-i-o-n s-a-i-d "I'-m g-o-i-n-g t-o . . ."'

'"EAT YOU UP."' shouted Mona.

She flung herself back against his chest and giggled helplessly. Florence looked on, displaying a touch of sourness.

'Let's do it again.' More giggles.

'No,' said Florence.

'The lion tore them limb from limb.' Rupert rolled his head and snarled. With Camilla as an audience, he as well as Mona was giving it all he had got. Acting on all fronts, he was displaying himself as good husband material.

'He ate black men and white men and pink men and blue men.'

'What about women?' Florence intervened with some hauteur.

'That is understood.'

'No it's not. Mrs D'Arcy always says persons at school. She made us write it in our think book last week.'

Mona turned on her furiously.

'Oh, tell your own story,' said Rupert.

'Please go on.'

Rupert rose to his feet, shunting his niece to the floor. Mona began to cry.

'Mrs Mackiedoodle and the strawberry jam avoids all polemics as far as I can remember,' said Camilla.

'They'll find some.' Running short of

patience, he began to make his way to the door.

'Once upon a time there was a Mrs Mackiedoodle. She lived in a white house with a green door and a black cat. One day she—'

The girls looked at her dully, then turned their attention to the golden retriever who had just blundered into the room from the garden. He let himself be hauled by his collar to Camilla's feet and slammed his head on her knee. He had long ago relinquished a dog will of his own.

'Well,' said Camilla, 'someone's interested.'

'It's what you do best,' said Rupert affectionately. 'Pouring oil on troubled waters is your forte.' And not just on theirs but on mine.

Watching her from the doorway, he thought for the umpteenth time that she was just what was needed to calm him. Big—all of five feet ten inches—heavy-boned, sensible and capable, an unreconstructed Sloane and a secretary, she was truly one hell of a relief. Looked at from another way, she might seem a blissfully boring bunker, but that was a relief too. Thank God for the rebound factor which could always be relied on to produce a wife at the right time. Or maybe it was just the time that had produced the right girl.

Whatever, there could be doubt he'd needed something. The last couple of months had been awful and almost dumped him. His highly leveraged fund had suffered large losses. He had bet on the future and it had failed him. None of his risk management models had helped him, nor had they saved him from the vituperation of a few of his clients. 'Who stuffed it?' they said. 'You did,' and he had to admit they were right. He had stuffed it all round.

In the past he had always prided himself on having the strength of character to take losses, on his ability to take them and walk away. But this time, coming on top of Kristina, he had been shocked and ashamed by the power of his own emotions. He had not bottled, nor had he cracked; but for the first time in his life he had not escaped unscathed and it was that which had really frightened him. For a month he, Rupert, normally so low-key and relaxed, had suffered night sweats, eczema and palpitations. It was shameful and all so horribly recent that he was afraid it would come back.

No surprise, perhaps, that it should turn out to be Camilla who provided the answer. Dear old dependable Milly, whom he had known as a safety net for two years. Good old faithful Milly who worked in the lower echelons of the same bank; healthy in body and mind, uncompetitive, unencumbered with a higher education, a peach. A rotten linguist and a great cook: how different from Kristina. No beauty admittedly, but who cared when a wife was a wife. Her parents had a garden in Dorset which they opened every year under the

National Gardens Scheme. She could not wait to escape to the same style of life herself. Rupert was quite tempted himself. 'As soon as we've got a home and are married,' he promised, 'we'll put up a nice smug notice beside the drive saying "Slow 5 mph. Children, dogs and horses".' They were living at present in his house in Clapham. He would just have to wait for a bit and so for that matter would she. But life in the five miles per hour lane looked blissful.

Smiling, he crossed the hall, fell over a pushchair and opened the door of the kitchen. A haze of dried flowers which were suspended inconveniently from the ceiling blocked his view to Meredith on the other side of the room. He sniffed hoping he would detect a nice roasting smell, juice or gravy, a barbecued sausage at the very least, but his nose knew at once there was nothing.

'Here,' said Meredith, 'want one?'

She passed him a lonely gingerbread man.

'Thanks,' said Rupert. 'Shall I put on some sausages or something?'

'I thought Camilla could help me with these doodahs.'

She was putting a flash of red pepper on some *smørrebrød*, the finishing touch on what promised to be thin gruel. They looked very cold yet the evening was chilly for summertime. His body was psyched up for some hot food: it had targeted sausages.

302

'Milly's busy with your kiddies. She's telling them a story. I don't suppose you have any sausages, do you?'

'Not like Kristina is she?'

'No. Much more suitable.'

'What happened?'

'She shoved off. Shut up.'

'Pity. We liked her.'

'You'll like Milly.'

'You don't think she'll be a tiny bit boring?'

'No. Unstressful. Kind. Calm.'

'A bit big isn't she?'

'All the better for having children.'

'Ah well, if it's a question of hips, I agree.'

'You know Elfie's having a baby?'

Meredith put down the butter knife and stared at her brother.

'Didn't they tell you?' asked Rupert.

'I haven't seen them for months. You know Pa. He never keeps in touch with me.'

'It's in September.'

'Christ, that's no time away. I don't understand it. I remember you saying a year ago in this very kitchen that Pa didn't want one.'

'He didn't. Changed his mind or perhaps it's an accident.'

'A second family at his age. Well, who would have thought Pa had it in him.'

'Maybe he doesn't.' Rupert regretted it the minute he had said it. He slammed his mouth shut against further conversation, but Meredith was staring into him. She was peering upwards, her fair fringe trailing across her eyes, her cornflower blue eyes like arrows.

'What do you mean by that?'

'Nothing.'

'Are you inferring something?'

'Of course not. I don't infer. You know me, a straight talker and I'm hungry. Can't we cut this crap and have something cooked?'

'Rupert, this is important. Pa is going to have a new child. That'll affect everything for us. Things will get divided up.' Meredith put her hand to her head as though the division sums had suddenly struck. 'If you're implying it's not his child, shouldn't we know? Him too?'

For a split second Rupert hesitated, then wiped it, though he knew that this atom of time had already conveyed a fatal doubt.

'Forget it, Merry. I meant nothing. And even if I did, you're well provided for and so am I.' It was ill-advisedly expressed, as he realised.

'So you did mean something.'

'No I didn't. Not at all. I was simply explaining that if I had, it would be irrelevant.'

She continued to look at him stubbornly and with stubborn doubt.

'Christ almighty. Leave it alone will you? We come out here for a nice unstressed evening and you get some crackpot idea in your head. So much for a stress-free visit.'

'Mona very stressed out,' said Mona from the doorway. She padded forwards to stretch

304

up for a gingerbread man from the table.

'And my life's no bed of roses either,' said Florence from behind.

'How did the story go?' Rupert asked Camilla. 'A bit short wasn't it?'

He shot a warning glance at his sister.

'Short on stamina,' replied Camilla. 'Bored. We came in to—'

She looked expectantly at Mona whose mouth was stuffed with the biscuit. 'Eat you up,' said Camilla glumly.

CHAPTER TWENTY-SIX

'How many years is it?'

'Twenty-seven? Twenty-eight?'

It was not lodged so clearly in her mind that she could be confident of being exact, but it must be all of that length of time since Susan had seen Colin Harmsworth. She had known him as a girl at a period when she was always in love with someone, though never, it was true, with Colin. This omission had not stopped her from agreeing to meet him this evening. After all he must have pursued an assiduous trail to find her and it was courageous of him to have followed it up. As a result she had even felt a tiny bit hopeful, though his letter should have served as a deterrent. 'A voice from the past' rarely bode well.

'Another drink?'

'Thank you.' She handed him her glass of Aqua Libra and began to leaf through *Horse and Hound* in his absence.

It was the very early evening and they had met in the green drawing room of one of Burford's most chintzy and comfortable hotels. They took up positions side-by-side on the sofa, upholstered in a style to seem like home. They were alone apart from another couple at the other end of the room, not side-by-side on cushions but face-to-face over a small oak table. Despite the vase of roses placed between them, their position conveyed the confrontational.

It wasn't, thought Susan, that she had expected so very much from this evening, but she had hoped for just a fraction more than she was receiving. After all, some people were late developers, weren't they? She recalled that the Colin Harmsworth of half-a-lifetime ago was a fringe-member of the little party-going gang she had frequented in her youth. Tolerated at its edge, he would have been roughly ejected from its centre had he presumed to invade it. It wasn't that he was undervalued, but rather valued for the wrong things: for his ability to run errands rather than fun. He was part of their infrastructure and, like roads and concrete foundations, he was boring but necessary. It was all terribly unfair for he was actually quite nice-looking with crinkly brown hair and round spaniel eyes. But even in that less discriminating era, there was a glass wall between the boys one slept with and those one asked to mend one's bicycles, and Colin had never managed to breach it. As a result he had once spent a whole evening mending a puncture to one of her tyres. Awful really to think how ill she had used him. Remembering the occasion, Susan now thought it was a fallacy that one married handymen: her generation had just kept them as handymen.

'Here you are, Susan.'

He was back at her side. She took her glass.

'I must say, Colin, your letter was rather a surprise. Why did you get in touch?'

'I heard a while ago that you had some bad luck. And then my own divorce came through last year. Hello, I thought, we've got something in common.'

'Ah.'

'So I thought I'd run the old Jag down here to meet up. Not that it's old, of course. It's a demonstrator model. Not new either, but only 300 miles on the clock.'

'That's good,' said Susan, rising to the spirit.

'It isn't silver. That's another good thing about Jaguars. You can tell most demonstrator models miles off because they're silver.'

'Of course. How silly of me.'

She took a swig of the sweet, strange water. Her two-tier earrings bobbled as she dipped her head. She had donned them to give a sense of occasion but she thought she might as well slip them back in her bag. She began to unscrew one then stopped, thinking this could be misconstrued as a step towards self-abandon. In *Frenchman's Creek*, which she had loved at the age of twelve, Daphne du Maurier had removed her heroine's ear-drops as a prelude to sex with the French pirate. Nowadays the sequence was extended: earrings, belt, skirt, shirt and pants.

'What do you drive?'

'A Ford.' It emerged like a yawn. Her jaw muscles were a little depressed, nor could she blame them. It wasn't just Colin. She was watching the couple on the other side of the room. Pugilists: tense, agitated and in imminent need of a lawyer.

'My first wife drove a Mini.'

'What happened to her?'

'She went off with a sales manager at Cadbury's.' His brown eyes, still dog-like, swivelled towards her. 'Don't worry. I've still got the house in Putney and the flat in Majorca.'

So that's it, she thought. He has come to tell me what his dowry would be if I took him on. Thirty cows, a herd of goats and a couple of spears, or to be precise, a big car, one town house and a flat in the Med.

'Susan, what do you say? Why don't we drive out somewhere nice and have dinner. I'm on my own, you're on your own.'

She fell silent. From the other side of the

room, the woman's voice rose in tearful protest. 'I am very proud of our children too.'

Oh God, thought Susan. A cameo of this evening flashed before her, indeed of a life married to someone like Harmsworth. Her alas and goodbyes to him began to take shape within her. She was resigned to the alternative that lay ahead tonight: there were two fish fingers in the freezer and a half-finished novel on the bedside table, the usual tale of a woman wistful for a better life. Together they amounted to the familiar punishment for a false start with a man. For the illusion (why wouldn't the damn thing lie down and die?) that shared hurt and kindness would be sufficient for a happy future.

*   *   *

'I thought you were going out,' said Nick when she arrived home.

'I was. He was sad and a bit awful. There was another couple in the place too and they were also sad and awful but in a different way.'

She felt infinitely depressed. At least his old spouse was out there, albeit with a Cadbury's sales manager, and not dead like hers.

'Well, I'm going out,' offered Nick.

'That is obvious. Who is it?'

He hesitated. 'Tabitha.'

She might have guessed. He did not look or even feel like Nick, but like a waxwork model.

He was wearing his sexual plumage: old gold cotton trousers, sneakers and a cream ribbed sweater, all new but carefully broken in. He had the self-conscious smell of cologne.

'At last,' she said.

'At last. In fact I've got a second piece of news too. I got offered another job. At the auctioneer's. I turned it down.'

She opened the freezer and reached for the packet of fish fingers. She checked there were two left, then shut it again and went to the whisky bottle from which she poured an unaccustomed and costly two-inch slug. She was thinking that perhaps it might be a good idea if he took the job. The triangle of Elfie, Philip and Hugh prowled around her head. Somehow she feared it could threaten hers and Nick's jobs. It was the secondary reason she had accepted Colin Harmsworth's invitation this evening. She had a feeling she should explore other avenues and the feeling had gnawed. Now here was Tabitha as a further unwelcome link.

'Mum. Are you OK?'

'I'm OK. Just sit down for a moment.'

He looked at her in surprise. His mother did not usually sound so serious when she asked him to sit down. He pulled out a chair and lolled into it. She noticed his demeanour had changed. He was in Tabitha's orbit.

'I am not trying to spoil anything but please take care.'

310

'For God's sake, Mum. I'm nineteen. Where do you think I've been all my life?' Fancy her talking condoms as though he were a fifteen-year-old.

'I'm not referring to what you think I'm saying. I'm talking about your possible involvement with her.'

I'm depressed this evening, thought Susan, I mustn't let it colour his life; but she persisted.

'I'm not easy about you're getting involved with her.'

'Don't interfere. I'm not a kid.'

'I'm talking to you as an adult which you used to be.' Susan paused, seeking an uncompromising explanation. 'Her family has problems.'

'Doesn't everyone's? The Queen's? Ours?'

'No need for lip. Her mother is vain, shallow, neurotic too probably. I don't like her. Look at the mother and you know how the daughter will turn out. That is a tried and tested maxim.'

'I'm not involved with her mother.'

He got up, leaving his chair out in the middle of the floor to express irritation, and prepared to leave. 'Right? That's it?'

'It is not it.' She caught hold of his arm. 'Nick, I am serious because I'm worried. Please leave her alone.'

He started to walk out, in an adolescent fury at being baulked.

'Nick, this is strictly between ourselves. That family is a hornet's nest. It is not surprising that

311

with a wife like that, it is rumoured that Philip has looked elsewhere.'

He turned round startled.

'What do you mean?' He remembered that Walter had also hinted.

'All I'm saying is it's better not to get too involved.'

'Who is it?'

'Nobody you or I know,' said Susan firmly to block an avenue.

'Anyway, I can't see what bearing it has on Tabs.'

His face, alert for a moment at the spark of scandal but now dowsed by the lack of information, relapsed into sulkiness. It was impossible living with his mother. He had accepted because he knew she had needed him, because it was cheap too. But she was fiddling with every area of his life. He picked up his cotton jacket that he had slung over the back of the chair.

'I still don't see how this affects my seeing Tabitha this evening.'

I cannot warn him without blurting out the facts, thought Susan. She hesitated on the brink but drew back. The young were too unreliable to be trusted. She decided to approach the problem from another direction.

'That job at the auctioneer's. Is it still open?'

'Why?'

'It sounds interesting.'

'More than this? I'd just started a bit of

dealing here. It seems foolish to switch at this stage.'

'I've a feeling that this place may be a cul-de-sac for you. Hugh's getting on. He won't want to keep the place running for ever. Especially with a child now.'

Nick stood there undecided, his coat swinging from the index finger of his right hand. The phrase cul-de-sac worried him. He lived in one. He was hemmed in by one. Oddly the point had been driven home to him as recently as this morning. It had been sunshiny and showery when he left home to drive to work. As he took the van along the lane, he noticed a summer rainbow. Its left foot was planted in Dennis Thompson's field and its right in Edgar Easom's. Even the range of Heaven's bow was a cul-de-sac. Tabitha had represented an exit.

*   *   *

When Nick arrived, she was lying in a hammock on the front lawn. It was as big as a Wendy house, rectangular and wooden like a four-poster bed with a dark green and scalloped awning which was fluttering in the light breeze of the summer evening. Having located her, he scrunched across the gravel drive self-consciously; last time he had been the delivery boy, this time the suitor, but the transition was not entirely complete.

'Hi,' he said.

'Hi.' She looked up from the book she was reading. A Moghul princess, she leant towards him on a pillow. She was wearing a long, loose ankle-length dress, a totality of coverage.

'OK? Shall we go?'

'Oh Nick. You couldn't do something for me before we leave. My car's making a funny noise.'

'We're going in mine.'

She wrinkled her nose and put the book down. 'I'm worried. It doesn't seem to have any power.'

'Can't you get it fixed?'

'It's just happened. I need it for tomorrow.'

He frowned. He didn't want to tinker about with an engine at the start of an evening.

'Nick, you'll know what's wrong with it. Do. Please.'

He succumbed. She wriggled to the edge of the hammock bed and put her feet to the ground. He saw her toes flex as she stood up. She led him to her car standing beside the house. It was red and one of the those shiny, compact, little-girl cars. Chaste nymphets drove them in television advertisements, girls with long hair and tight high breasts and legs supple enough to wrap around a man's neck, dolls who pretended to be daddy's daughters.

'How does the bonnet open?'

'I'm not sure.'

He slid into the driver's seat, found the

manual, read it for five minutes and then pulled a lever. All the while, she leaned attentively on the door. He propped open the bonnet and regarded the engine. It was obvious to even an amateur glance that the inside looked oily.

'Perhaps the plugs are affected. When did you last get them changed?'

'Do I need new ones?'

'Well, they could be cleaned I suppose.'

She opened her slanting eyes in a flattery of gratitude.

He tested the engine to confirm the misfiring and began to disconnect the lead. He then started on the plugs, but they were as if welded into the engine block and he had to strain to release each one. There was no space to manoeuvre and he noticed a streak of oil on his trousers.

'Start the engine,' he told her.

She went to the driver's seat and sat there long enough for him to test and then clean the first one. Halfway through the second, this had become boring so she slipped out of the car and started back to the house. Nick was by now engaged in a long and lonely tussle with the engine, man gripped by machine. His knuckles had been squashed and scraped, his eyes and biceps were pumping. He noticed that Tabitha had drifted back to the hammock. Grimly he cleaned each one, adjusted the gap and tested them for a spark before screwing them back.

No good, so he repeated his efforts, back and forth. It was late by the time he slammed the bonnet shut and returned to the driver's seat. He was furious. The job had taken an hour and a half and reduced his lust to floor-level. As he started the engine for the umpteenth time, she looked up, put down the book and ran over to him.

'It's your car. You might take an interest,' he said intemperately. He could smell the cologne with which he had anointed himself two hours ago. He was now covered in grease and his right knuckle was bloodied.

She did not answer, but he saw her looking at the oil he had transferred to the driving wheel. In the silence they both listened to the noise of the engine.

'It's still wrong.' She frowned with irritation. 'Shit.'

He wrenched the key out and stared at her from the driver's seat. 'Is that all you've got to say?'

'Sorry. It's terribly kind of you. Thanks. It's just a bit annoying, that's all. I wanted to use it for tomorrow.'

He felt incensed by this scant appreciation. 'Aren't you going to ask me in for a drink before we set off?'

'I've brought you a beer.' She handed him a can of lager and a glass. 'But it's a bit late to go anywhere now, isn't it?'

'I thought we agreed to spend the evening

together.'

'I don't feel like it now.'

'Oh don't you?'

'It's exhausting fooling about with an engine.'

'I'm not aware you did much fooling about with the engine.'

'Don't be boring.'

'I've wasted half the evening, got covered in oil and you say that I'm boring.'

'How was I to guess it would take this long? I thought you knew about vans and things.'

'You mean the delivery boy.'

'Well, I don't know what else we'd have done. Not screwed if that's what you're thinking.'

'I wasn't thinking that.' He stopped for a second but, now that the word was spoken, felt the challenge and his thoughts went arms-akimbo. 'Though now you mention it, why not?'

'Because I don't.'

'You don't?'

'Girls like me don't.'

'What about Adam?'

'He's different.'

Oh, he doesn't know about vans and things. A blood-bath washed inside his head. He shouted through its roar, 'Jesus, you're more fastidious than your father, I'll say that.'

She whipped round and stared at him. 'What do you mean by that?'

317

'Ask Walter. Your dad's the talk of the town.'

She looked at him poisonously for a second, then turned and walked away towards the house.

Christ, thought Nick, what the hell have I done. He began to run after her. 'Tabitha,' he called. 'Forget it, I didn't mean it,' but she had closed the door.

*   *   *

It had grown chilly this evening, though Elfie and Hugh had sat and talked on the seat beside the goldfish pool until the sky had turned a gnarled pink and grey. They then returned to the house. Now they were sitting one behind the other on the big faded carpet in the drawing room. The dogs, delighted to find that the leaders of their pack had sunk to their level, were still smothering them with a welcome.

'Bugger off,' said Hugh. 'OK, try it again.'

She sat with folded legs in the cobbler's position practising deep-breathing techniques. She inhaled to her toes, feeling her diaphragm lift up and out.

'One, two, three,' he counted, grasping the sides of her ribcage. 'Now, hiss it out. One, two, three, four, five, six, longer if you can. OK? Do it again.'

'That's enough,' said Elfie. 'I'll move on to panting now. Ready? Oh God, not with Bertie, he'll go mad with ecstasy.'

She pushed the little whippet away and was just about to start the sequence of quick, shallow breaths which she had been taught to practise for contractions, when the phone rang.

'I'd better answer it,' said Hugh. 'I'm expecting a call. New York, most likely.'

He creaked himself up from the floor and tottered over to the telephone, his knees cracking like twigs in a storm. He found all this empathy business quite exhausting.

'Who?' Elfie heard him say. 'Ah Martha, how nice to hear—What? Look, steady on a moment.'

Elfie stopped panting and sat forward, suddenly alarmed. A flood was seeping from the receiver.

'I don't understand. When did you—? What? Wait, Martha. Martha? Are you there?' He stood staring at the telephone. 'She's gone,' he said, his eyebrows propped up with amazement.

In a panic Elfie tried to get up from the floor but the unwieldiness of her body left her wallowing on the rug. She was two stone heavier than she had weighed at Christmas.

'What?', she said, 'What's happened? What is it?' fear fighting the compulsion to know.

Hugh replaced the receiver and turned round. 'She sounded potty. She wants me to sack Walter.'

'Sack Walter. Why?'

'I think she's hit the bottle. Something about

him spreading rumours about her husband.'

'What rumours?' She was leaning forward, rigid, her relaxation techniques deserted just when most required.

'She was nearly incoherent. Mind you, I never liked Dacre. Untrustworthy type. Always out for the main chance. Always—'

'She's mad. Don't listen to her. Walter's harmless. He would never hurt anyone.'

By now Elfie had managed to struggle to her feet.

'I thought she mentioned Nick too.'

'Nick? Nick?'

Oh God, she thought, not Susan, it couldn't be Susan who had effected a leak. That morning in the studio, submerged fathoms deep, arose to haunt her. Successfully sunk like so much else, it bobbed to the surface and floated.

*　　　*　　　*

It was the late afternoon of the following day when Philip returned to his home. He parked the car as usual in the long stone-roofed barn and stepped out. Martha's Range Rover was not there; she was probably still playing golf. He stretched his arms and put his head back. It had been a protracted drive of fumes, lorries and motorway bad temper. He savoured as always that first true smell of the early-evening garden: of warm earth, green leaves, of musky moth-pollinated flowers starting to open. The almond scent of heliotrope floated in the air. He traced it to a pot on his left. He closed his eyes and felt some peace. He slipped his hand in his jacket pocket and took out the key, intending to go into the house and drop his case off, but halted halfway on the gravel, deciding to walk round the garden first. He left his possessions in the middle of the drive, loosened his tie and unbuttoned the neck of his pale blue shirt, moving his head from side to side as he did so. His jaw muscles still felt tense. Instead of keeping to the path, he crossed the soft level lawn and rounded the house. Past the dark canal pool on his left which he was glad to note had been kept topped up with water. Fish stirred in its depths, one or two coming open-mouthed to the surface in the expectation of crumbs. Down the axial path at the back of the house which ran under the three iron rose-arches. Here he stopped for a moment, under the middle one, a festoon of weeping blossoms about his head, a froth of catmint and lavender at his feet. As he looked around him, he thought that the garden had never seemed lovelier. Long fingers of shade had started to stretch across its breadth and in their violet shadows, groups of milky Oriental lilies arched in sheaves. As he crossed the grass to sniff them, he noticed with a smile that there was a scatter of honeybees in the cups of the white mallows. The very sight of them slowed him down. Each pattered its circuit around the pollened arrow of the eye, a clockwise movement dipping on the right, rising on the left, again and again, dizzying. In a couple of weeks it would be time to draw the honey crop. More than ever, he felt that the flowers and the bees mattered to him.

For a moment he stood watching the workers hum from cup to cup, then turned and continued. On past the swimming pool enclosure to his right, where he didn't stop, and the white garden on his left. Here it was full of the scent of tobacco plants, tall candelabras waving over the somnolent and superfluous sphinxes at the exit. Then on under the cherry trees overhanging the path, and out through the beech hedge. Expectantly he glanced ahead, then paused in puzzlement. The path had grown muddy; not just crumbs but lumps of earth were scattered over its surface. Strange, he thought, when everything else was immaculate. He took a few more paces forward. A clod had stuck to the sole of his shoe, odder still when it hadn't rained the last few days. As he looked round for a twig to dislodge it, he saw the beds of his seedling roses, at least he thought he saw the beds of his seedling roses, though they were no longer orderly beds but, he stared in shock, a madman's terrain. Some decapitated, others half axed with a spade, a few dug up, lying on the far path, their young roots dried out in the sun. He picked one up and looked at in helpless bewilderment, touching its faded, flattened petals. Someone had stood here and flailed. Today? Yesterday? Not even when but who? Some lunatic? Did Martha know? Was that why she was out? He stood frozen among the dying roses, paralysed until a second fear struck him. In sudden panic, he ran over to the hives. Indifferent, self-absorbed, the stream of workers cascaded into and out of the doors. Unharmed and aloof, a flower more or a flower less was of little importance to them. They were glutted by summer.

He went back to the roses and stood looking, a nerve working in his jaw. A cold anger had begun to seep over the first shock. Then he turned and walked back to the silent house. Deliberate in his movements, he picked up the suitcase and jacket he had left on the drive and put his keys in the lock of the iron-studded door. He crossed the cool flagstone hall, noting that the post had been neatly stacked on the table. He put the case down and leafed through it. Catalogues, notices of exhibitions, cold-mailings from charities, his old school asking him to its annual dinner, his old college soliciting a covenant. At the bottom he found what he was looking for. She had made him wait. An envelope, white, but recognisably one of their own, blank, without even his name on it, depersonalised. He slit it open and stood reading, though what it said could be encompassed in a single glance.

CHAPTER TWENTY-SEVEN

'You must accept,' said Hugh, 'I'm going to have to ask Nick and Walter what this is all about. I can't put it off any longer.'

It was the evening of the following day. Elfie lay on the crewel-patterned sofa, her feet propped up on its arm. She chose to look at the ceiling rather than Hugh. She lay outwardly at peace, inwardly in turmoil.

'I don't accept it. I've said again and again, it's wiser not to meddle with these things.'

'Elfie.' He started pacing round the room. 'I can't ignore it. Two men in my employ go into a customer's house and are the subsequent source of slander.' He paused for a second, in search of a clinching phrase from his past. 'It's very *fons et origo*,' he added with relish.

He looked across the room to his wife. Her skin was browner, the pigmentation forming a sort of butterfly mask across the wings of her cheeks like tribal paint. He wished she would say something.

'You wouldn't prefer to speak to them yourself, would you? You're closer to Walter than I am.'

'No,' said Elfie.

'You understand that if there's anything in it, I'm going to have to get rid of them?'

'No.' She sat up, ignoring a severe pain on her right-hand side just below her breast. 'No, Hugh, you can't do that. Nick's got nowhere to go and Susan depends on his income. As for Walter, we agreed to keep him because Maisie's foul to him at home and he's too old to work for anyone else.'

'Precisely. He's useless.'

'We need him. At the very least in the garden.'

'He's too old to dig. We need a digger. A lifter at work and a digger at home. How old is he? Ancient anyway.'

'Seventy next year. Only four years older than you are,' said Elfie spitefully. 'Are you pensioning yourself off?'

'Do lie down again,' said Hugh, refusing to rise to the bait. At this stage of the pregnancy he was keen to defer to his wife's agitation. He continued more gently, 'I do of course realise that I'll have to speak to Susan before I talk to Nick. I can't do this behind her back.'

'No,' said Elfie, attempting to sit again after briefly lying back.

'For Heaven's sake, what's the matter with you? It's a moral obligation. I'd have thought you'd agree.'

'It'll upset her.' It sounded feeble.

'It'll upset her more if I do it without her knowledge.'

'It's Nick's business. You can't tittle-tattle to his mother.'

'Look, she manages the showroom. Even if she weren't a mother, she's got to be told what the employees are up to. If they lose us

325

customers through some indiscretion, she'll have to know. I can't shield her any more than I can him.'

Testy from the effort of controlling his temper, he had begun to crave a cigarette. There was a half-finished packet from nearly eight months ago in the little brass box with dragons that stood on the left of the chimney-piece. He could visualise it now. He had not had a single puff since he knew she was pregnant. He tried to imagine the nicotine penetrating his body, down, down, down. It didn't work. He looked piteously across to his wife. She had shifted her position. She was sitting bolt upright, having swung her feet one after the other to the floor. Her hands were linked across her upper belly where the mound sloped back to her breasts. She was wearing her pale blue cotton kaftan with its navy butterflies around the neck and hem. He remembered her in it that winter night when she had flung the sugar on the fire. He suffered the conflict between caring and irritation. He began to fidget, his right leg pumping up and down. Damn her, she could be so stubborn. Why was she so obstructionist?

'I'd better talk to her.'

'What do you mean?' he said grumpily, the *volte face* catching him unprepared.

'*I'll* speak to Susan.'

'*You'll* speak to Susan?'

'*I'll* speak to Susan.'

326

He stared at her in surprise and relief.

'What a good idea.' He gave a large smile, greatly relieved to be reprieved from this little intimacy. 'See her here since you're not coming into the studio now.'

'Oh no, not here.'

'Yes, yes, much better. First thing tomorrow. Get it over with.' He began to edge towards the door, itching to scamper off in case his wife changed her mind. 'Some lemon and ginger tea? Your favourite pot? Why don't we get a cushion for your back?'

*　　　*　　　*

'How well you look,' said Susan conversationally. In fact she thought otherwise. Even the brown pigmentation could not mask the pallor of Elfie's face. She wondered whether she was all right.

'It's not long now is it?'

'Two weeks.' It sounded curt. Elfie was clearly reluctant to indulge in irrelevant chat. She was wedged, huge and immobile, in a chair on the terrace behind the stone house. She placed the cup of coffee untasted on the slatted wooden table.

'What are you going to call it?'

'We still don't know.'

'Sorry, I forgot.'

'We'll wait till we see it.'

I don't want to talk, thought Elfie. Behind

327

the prattle, the invisible ink of question and answer persisted. She realised it was the first time she had seen Susan alone since the awful morning of Philip's visit. Had she heard or not? Beneath the shiny veneer of office manners, the question and answer had continued in Elfie's mind, an argument doomed to silence because it could never be shaped into words.

'Hugh asked me to talk to you.' She spoke looking out on the grass. Beside her Susan was doing the same. Profile paralleled profile. A third part would have guessed they were watching a cricket match.

'On Monday evening,' continued Elfie in an abnormal monotone, 'Martha Dacre rang in a state and told him to get rid of Nick and Walter. It seems that Nick said—'

'I know what Nick said. He's admitted everything to me.'

But who told him? Was it you? Elfie asked her silently. And what did you tell him? Did you hear?

I heard, said Susan voicelessly, but I didn't tell him. Trust me.

'Hugh says,' mumbled Elfie, hiding behind the formality of her husband the employer, 'Hugh says he can't have them going to a customer's house and spreading rumour.'

She felt heat boil up her neck and mottle her cheeks. It was a warm morning and even though they were shaded by the large cream umbrella, she began to fan herself with her hand. Her companion failed to respond. In the silence, Elfie was paralysed by a strange sense of remoteness. She had known this woman for seven years, indeed seen her for most days of that period, yet she was speaking to her from a far distance. Just beyond the fringe of the umbrella, she could see a buzzard drifting in the August morning on a high current of air. For a moment she imagined herself in his position, looking down. She had a bird's-eye view of the foreshortened house chimneys, the patchworked garden, the top of their umbrella, their feet probably sticking out.

Susan still sat in silence.

'I don't know how rumours start,' said Elfie despairingly, 'but they are so often deeply wrong.'

'Of course,' said Susan.

'They can't be spread.'

'They haven't been.' Susan's posture had not changed, she was still watching the cricket match; but something had shifted. *They haven't been*. It was the nearest she had dared broach the specific. She had camouflaged it in the general but she hoped it would do. Trust me, she willed silently.

Elfie felt the shift. They continued to sit for a few moments, neither speaking yet each travelling through the lull, at the end of which some equanimity emerged, the harmony of being on the same side.

'Hugh says he'll speak to them but won't do

it behind your back.'

'What exactly will he say?'

'He was going to ask them if Martha had misrepresented what they said. If not, he thinks they'll have to leave.'

The equanimity splintered.

'He'll sack them.'

'I've told him he mustn't but he's adamant.'

Elfie put her hand to her forehead in a gesture of despair. It's my fault, she thought, I'm the start of all this.

Susan did not notice. She was lost in her own guilt. She recalled the other night. I caused it, she accused herself. See no evil, hear no evil, speak no evil; she had kept to this, yet she had still trespassed: she had inferred and a half-indiscretion was worse than a whole one.

She could see only one course.

'If they go, I must go too,' she said flatly.

Elfie turned to look at her for the first time. She was aghast.

'Not you.'

'It's only fair.'

'But you can't. What will you do? You haven't got another job to go to.'

'Never mind,' said Susan, gambling hard. 'I'll find something. It's the honourable thing to do. Tell Hugh before he talks to Nick and Walter that if they go, I go too.'

Maybe, just maybe, thought Elfie, switching suddenly from aghast to relieved but not showing it, maybe Susan and I can salvage something.

*   *   *

'For Christ's sake,' said Hugh, 'We can't do without her.' He paused and took a deep breath. 'She's sharp, I'll give her that.'

'It's not sharpness. It's her sense of honour.' Or both probably, thought Elfie.

'What honour? How does honour come into this?'

'Never mind.' She realised she shouldn't have said something that was impossible to explain.

'You are pitifully naive,' he yelled down the telephone. 'This isn't self-immolation. She's using herself as a hostage.'

'You don't understand. And don't shout at me.'

'I'm not shouting at you. I'm just exasperated, that's all.'

He flicked an imaginary speck of fluff off his jacket with irritation. This whole mini-tempest summarised the trouble with small businesses: they required inordinate attention to minutiae. He had a quick pang for the old days of schemes, strategies and human beings pinioned at a safe distance by the personnel manager.

'It's perfectly simple,' Elfie was saying at the other end of the telephone. 'We've got to keep Susan, especially now I'll be out of action for several months. Give Nick and Walter a wigging, that's all, but don't you dare upset them.'

'Waving a finger isn't enough for what they've done.'

'Then wave a small stick.'

'You've put Susan up to this.'

'Absolutely not. I'm as horrified as the next man,' said Elfie trying not to smile. 'I also admire her and so should you.'

I was a fool, thought Hugh, to let two women put their heads together, two make a flaming sorority. A good clean public-spirited sacking is what's required, a male clearing of the decks. He realised that the last time such an event had occurred was when it had happened to him.

*   *   *

'Put that looking glass down and come in here.'

Nick wedged the gilt-gesso mirror which was destined for Holland, against the wall and raised his eyes to Walter who had just shambled in. 'Not you,' he mouthed.

'Oh most certainly yes,' said Hugh, 'him too.'

They followed him into the office. Hugh strode round and sat the other side of his partner's desk, the priest behind his mahogany altar. At his own sacking the scene had been much the same; it was reassuring to change roles. He clasped his hands together and his caterpillar eyebrows met, as he prepared to embark on his text.

332

'It has been brought to my attention that the pair of you have slandered one of my best clients.'

Walter looked at Nick for help. He had pulled off his cap, feeling the presence of God, but this had become a shade technical for his co-operation.

'What do you have to say?' asked Hugh.

'I made an error of judgement,' replied Nick. 'It wasn't Walter's fault.'

'What happened?'

'I implied to Tabitha Dacre for reasons I don't wish to go into that her father was looking at other women.'

'Unforgiveable on your part,' said Hugh. 'What other women?' He felt ravenous with curiosity. The bugger was having a run-around.

'She's—' Walter mumbled.

'Shut up,' said Nick. 'Walter's blameless. It was all completely vague and no one was ever named. It's all my fault and even though it won't happen again, I'm ready to pay the price. I'm leaving before you sack me. I'm going to work for Berry, Withers and Todd.'

Hugh entered a state of shock. 'Berry, Withers and Todd?'

'They'll train me. I'll be pricing and assessing.'

'You can't leave,' said Hugh competitively.

'I thought you wanted me to.'

I did, thought Hugh, sod, that's torn it. There'll be no stopping his mother's

333

martyrdom now. He unclasped his hands, waved them helplessly in the air, then scratched his forehead, all attempts at a posture dissolved.

'What's wrong with this place?'

'I know you've let me do a bit of dealing, but it's not enough, I've got to give up the delivery if I'm going to pick up real skills.'

'What would you want to stay?'

Nick stood square. He glimpsed an opening. He was running with the rugby ball in his hands, a roar behind him like the fire-launch of a rocket.

'More dealing. An increase in salary after three months. I could be of serious use to you. And, oh yes, Walter will have to stay on.' He felt himself to be bursting and hid it by looking across affectionately at the old man.

'I'll think about it,' said Hugh. His horse had slipped from beneath him. He regained his seat by discharging a fresh round of strong moral disapproval. 'You realise what you've done is disgraceful.'

'I know,' said Nick.

'Honesty doesn't exonerate you. You understand that.'

Nick nodded. He had been genuinely ashamed, but having scored a touch-down, now knew it behoved him to look abashed too.

Christ, thought Hugh, and I was going to sack him. It now seems I'm about to promote him. He got up and shuffled his papers for a moment to allow a decent period of mourning for a lost purpose.

'She's left him,' erupted Walter, at last finding his opportunity. Sufficiently airborne, he could now drop his bomb. 'I went to check the bees and she's left him. She did his roses in too.'

'What?' exclaimed Hugh.

'She smashed his roses.'

'Christ, she smashed his roses?'

'Slashed 'em. Dug 'em up.'

'His roses.' Hugh felt squeamish. Any shred of envy for Philip took a dip. The sulphurous whiff of adultery had been seen off by shades of the madhouse.

'Christ,' he repeated. 'No fury like a woman scorned. Though he deserves it of course if what you said was true. Was it? Is it?'

*   *   *

One must walk by on the other side, Elfie had decided, but her resolution seemed to be failing. She stumbled slowly round the kitchen harrowed by guilt. It was half an hour since Hugh had rung with the news. 'She did for his roses,' he had said. 'Hacked them down and out. Bit deranged, isn't it?' But it wasn't, thought Elfie, not mad at all. It had its own hideous logic, that of consequence.

She sat down exhausted. Twice she put her hand to the telephone, then twice drew back.

335

The third time she rang his office. She recognised the silky, brainless voice of Ellen, the telephonist, she remembered her joined-up prattle. 'Mr Dacre isn't here he's on holiday this week do you want his secretary?'

She declined and cancelled the call, but the contact had given a boost to her momentum. She hesitated briefly, then pressed in the local code and digits. Small likelihood of a response, but she sat tensely and began to tremble. What was she afraid of, she wondered. Discovery or abuse? Both seemed equally deserved. By the tenth ring she had decided to hang up when he answered.

'It's me, Elfie,' she said quietly. 'Are you able to talk to me?'

There was a long aggressive silence, whilst she heard the surf of blood in her ears. She tried again. 'I didn't want to ring you here. I phoned you at the office.' She resisted the temptation to apologise. Take it or leave it, there was no other option.

'I didn't think I'd get much done this week.'

'Walter's told Hugh who's just rung me. I couldn't not speak to you.'

He paused, then spoke rapidly. 'I'd like to come over and see you.'

She recoiled in alarm. 'Not very wise.'

'Are you on your own?'

She hesitated. He read this as an admission.

'I'll be with you shortly. I've something to give you.'

336

'No.' She panicked. 'I think you'd better not.'

*   *   *

'I've forgotten,' he said, shocked by the clumsy change in her appearance, 'how big a woman gets at the end. It must be hell.'

'It is.' She added, 'You can't stay.'

'I shan't. I came to apologise. It won't take long.'

'No, it's my—'

'Shut up. I've spent the week allotting blame, and plenty of it, I might say, to you. And now I'm sick to death of it. I wanted to tell you this before it was born. The second thing I wanted to say was that Martha knew—and knows— nothing about you. There's a third thing. A question. Can the vague rumours of which I was accused be traced back to Susan?'

She coloured, the red flushing beneath the hormonal pigment of her cheeks. 'All I can tell you is that if she overheard that morning, neither I nor anyone else will ever know. She is trustworthy.'

How she hated this sordid complicity.

He put his head back and inhaled sharply. 'I came to tell you something else. I didn't mean it, that day. It was a dreadful thing to say.'

She felt tears pricking her eyes. To be returned innocent when she was guilty. And him the fall-guy.

'I'm so sorry,' she faltered. 'So terribly sorry. She's left you. And then the roses. She tried to kill your roses.'

'Some women smash the furniture. She was cleverer than that. It was the massacre of the innocents. She wanted to wound me where it would most hurt. I've been over things again and again this week. I've come to realise mine wasn't a marriage that could ever have endured. It was always bound to founder on envy.' He leant forward and touched her hand briefly. 'Not like yours. Yours will last, won't it?'

She nodded, unable to speak. It would have foundered without you, she thought.

'Well.' He stepped back. 'That's that. I've talked an awful lot, but then I haven't had anyone else to speak to this week apart from the lawyer, and at three hundred quid an hour you prefer to keep quiet.'

She looked at him. She felt exhausted, the veins in her leg aching, a pain in her groin. She backed towards one of the hall chairs. A thin Jacobean upright, it was too narrow for her now so she collapsed on its edge.

'I suppose I was the catalyst.'

He was momentarily startled by the word. In his own world, it would only be applied to detergents. It was a reminder that they belonged to such different ways of life. 'A good old-fashioned antique catalyst. A bit much, isn't it, for someone who put in such a brief

338

appearance.'

She shook her head slowly. She suddenly recalled Anthony. How funny, she thought and she almost smiled. All those four years I spent with Anthony. I could have used being a catalyst then. They fell silent. He regarded her closely as she sat thinking, her head tilted downwards, her hair lank, not as fair as he remembered but darkened with sweat perhaps. Those strange brown marks on her face—he could not recall such symptoms with Martha. Her vast pyramidal form, legs splayed out to brace her weight. He thought he could smell her, a not unpleasant musky smell like earth and strawberries. To anyone else she would have seemed ugly, but now that he had adjusted to the change in her looks, he found her quite beautiful. He had no wish to touch her, yet felt so close he might be buried inside her. As indeed I am, he said to himself. He allowed himself the luxury of looking for a second longer, reluctant to shut the door with his final words, knowing it was unlikely he would see her again.

'There is one more thing,' he said.

She lifted her head.

'I've brought you this.' He returned to the doorstep and picked up a potted plant. 'It's one of the seedling roses from the cross I made last summer. They all died except for this one. The roots of the others were too young to survive. They dried out in the sun.' He passed it to her.

'See? It's flowering. I said it would be purple, didn't I?'

Elfie took the plant and sniffed the dark velvet interior of its flowers.

'It's beautiful.' Sad it should be so perfect.

'Keep it. It's yours. It'll only be sold with the house otherwise.' He paused, suddenly doubtful of her reaction. 'Don't put it in the dustbin.'

He suddenly realised he had blundered. What hubris. She would not want it as a reminder. In any case, she would have the child. What meaning could a rose carry for her when she had expunged him from the child.

She shook her head. She was longing for him to leave. She recognised that she had not been equal to his gesture of sympathy. It was unfortunate but she was too nervous and physically exhausted to carry it through.

'Well,' he said with a degree of formality. 'It was kind of you to see me.'

Revitalised by a shot of shame, she struggled upright, pulling on the wooden arms of the chair. He could not approach her directly because of the barricade of her stomach, but came to her side. They touched cheeks briefly, though he kept his body apart. He knew he had avoided looking at her belly during the entire meeting and had no wish to touch it now. What was in her future was in his past.

She watched him walk to his car, jerk open the door, and start the engine. He looked back, gave a small formal wave, then reversed and drove away. She gave a sighing breath. Despite her relief, a strange sense of loss flooded her that unfinished business should have at last reached its close. She left the big grey oak door open to allow air into the house and walked to the sofa in the drawing room. All over. Silence. She lay down. A minute later she heard the noise of wheels on gravel. Not him again, she prayed. There was the sound of footsteps, a quick excitable tread, surely not Philip's, and of something being knocked over in the hall, accompanied by swearing which she recognised as Hugh's.

'Elfie?' he shouted. 'Elfie?'

'In here.'

He erupted into the room.

'That was Dacre's car coming out of the drive, wasn't it? What's he been doing here?'

Oh God, she thought, Hugh back early. She was reminded of a French farce. She kept her eyes closed, too tired to worry except for the child.

'Please, Hugh. We owed him, Martha anyway, an apology. I rang there because I knew you wouldn't. He dropped by to say he bore no ill will.' She did not stumble. She was using words like stepping stones. At any other time she would have felt shame at her own sure-footedness.

'Ill will. I'll say not. The bugger's the guilty party.'

'We don't know who's guilty. Anyway it's not our business.'

'And what's that rose doing in the hall?' he asked suspiciously. Elfie kept her eyes closed.

'Elfie, answer me.'

'From the noise I heard, it's not there any longer.'

'There's earth all over the hall. It needs a woman's touch,' he said crossly, helping himself to the polished steel shovel and brush that stood by the fireplace. 'Elfie, why's it there? Did he bring it?'

'It was the only one that survived the fracas.'

Hugh subsided into a chair and looked at her closed impenetrable eyelids.

'But why should he give it to you?'

'Hugh,' said Elfie, and she gasped suddenly as a pain dragged at her abdomen. 'I don't feel very well.'

But why should he give it to you, he thought again as he went over to help her.

*   *   *

Walled in by his own thoughts, Philip had not noticed Hugh. He drove back and entered his empty house, lost in his own ruminations. It had been some relief to see her, though he wondered whether that was due in part to his need to take some, indeed any kind of precipitate action. In the last few days he had been alarmed by his mood swings, veering

342

between ease at his freedom, and terror at finding the ground so stratospherically far from his feet. Still, the sense of rightness in their meeting persisted, whatever its outcome and however painful the inequality in their positions. There were ways of parting and the last ugly memory had at least been erased. It was his desire for this that had catapulted him into seeing her once more. Unable and unwilling to repair the larger breach of his marriage, he had turned his attention to the smaller one instead.

You used me like a stud. The poison of the accusation was now dispelled. To help her he had told her he hadn't meant it. This wasn't entirely true, but if he did mean it, he thought he had now come to terms with it. At least last night he had thought so. He had been standing in his study, scanning the shelves for something helpful to read. He rejected *Pilgrim's Progress.* Nothing too lofty or sagacious. Instead, idly, he had picked out his little copy of *The Life of the Bee* by Maeterlinck. He had turned over its ancient flimsy pages, seeking a passage that had struck his eye earlier in the year. Where was it? He flicked through chapter 1, then on to 2. These things were always so damned elusive when you needed them. Perhaps he had imagined it. No. Here it was, this was it.

It is to the future, therefore, that the bees subordinate all things, and with a foresight, a harmonious co-operation, a skill in interpreting events and turning them to the best advantage, that must compel our heartiest admiration . . .

The words began to blur. He had closed his eyes, then the book and put it back on the shelf. Perhaps, below the level of her subconscious wherever that was, she too had been driven towards her future. *A skill in interpreting events and turning them to the best advantage, that must compel our heartiest admiration . . .* My admiration, Elfie, he had thought wryly. Yes, he had come to terms with it. He could now see it more coolly from a distance. After all, human beings were only genes which needed to reproduce themselves. What was that famous line? A hen is only an egg's way of making another egg. Poor Elfie. Yet he could not deny that a part of him—a gawky and remote ghost from his youth, beyond all adult reasoning— that part of him had still hoped during their meeting this afternoon that the citadel of her marriage would crumble. 'Leave Hugh,' and she would say yes. 'Choose me,' and she would give him his future.

CHAPTER TWENTY-EIGHT

The hospital was housed in two separate blocks: a nineteenth-century brick infirmary for the sick and the dying, and a new concrete maternity unit, purpose-built for the eighties. Thus cradle was in theory insulated from grave.

In delivery room 5a, the senior midwife who was called Aileen Smailes and her assistant were attending the first routine birth of their shift. Mr Smailes was a stock farmer, and as it happened, Aileen had already brought a bonny Charolais calf into the world that same morning. She was in agreement with her dentist friend, Meg Mcgrath, who pulled horses' teeth, that the distinction between humans and animals was finer than usually supposed. But she did prefer the alfresco conditions on the farm. She had never got used to the heat of the delivery room which was kept at 21° centigrade.

'It's stifling in here,' gasped her assistant, a student who was wading through her requisite number of deliveries to qualify. She looked beseechingly at Aileen who was adjusting the temperature of the small white room in readiness for the final stage of labour.

Above the radiators, the sunflowered cotton curtains at the window shifted slightly in the heat-haze. Overhead the lights had been dimmed for the birth, and in the background, the patient's favoured tape of jungle music pounded quietly on.

'All right Dawn?' said Jenny, the student, handing the body on the birthing-table a fresh mug of tepid water to sip. 'Now try and relax that pelvic floor between contractions.'

'I'm gonna die,' the girl grunted.

'Nonsense, you're doing splendidly, isn't she?' Aileen enquired of Jason, the pale young garage mechanic who stood at the head of the birthing-table to give moral and physical support to his girlfriend.

'Oh Dawnie,' he contributed wanly.

He felt queasy and debated whether to go out. He decided against. The fathers' room was only down the corridor but the male team spirit was under threat from an element of machismo. He had noticed that joshing was reserved for fathers who flinched and fled. Jason decided to stay with the women. He resolved to keep his eyes averted from the helpful mirrors positioned to reflect every nuance of activity at Dawn's nether end. 'Look,' Jenny, the little student, had said, but one glance, he knew, would put him off sex for life.

'Aaah,' screamed Dawn.

Twenty years old, Caucasian, unmarried and a waitress, Dawn was also a primagravida possessed of a steady pulse rate and A1 abdominal muscles as a result of which she was making admirable progress. In the mirror, a dark matted head was beginning to protrude from the split between her legs.

'Good girl, well done,' encouraged Aileen. She kept her sterilised rubber fingers on the surface of the head to monitor and ease its descent. An expulsive crowning could increase the risk of laceration.

346

Jason stroked his girlfriend's face and avoided the mirror, as she gave two more terrible shrieks at the ensuing contractions. The sound curdled his blood and his stomach. He winced and concentrated on not fainting. Poor little Dawnie, he thought: what pain she was forced to bear.

'Look,' said Jenny, 'the head is out.'

'Is it a boy or a girl?' he gasped and then flushed at his stupidity. He hadn't told Dawn, but he hoped it would be a boy. Down at the garage, the other mechanics would be sour with envy.

'Too early to tell,' said Jenny kindly.

Beside her, Aileen's expression was invisible as she bent towards the workface, where the head had begun almost immediately to turn from its position facing the rectum to its successive stage of looking at the thigh. Aileen seemed to be on automatic pilot, clearing the excess mucus from the baby's mouth.

'Do you need help?' offered Jenny but unusually there was no immediate reply.

'No,' said Aileen after a little, deciding to stall and keep her head well tucked down.

Oh, she thought, oh dear, oh deary me, oh dear, oh bloody hell, oh dear, we have a problem here, oh me, oh my. Nice to think it wasn't a problem, but that would be pie in the sky. She wished she was back on the farm. Charolais, Limousin, Friesian, Hereford, Aberdeen Angus, each and every one no

347

problem. What was the best way of dealing with this now?

'Can you see the head?' said Jenny to Jason. Aileen glared at her, being tempted for a second to push the head back whilst she thought what to do. She made a mental search through her counselling course but emerged empty-handed. She offered a little prayer for inspiration. She remembered the words of her textbook. 'The moment of birth is both joyous and beautiful. The midwife is privileged to share this unique and intimate experience with the parents.' How passionately she believed it. Tanked up but less than aglow with these positive thoughts, she concentrated on clearing the baby's wet crumpled little face during the few minutes' pause before the uterine contractions that would expel him into what she hoped would be a welcoming world.

Perhaps Jason knows, she prayed, but instinct and experience warned her otherwise. He was still avoiding the mirror, but the moment of truth was irresistibly near.

'Aaargh,' groaned Dawn.

On cue, the music gave a triumphal thump.

'There,' said Aileen. The shoulders had slipped out. She hooked her fingers beneath the baby's armpits and lifted him tenderly onto Dawn's stomach.

'A wonderful boy,' said Aileen. 'A joyous birth.'

He looked indeed a perfect child, strong as a

calf, beautifully formed and with the noisy lungs of an athlete. Faultless in every respect, apart from the fact that he was clearly not Jason's, since he was decidedly black.

Dawn levered herself up against the pillow in expectation. There was the rush of indrawn breath.

'Oh Gawd,' she said. 'Oh my Gawd. Oo'd have thought it. It was only a one-night stand in Lanzarote,' she said pleadingly to Jason before falling back.

The two midwives blinked.

'Fucking hell,' said Jason. 'You rotten little swine. And you told me it was mine.'

He plunged from the cubicle, bolted down the corridor past the father's room and vanished out of sight.

'Not very supportive,' said Jenny. 'Is he?'

'Oh dear,' said Aileen, near to tears. 'I think a little counselling is in order.'

*   *   *

At nine o'clock the same night, Elfie and Hugh were about to go to bed when her pains returned. They stopped at the foot of the old oak staircase.

'It must be for real this time,' he said hesitantly.

'It might stop like this morning.'

'I think I should drive you to hospital now.' He was surprised but he had begun to shake inwardly. He concealed this from his wife. He had been in an anxiety-state all day.

'They'll send me home again if I'm too early. It's not due for ten days after all.'

They returned to the room to sit it out for another hour or more. He stared at her, glancing at the clock to time her discomfort. The arrow of the second hand tripped insistently over its brass face, measuring the pains.

'They are more frequent,' he said.

'Yes. They are.'

'Regular too.'

'Very regular.'

They exchanged prolonged stares, as though awaiting the other's starting-pistol.

'Is your bag packed and ready?'

'Both of them.' She had prepared one for him as well as one for her and the child three days ago.

'Well?' She had begun to shake too.

'We are a fine pair,' he said. It was a relief to move. She phoned the hospital and Judith whilst Hugh started the car. He squealed out of the gate, then calmed down and tried to drive at a steady pace to maintain outward equilibrium.

'Look at the moon,' she said.

She felt they were floating in a space capsule. In the darkness, a huge melon pink harvest moon had risen and now hung in its self-created haze in the south-eastern quarter of the night sky.

'What did you tell me about moon-gates?' she asked.

'They were Chinese. A focus for meditation whilst the moon passed through their curve.' He stammered on the 'm' in meditation and moon.

'Oh Hughie, your teeth are chattering.'

'Sorry.'

She put a hand over his on the wheel.

'I've forgotten a vacuum flask,' she said.

'My book?' He had decided to have another stab at *War and Peace*. He hadn't made much headway the first time.

'It's in. But what an awful choice. How long do you expect me to be stuck there? Three years?'

'Vaseline for you? Are you OK?' he added anxiously as she tensed in a spasm.

'Yes.'

'Facecloth?'

'Yes.'

'Leg-warmers.'

'And hot water bottle.'

'It's August.'

'Doesn't matter. It's on the list.'

'Nappies?'

'Nappies.'

Somehow the item came as a shock, odd when it had been so throughly rehearsed.

'When we come back,' said Elfie slowly, 'there'll be three of us in this car,' and they both fell silent, hand clasped over hand. He parked the car outside the hospital in the brightly lit forecourt. As he unhooked himself from the seatbelt, she reached over to him and kissed him on the soft leathery part of his cheekbone above the shaving line.

'Goodbye,' she murmured.

'I'm staying with you,' he said, though he recognised she was saying goodbye to her old self as much as to him.

He was wrong in thinking he would stay with her, for ten minutes later he had been despatched down the corridor for half an hour in the fathers' room whilst his wife was prepared. Over my dead body, he thought, after one look round the door at the inmates. He had not bonded with the fathers at the one and only ante-natal class he had attended and now was no time to start. There was no doubt about it, she should have had the child in the Lindo wing of St Mary's, a sensible little private start to a life, but he had been strapped for ready cash and anyway she had insisted it had better get used to belonging to the human race.

Nervously he went back to the car and sat in the private darkness of his own territory. Here it was quiet and familiar but it was also a mistake, here in the darkness. Here, he stopped shaking but started thinking thoughts he had put off from earlier in the day. They were waiting, alert and ready for their summons. In a second, all his free-floating anxieties had suddenly converged upon a single stage. The morning's events flooded his senses. He smelt the perfume of the rose. It occurred to him that presumably he had not yet managed to rid it from his nostrils. He concentrated on Elfie, but all he saw was a pattern of events that centered concentrically upon her. The thread took him by the hand and led him from one circle to the next, from the start of Martha's telephone call about Dacre to discovering him at his house. He tried to drop the cord but it seemed stuck to his hand like a figment from a bad dream. To struggle only entwined him yet further. Dacre on my territory, he thought. On my territory, with my wife. My wife and Dacre. I should see him, ask him what's gone on. His mind began to spring back in time, landing on first one prominence and then the next. Slithering out of bounds, it scavenged through the memories of his first marriage. His heart started to thud, preparing him for disaster. 'Stop this at once,' he told himself. 'Stop now.' He tried to breathe deeply, borrowing the relaxation techniques of his wife. The irony of this was not lost on him and with it, a degree of sanity and self-interest was somewhat restored. He realised that to confront Dacre would mean the foolish and fruitless exposure of himself. These are night terrors, he thought, I am a typical anxious father, and he got out of the car to keep his worst foolish fear at bay.

It seemed an endless night to Elfie. She tried to keep moving so she walked, she knelt and she squatted. At the bad times she lay down and plunged the gas and air mask over her face. Light-headed after one of these sessions she had the sensation of helplessly tossing within an active sea, swaying rhythmically, plunging to sixty feet and then breaking open on a rock. 'Stroke me,' she said at one point to Hugh and he leaned forward to brush her face and her stomach. It was hot and she crushed an ice-cube against her tongue. She tried to imagine the reluctant child stirring in its bed of soft tissue and bone—its large head, arms folded secretively across its chest, the cord tucked around the legs. She thought of its closed eyes and mouth puckered ready to cry, but it had neither a face nor even the anchor of a name in her thoughts.

'My insides are old and slow,' she told the midwife.

'They are in fine fettle and normal,' the midwife replied who dwelt only in the kind bright world of praise.

Opening her eyes reminded Elfie of the shadowy silhouettes that passed continuously behind the curtains screening her bed. Teenage girls reading *Jackie*, the bank manager expecting his 1.8 children, fertile Catholics and costive Anglicans, all of them awaiting deliverance. It seemed terribly surreal. At one point she heard a whisper that it was only a one-night stand in Lanzarote. How intriguing, she thought, before pain engulfed her. She wished they would push back the screens so that she could stare into these lives which would give her a further horizon beyond the suffocating repeat of pain, gas and air. All she could see above the curtains was the top of a tall window on the opposite side of the ward where a creamy blue sky marked the start of another hot day.

'Any message from Judith?' she muttered to Hugh.

She had arranged that Judith should drive over to the house at first light.

'She says grunt if you feel like it.'

'Oh Hugh, how terribly like Judith. Give me the cold sponge.'

Hugh mopped his own brow before attending to his wife's. Sleepless, sweating and grey, he felt nervous. He wondered if the strain could induce a cardiac arrest. Their local MP had been rushed into hospital after an all-night sitting.

'How big am I now?' Elfie asked the new monitoring midwife. She liked her broad outdoors face.

It was Aileen who had just come on duty. She held up eight encouraging fingers to show the degree of dilation.

'Nearly there,' she promised. 'You're both

coping awfully well.'

*   *   *

Walking outside in the cool green of that morning, Philip noted that the workers had already begun to fling out the drones. Summer was over. This year at the same time as last year, the first clusters had been judged and executed and they littered the grass beside the hives. Long forgotten because never needed, the lines of verse lifted within him:

> This passive place a Summer's nimble mansion
> Where Bloom and Bees
> Fulfill'd their Oriental Circuit
> Then ceased, like these.

He walked back through the garden. Mopy and full of ill humours, he closed the house, took the car keys and drove back to London to escape the enfeebling presence of elegy.

*   *   *

I must lie down for twenty minutes, thought Hugh. He had escaped to the car, but the area where it was parked was electric with anxieties. His night terrors were shed but they had left him fractious; the infirmary loomed over him like a grave and the coming and going of ambulances made him nervous. Exhausted, he returned to the maternity unit, bought himself a cup of hot sugary tea from the vending machine and peered cautiously round the door of the father's room. With any luck it might be empty of youths. There were some Ercol-type chairs with wooden arms in there and he could rest in clinical isolation. One look, however, warned him he would have to compromise though it wasn't too bad. There was only a lone father with his head in his hands so Hugh decided to brave it. He could use his first volume of *War and Peace* as a shield.

'May I disturb you?' he said in the voice of assumption.

The man lifted his head and nodded.

The pair sat for a moment in silence. Hugh took a few gulps of tea and opened his book at random. He could not remember how far he had reached. Chapter XVI seemed as good a starting-point as any.

'My dear Boris,' said the princess as the carriage that the countess had placed at her disposal rolled over the straw-covered street and into the courtyard of Count Besoukhow's house. 'My dear Boris,' she repeated and she put out her hand from under her shabby cloak—

'It's your daughter in here is it?' asked the man, apparently undeterred by the book.

'No,' said Hugh stiffly and prepared to return to his text.

357

'Sorry.' The man made a gesture of apology.

'It's my wife's first.' Hugh had not meant to proffer information but the tea was thawing his reserve. Besides there was something familiar about the fellow, or perhaps familiar about his type. Short, stocky with a bald head and a rotund voice. A voice used to compelling attention, possibly suited to the courts. Hugh wondered if he was a barrister.

'She's OK?'

'I slipped out for twenty minutes rest, but the midwife was complimenting her when I left.'

'They always do. They say you never forget the midwife who delivers your baby.' An infinitesimal spasm crossed his face.

'Your first?' said Hugh, drawn into an exchange. He let his book relax below the angle of 90° which was a sign of submission.

'Our second.'

'Ah well, you're all right then.'

'Not exactly.'

'Ah,' said Hugh, hoping he wasn't going to run into a problem here. He realised that the chance to prop up his book had just passed. Thoughtfully, he chewed his last mouthful of tea. His breath, already foul, was now coated with tannin.

His companion rose and walked to the window. Thin, unlined, turqoise curtains of rayon or polyester hung limply to either side. There was a box outside of red pelargoniums in violent need of hospitalisation.

'They sent me out because I was getting too nervy to give support.'

'I'm sorry to hear that.' Hugh hoped he would clam up. His new friend was getting perilously close to self-display.

'We lost our first child at birth.'

Oh God, thought Hugh. He placed his empty plastic mug gingerly upon the plastic table. He should have known better than to risk the fathers' room. It was simply dreadful, of course, and he felt terribly sorry for him, and compelled to offer words of comfort but all he could think of was 'my dear Boris'. He wished he could tip-toe out. The inability to do so produced a spurt of unwarranted aggression that he knew was utterly appalling. But wasn't it a tiny bit self-absorbed of this poor fellow to burden a stranger with his agonies? Especially an ageing father awaiting his wife's first child? Didn't he realise that human problems could contaminate? They were as infectious as the plague.

'They said that if it had lived it would have been brain-damaged, starved of oxygen. They said it was a kinder thing for it to die.'

Hugh felt slightly faint. 'I'm deeply sorry.' He spoke in a shocked attempt to sedate them both. 'But they're so experienced that you must believe it.' Why, he wondered, was the bromide 'it's all for the best' only applied to the most frightful situations?

His companion still had his back towards

him. Motionless he seemed in the eye of a trance.

'Rationally they were right, of course. But that doesn't come into it.' He dipped his head. 'We would have loved our child unconditionally. You learn quite late in life, often too late for it to operate, often only when you've lost its object, that real love is by its nature unconditional.'

Hugh sat still on the chair. He did not answer, could not indeed speak. A moment later he did something he had never done in his entire life. He got up, crossed the little room and put an arm around the stranger beside the window. Silently the pair stood locked together like brothers. In the corridor outside, a wheelchair rolled by en route for labour room 5a, but the men stayed standing side by side.

*   *   *

On arrival, Philip flipped listlessly through the papers on his desk. As always in his absence and as always on his return, they seemed meaningless. He tried and failed to immerse himself in changes to state aid for German exports. He felt unwell for he had eaten mechanically and without appetite for days. Having left home in the hurry of escape, he now longed to be back in the cool of the garden. He realised, too, that in his haste he had forgotten to prepare the hives for the autumn. He rang Walter. He didn't expect him to be in, but Maisie went without demur to fetch him from their front garden.

'Thought you'd be working, Walter,' he said curtly.

'We got the day off. She's having the baby.'

'Who?' asked Philip, but it was for show. He stared blankly at a profile of the Hong Kong Trade Development Council.

'The missus. Elfie.'

She can't be, he thought foolishly. I left her only yesterday. The room appeared to be tilting so he closed his eyes but the spinning vision persisted.

'I rang to ask you if you could start feeding the bees and put the winter doors in.'

'Right-o,' said Walter, glad that the show was still on the road. Normal service seemed to have resumed.

Philip rang off and went to the window, the same one through which he had seen and heard the flute player. The boy had not returned. He had taken up his impermanent musical abode elsewhere. Blindly Philip stared through the glass. He felt breathless. What did I expect? That it wouldn't come out? Was birth—like death—however much awaited, a shock?

Apparently. It was indeed a shock that those two ghostly nights so long ago had now produced his flesh and substance. It had a face. His face? Down on its arms. His down? The room span again. He realised that his efforts to be rational had not been entirely successful. What do I do? he wondered. Elfie. She had been the instrument through which he had lost his marriage and family, and at this very moment she was giving birth, thereby establishing her own marriage with his child.

He looked at his desk and felt a revulsion for everything he did. He had married for status and money, he worked for status and money. Clots of both stuffs had stuck to him with the result that he had become a moderately rich man. But what had once caused him much satisfaction was now starting to revolt him. He felt the need to divest himself, not to leave all the divesting to Martha. He was surprised by its force—such a basic urge, like the need of the unwashed to cleanse themselves. He suddenly remembered from his school assembly St Luke's parable of the rich man who intended to pull down his barns to build a larger one to house all his fruits and goods so he could tell his soul to eat, drink and be merry. Even now over the years, he could recall his headmaster, a zealot, dressing himself in the words of God. *'Thou fool, this night thy soul shall be required of thee; then whose shall those things be, which thou hast provided?'*

He sat down. 'Thou fool,' he said to himself, and then over and over again, 'Thou fool.' Then, as his thoughts began to clarify a route in his mind, he started to feel a little better. 'Thou fucking idiot, more like it,' he said out loud. He went over to his desk and, from a great height so that he could enjoy its thud, he dropped the paper on the Hong Kong Trade Development Council in the waste paper basket, and covered it up with the notes on change to state aid for German exports. He picked out a fresh sheet of paper from the left drawer of his partner's desk, took up his slim gold Pelikan pen, then laid it aside for a leaky biro and wrote Dacre's Roses as a heading. He underlined it and began to make lists: Floribundas, Gallicas, Damasks, Albas, Centifolias, Moss Roses, Chinas, Portlands, Bourbons and Hybrid Perpetuals. He covered two pages, then took up a third and gave it a fresh title: *The Breeding Programme*.

*   *   *

'Oh, my darling Elf.' Hugh leaned over her in the delivery room.

'We tried the father's room. We called for you everywhere,' said Jenny, the student nurse.

'I must have been in the car at that moment.'

Hugh felt he was near the point of weeping with remorse and nervousness.

Aileen surveyed him. Some fathers did a bunk at the climax.

'You're sure you want to stay?' She had been told he had failed to attend his pre-natal lessons.

'Yes.' Hugh pulled himself together. 'I'm not afraid of blood.'

363

'Good,' said Aileen. 'You haven't missed it. Nearly there. No obstructions.'

'Christ,' gasped Elfie, her head thrown back in agony against the upright pillow of the birthing-table.

'One more push,' advised Aileen, sterilised surgical gloves exploring. She hovered, waiting to introduce the infant to its new terrifying world of light, noise, air, gravity and tactical stimulus.

From the other end of the bed, Hugh stood motionless, staring transfixed and intent at the mirror. The head, dark and sticky, had started to emerge. It seemed to have plenty of hair.

'It's coming,' he said. 'Little Elf, it's on its way.'

Aileen was bending low, assessing the situation. No need for an episiotomy, no need for forceps. This primagravida was in remarkably good shape.

'Push now,' she said unnecessarily as Elfie's insides underwent a spontaneous contraction. It lasted five seconds.

In the mirror, the head could be seen breaking through. Aileen eased the face delicately as she wiped the mucus from the mouth, taking care to avoid the nostrils. She checked that the cord was not wound around the neck.

'You can touch it,' she said.

Elfie reached down.

Not daring to move, Hugh watched in the

mirror his wife's fingers exploring the face.

The infant began to rotate, taking up its sideways position facing the thigh. Still housed, its slippery shoulders were twisting. Aileen placed her hands on each of its tiny flat ears. She began to drag gently and intuitively, so that first one shoulder slid out and then the next. She grasped the warm wet trunk.

'There,' she said, lifting the child.

A gush of liquor followed its release as she placed it on Elfie's stomach.

'It's a girl,' said Hugh. 'A girl, oh my darling Elf, it's a girl.'

He bent down, not daring to touch the downy damp skin.

Almost immediately, the child had begun to breathe, stimulated by its introduction to the comparatively cool air. It protested loudly. The noise of its crying erupted on the waiting audience.

'Is she all right?' gasped Elfie.

Aileen was engaged on her assessment, scoring heart rate, respiration, muscle tone and reflex response to stimulus and colour. She waited until she had finished.

'Very good,' she said. '9 out of 10.'

'Is that all,' said Hugh. Agonised he peered downwards. Was there a toe missing?

'It's excellent. Nobody gets 10 out of 10.'

She smiled, knowing she would repeat the test in five minutes time. Meanwhile she clamped the cord securely.

'You can cut it if you want.'

'Do you want to?' asked Hugh shyly.

'You do it,' murmured Elfie. She just wanted to lie still with the child folded within her arms.

Aileen handed him the cord scissors. Gingerly he applied them. Ridiculous but he was fearful of hurting his new daughter.

'Firmly,' said Aileen. Only this morning she had watched the breaking of the cord between a Charolais cow and her calf.

Hugh re-applied himself, pushing his spectacles back on his nose as he bent forwards. As he straightened up, he noticed the child had a small dark red mark on the nape of her neck.

'What's that?' he said pointing to it.

'What?' said Elfie, alerted to a strangeness and alarmed. She could not see from her position. Only the infant's face, squashed, vulnerable, hers. She had not imagined it like this.

'That,' said Hugh to Aileen. 'That mark.'

'Oh,' Aileen looked. 'That's nothing to worry about. It sometimes runs in families. We call it the stork-beak's mark. It's blood vessels. They usually fade.'

Hugh stood still, thinking, remembering. All those years ago. Thirty-five years ago. The memory, faint at first, no more than a silhouette, began to take shape and colour.

'Rupert had it,' he said to Elfie. 'Rupert had it.' He began to laugh until the tears that had

366

been standing in his eyes brimmed over and ran down his cheeks. 'Rupert had it.'

'The stork-beak's mark?' Elfie turned the infant over. Who knows? Behind its closed lids, the child's eyes would be dark blue-grey. The light, although dim, must hurt them. My own dear darling, she thought. Not Philip's, not Hugh's, not even mine now it's outside in the world—but itself and brought by the stork. She too began to laugh.

'Hugh,' she said.

He stood beside her, one hand on her head and the other on the child's shoulder.

'What?,' he said.

'Just Hugh.'

Later, as they left the delivery room for the post-natal ward, Hugh stopped in the corridor outside the father's room. He hesitated, opened the door and looked round. His friend had gone. He stared at two youths who had replaced him. 'I don't suppose you know what's happened to . . .' He realised he didn't know his name. Boris, he thought. The youths gazed at him blankly, wearing jeans and kickers. One of them was chewing gum. He closed the door. It runs in families, Rupert had it, he thought again. He wanted to shout it as he ran to catch up the wheelchair with his wife and daughter. Rupert had it. He would have loved them unconditionally, but in all honesty thank God that no such act of faith was required.

CHAPTER TWENTY-NINE

Lydia replaced the telephone receiver but remained seated for a moment in her armchair beside the small table. Her right cheek was flushed with emotion, her left chill and pale as always. She looked down at Ben, sleeping and twitching beside her feet. 'She's had a little girl,' she announced, but the dog was now fully deaf as well as blind in one eye. She stubbed him with one toe but meeting no response, she picked up the holiday photo of Ronnie standing in front of some tastefully decayed remains. Taken fifteen years ago, it marked their architectural cruise phase that had flared briefly after his retirement.

She stared at the laughing image. 'We have our third grandchild. You old bugger, couldn't you have hung on a bit longer. Typical. You always did leave the greetings to me.'

She replaced the photograph tremulously on its stand beside the bowl of pot pourri which had exhaled its last sigh several years ago. She then rose with deliberation to her feet. Immediately after his death, she had been reckless of her own welfare; now, especially of late, she was careful in all her movements, fearful of falling, though fear of life was not, in fact, the origin, but rather fear of extinction. It was, she knew, a sign of wanting to live a little longer, to be granted the widow's right to a span.

On the telephone just now, Judith had promised she would come and take her to see the child as soon as Elfie was home which would be in a couple of days. Impatience and curiosity fluttered excitedly within her, further signs of returning life. Her sense of occasion spoke out for immediate celebration, not one to be postponed for a few days. Frustrated by her only companions, a moribund dog and a husband immured in his photograph frame, she looked round for an outlet. She walked to the window and stared out at the parched grass. In the distance she saw that a sunbeam had picked out Ronnie's young chestnuts where she had thrown his ashes and they had fallen, mingling with snowflakes in the wintry beginning of the year.

She left the window, hauled Ben into the kitchen, took the car keys from the kitchen drawer and locked the house. Summoning up her nerve because it was an unaccustomed journey and therefore required gumption, she drove doggedly to Croft Castle. Late August, so of course the car park was full with family cars. She decided to advance to the area for the disabled which was nearer her quarry. She lacked any certificate of disability, indeed would disdain it, but was confident her age, white hair and walking stick would be ample qualification.

Having parked the car, she walked slowly over the gravel, onto the dry grass around the

369

ancient stone castle, then through the wooden latch gate and across the field. It would be a long walk for her. The ground was hard and unyielding and she stumbled several times on hillocks. Unnoticed, thistles tore at her old woman's remedial stockings. Fixing her eyes on the horizon, she could see in the distance the single-flanked avenue of sweet chestnuts stretching for half a mile. Planted after 1588, the huge misshapen hulks reared out of the undergrowth of youngsters around them. At closer quarters, their details became apparent. The trees were so old, they seemed to have mutated into fossils. They thrust their huge membranes into the earth, their limbs lifted in jerky agonised shapes into the sky. A small, short-lived organism, Lydia stood under their August canopy of dark green and looked up. Ronnie, are you there, she wondered, as she put her hands over the grey fissured trunk. She recalled his voice saying hope is in the trees. Then she had not believed, but now there stirred the first glimmers of his faith within her. As she touched the living past, she felt his presence beside her, and also their grandchild stretching far into the future.

*   *   *

Three weeks later Rupert was also introduced to the new baby. Ill at ease, he lingered at the door in the wake of his fiancée who was meeting her stepmother for the first time. Listening to their female exchange, he engrossed himself in a cardboard cut-out of a pink pig suspended from the ceiling. The little pig flew. If you pulled the cord in its belly, its wings flapped. To occupy his hands and delay the encounter, Rupert yanked the string a couple of times. The pig squeaked as well as flew.

'Stop fiddling. Come over here,' said Hugh impatiently.

'Look,' said Camilla 'Say hello.'

Rupert crossed the room. Avoiding Elfie's gaze but smiling so as not to cause offence, he looked down at the infant cradled in her arms.

'See? Pigs can fly,' she said to him.

Nervous of his own reactions, he did not answer. The baby's hair was flat and downy, a brownish-black, its skin golden, its eyelids closed. Its small mouth moved as though words pushed against it. He had been prepared to meet a stranger, an alien, but, watching it, he felt a sharp flush of recognition. He pushed the illusion aside and continued to make his inventory. He noted the redundant limbs of the newborn, amorphous, except for the perfection of its oddly mature hands and nails.

'I've something to show you,' said Hugh.

He bent down and detached his tiny daughter from his wife's arms. He placed her face down over his right shoulder. The sight of his father with his child gave Rupert a violent

371

pang. Not wanting to look, he suffered a split second's nystagmus, his eyes involuntarily swivelling away.

'Look.' Hugh pointed with his finger. 'Come closer,' he commanded as Rupert still hung back.

He took a few steps forward and peered hesitantly. A sweet, clean and chalky scent hung around the child.

'You had one of these.' Hugh pointed again.

Rupert edged close and saw a pinkish-red blotch.

'It's a family trait,' added Hugh.

Rupert put his hand up to the nape of his neck where he kept his hair dipped down. 'I still have it,' he said slowly.

'I didn't know,' exclaimed Camilla.

She was delighted to discover a new idiosyncrasy. She went behind him and examined it.

'It's a family birth mark,' said Hugh. 'Like a signature.'

Rupert looked at his father. Something in his voice, perhaps the degree of affirmation, made him wonder whether he too must have suffered doubts about its provenance.

He surprised himself by replying: 'She looks like me.'

'She looks like me,' contradicted Hugh.

'You realise,' murmured Elfie to Camilla who had rejoined her. 'You realise that you will have to cope with a certain amount of family egotism.'

'Oh, I'll be the passive one,' said Camilla.

'You are a very sensible young woman.'

She remembered sitting in the summerhouse over a year ago surrounded by the roses. 'You think that action can solve everything,' she had told him. She remained uncertain whether it had or hadn't but no matter, the subject was now closed. She had folded her mind around it. Absolution could be accepted, even if unearned.

Later, as Rupert drove her away, Camilla sat thinking. She leaned over and stroked his neck.

'What a shy boy, not to show me.'

'It wasn't important.'

'Not important, and certainly not worth bothering to hide. It's quite common in babies, you know. My sister, the one who's a pediatrician, once told me.'

Rupert sat thinking. Eventually he said, 'Just shut up about this, will you? And don't repeat that to my father. Ever.'

Elfie was right, thought Camilla. Hugh and Rupert were such egotists. One day she would ask Elf how she coped.

*   *   *

After they had gone, Hugh and Elfie sat quietly in the sanctuary garden. It was the latter part of the afternoon. Between them and shaded from the autumnal sunshine, the baby lay dozing in a sling. From time to time, as though for comfort, Hugh stroked the downy nape of her neck. Returned to his own childhood, he remembered the Blenheim spaniels his mother used to breed, each bearing the sign of its lineage which was a brown thumbprint on the dome of its white head. He recalled Arthur and Nellie and Zozo and Frog.

Reminded by their names, he said: 'I don't really care for Adele. It's like some opera singer. It doesn't suit her.'

'I agree. I don't much like it either. How about our first choice. Nina?

'I've gone off that too. Rose.'

'Lily?'

'Rose. Rose Lyle. Rose. She looks like a rose. Pink with a darker pink rose on her neck.'

To her left, Elfie noticed the purple seedling rose had been planted at the back of the nearby flower-bed. Judith, no doubt, responsible and well-meaning as always. A disturbing presence, it would have to go. It was a threat to a closed mind. Then, she thought, no, stay, let it disturb. Let it administer the moral lesson that was deserved but not actually received. Maybe, she decided, that was always the case. In the end, you had to rely on yourself for punishment, be your own judge and jury. It was more often in children's books than in life, that people were taught a moral lesson. After all, fables were indeed fabulous.

'Is it agreed then?' asked Hugh. 'Rose Lyle?'

'Oh, I couldn't bear Rose, too dulcet,' she said, thinking that one hairshirt was quite enough.

'Perhaps the next time,' he suggested. 'Yes?'

Elfie looked at him and smiled. She raised her fingers gently to his chin and then down to the child. It seemed doubtful that the stork could be induced twice.